To

Memories of the Kurai

The Quest for Qieta: Book 2

Dr. T. Wu

MEMORIES OF THE KURAI

For information contact:
Website; http://www.thequestforqieta.com
Instagram/X/TikTok; @tinainqieta

Book Cover design by Antonio Cesar
Book Formatting by Derek Murphy
ISBN: 978-1-7395297-1-0

First Edition: July 2024

CHAPTER ONE

Nostalgia and Unfamiliarity

ALBERT GULPS AS HE STARES at the man in front of him. A man whose presence is so nostalgic, yet exudes an unfamiliar aura, which causes something to sink inside Albert's heart.

The man boasts a tall nose, a strong jawline, and thick dark eyebrows which arch above the two glowing amethysts of his eyes. Those violet jewels were once the gentle yet playful eyes of Brother Satoshi. Now, they are the cold, intimidating stones of Lord Azrael. Is this really the same man? Albert blinks hard.

Satoshi nods before a deep voice escapes his lips like liquid silk. "Albert Leon. Long time no see."

Liuana Pharlos briskly takes a few steps forward and points his staff at Satoshi.

"Stay away, Azrael!" the old man shouts. Liuana Pharlos concentrates his energy and gives a powerful swing of his staff. A bright glow radiates out from the blue orb on the end and an overwhelming blast of light shoots towards the man sitting on the porcelain structure.

Satoshi watches the attack come towards him, unfazed.

Albert is still in a state of shock. *Why is Satoshi here? Now?*

A second before the blue light from the orb hits him, Satoshi lifts his right hand; an invisible barrier forms around him to deflect the blast. The deflection crashes into the dome above them, causing the coloured glass to shatter into millions of broken pieces that scatter onto the floor, forming a rain of coloured dust.

Satoshi appears rather uninterested as the attack finishes and he puts down his hand. "My. That was not very welcoming," he comments, raising an eyebrow. He rises, before taking a few slow steps towards Albert and the old man. His footsteps create sharp echoes that bounce through the hall.

Liuana Pharlos drops his staff and bends forward. Gasping, he steadies himself with his hands on his thighs. The blast has taken a lot out of him. He squeezes his eyes shut and exhales a long, difficult breath.

Albert takes a small step back and his hands hover in front of him in defence. Satoshi is now right in front of him, his tall frame giving Albert the same strange feeling of nostalgia mixed with new and unfamiliar intimidation.

"Little Albert," Satoshi says, "haven't you grown up to be a charming young man?" He reaches out and ruffles his hand through Albert's short, golden hair.

Albert is as still as stone, his eyes wide and his breathing heavy.

Satoshi smiles. Suddenly, he strikes at Albert's neck with the side of his left hand.

Albert's instincts take over, and he grasps onto Satoshi's wrist in defence. His eyes are still round and wide, and he starts to shake.

"Hmm, good work," Satoshi says, acknowledging Albert's reaction. "A true first-hand guard you are, Sir Albert Leon."

Albert's grasp loosens and Satoshi withdraws his

hand. Satoshi turns his back and walks away, only to suddenly stop. He turns to face Albert once more. His amethyst eyes linger on the first-hand guard for a moment before his lips part.

"Sorry, little Albert," he whispers. The corners of his mouth turn up into a soft smile as he lifts his hand once again. An aura of elegance radiates out from him, and he gives a simple wave towards the left.

Albert is lifted off the ground and hurled out of sight with overwhelming speed. His back crashes into one of the ivory pillars and immediately cracks from the force. A small groan escapes his lips as he falls to the floor in an agonising heap.

The pain is astounding. He rolls forwards and manages to lift his head. Satoshi continues to walk away from him. The image of Satoshi gradually diminishes as Albert's vision blurs and a haze of darkness drapes over him.

Albert barely manages to whisper, "Brother Satoshi . . ." before he falls unconscious.

CHAPTER TWO

Stone Walls

ALBERT WAKES UP. IT IS terribly dark. He cannot see anything. It takes a while for his eyes to adjust to the darkness. Is that moonlight coming in from a window?

He tries to sit up, but immediately falls back down. He winces as his head impacts the hard ground. Where is he?

Albert tries to sit up once again, slower this time. An awful ache radiates through his entire body and seeps down into his bones. Perhaps he has fractured something.

He looks around once again. There is a small square of light high up on the wall, through which he can see the moon. His vision slowly starts to focus.

Albert realises he is inside a cell of some sort. His mind suddenly flashes back to the vision of Satoshi walking away just before he fell unconscious. There is a pounding pain in his head as he remembers the events.

What is going on? Albert thinks. He slowly gets to his feet. Pain gnaws at every inch of his body. He reaches out to touch the wall of the room. Rough stone. His hands trace over the jagged surface as he tries to map out as much of the area as he can. He wonders how he got here.

After a while, Albert deduces that he is contained within four stone walls and that he cannot seem to find any sign of a door. He has no idea how he got inside, or how he will get out. He slowly drops to the floor as weakness overtakes him and pain eats at him unforgivingly. His stomach churns and nausea rises in his throat as he collapses.

How long has he been here? *Why* is he here?

Albert closes his eyes as the pounding headache continues to throb inside his skull. How will he be able to send a Kaidara to Prince Takashi in this state? Where is Liuana Pharlos? Has Brother Satoshi been here in Qieta all this time?

What in the world is going on?

There are too many questions in Albert's mind, but his body is too weak right now. He wonders about his fate and whether or not he will be able to get out of here.

Ssssst. Ssssst. Ssssst.

What is that sound? Albert wonders. A very light scraping sound is coming from somewhere to the right of him, it seems. He tries to turn his head. Everything hurts.

Ssssst. Ssssst. Ssssst.

The sound comes once more. Is something scraping against a hard surface? Is the sound really there, or is he hallucinating? The memory of Emperor Takashi carving patterns onto a picture frame for one of Prince Takashi's very first paintings suddenly flashes across his mind.

It was a time not long after he'd been taken in by the Takashi family. He admired Prince Takashi's artistic talent and the emperor's practicality. These heart-warming moments with the Takashi family would often make him miss his own.

Why are these memories suddenly flooding into his mind?

Ssssst. Ssssst. Ssssst.

Albert falls unconscious once again.

CHAPTER THREE

Master Kinali

IN THE BUSTLING CENTRAL OF Ajisai Village, Satoru steps down from a royal cart. The sun shines brightly on the busy town as people make their way along the cobbled paths. Various men and women stand by stalls, selling goods and shouting for customers.

"A fresh box of strawberries! Five kudon only!"

"A bunch of lychees! Seven kudon!"

"Fresh bread! Fresh bread! Two kudon a loaf!"

Satoru adjusts his clothing and orients himself in

the right direction. Immediately, the citizens notice him, and excited crowds begin to gather. Today, the prince is wearing a crimson and golden robe. His hair is let down, and the beautiful, long strands drape loosely, adorned with various golden embellishments.

"Prince Takashi!" an excited middle-aged lady exclaims.

"Your Majesty," another man pipes up, "welcome to Ajisai!"

The shopkeepers stop waving for customers as they gaze wide-eyed at the handsome leader of Shinrin. They bow frantically. Somewhere in the crowd, a young lady faints at the sight of the prince.

"Good morning, my citizens," Satoru says. He politely makes his way through the excited crowd as he nods at various people who are greeting him. He is in a hurry. He reaches the aviary—a small, grey cobbled building on the corner off the main street of the Ajisai town centre. Satoru pushes the door open.

A man with light brown hair and a matching moustache is standing at the counter. He blinks through his round spectacles and bows immediately. "Your Majesty!" he says.

"Good morning, Tom," Prince Takashi replies.

"What might our royal leader be doing here on this

fine morning?" he asks.

"I've come to send a message to Qieta."

"Is that so?" Tom hurries out from behind the counter to greet the royal prince properly. He bows again. "Please follow me, Prince Takashi," Tom says.

Satoru follows Tom out to the back of the aviary, where a beautifully kept garden stands. Trees in various well-trimmed shapes and sizes surround its perimeter, and flowers of both pastel and vibrant colours bloom beneath them. There are many Ketu resting on the tree branches. A few are swooping around, flapping their wings in the warm morning breeze.

Satoru and Tom reach a tall, thin tree. A small, wooden birdhouse is perched on top of it. Tom whistles a short tune, one that is different to the call for a Ketu. Soon enough, a small, azure bird with black wings hops out onto the branch.

A Kaidara.

Satoru takes a small parchment from his sleeve and unfolds it in front of the bird. She hops closer to study the script with her beady eyes. She blinks a few times, hops a step backwards, and chirps.

"Tom, please send the message to Sir Leon in Qieta," Satoru says.

"Certainly, Your Majesty," he replies. He whistles

another short command and the Kaidara chirps again in response.

She takes off with surprising speed, soon disappearing into the blue sky.

✻

That evening, as Satoru prepares himself for slumber, something *tap taps* on his chamber window. As he makes his way across to it, a crimson bird greets him.

Satoru quickly unravels the small scroll it holds and scans the message. His eyes widen.

Prince Takashi,

I hope this finds you well. My wife and I are alive and currently residing at Akamatsu Infirmary. We are recovering, slowly but surely. I hope we can meet again sometime soon once I get better.

Regards,
Erol Kinali

Master Kinali, Satoru thinks. His heart beats hard inside his chest. His hands shake as he grips onto the piece of parchment. He is absolutely overjoyed to hear this news.

Akalin will be absolutely delighted.

But where is *Akalin?* Satoru wonders. Every Ketu Satoru had sent to him had flown back with the messages undelivered, suggesting that his second-hand guard is not in Shinrin. Satoru has no idea how he will be able to get hold of him.

Satoru decides he must visit Master and Mrs Kinali as soon as he can. A weight is lifted off his shoulders as he clutches the parchment tightly to his chest.

His master is alive.

✽

The next day, Satoru alights from his royal cart in the village of Akamatsu. He stands before a large, black-and-white building with a slanted slate roof. Etched in golden writing on a long piece of wooden board reads: AKAMATSU INFIRMARY.

Satoru enters.

The lady at the front desk immediately stands and bows deeply. "Prince Takashi!" she exclaims.

"Good afternoon, Milady," Satoru replies. "I am here to see Master and Mrs Kinali."

"Oh! Certainly," the lady says. "Please, follow me. They are residing on the third floor in the east wing."

Satoru follows the lady as they walk down immaculately clean corridors and up some winding wooden steps. Soon enough, they reach the door of a ward.

The lady gently slides it open and bows. "Your Majesty." She gestures for Satoru to enter. "Master Kinali is in the side room right at the back."

Satoru thanks her before stepping inside. He makes his way towards the back of the ward and peers through the small, square glass into the side room. Inside, a gentleman is propped up on a bed, looking out of the window. His silver hair is long and loose.

Satoru knocks lightly, causing the man to turn. His eyebrows raise in surprise as Satoru slides the door open and steps towards him.

"Master Kinali," Satoru says. A watery film spreads in front of Satoru's eyes. He opens his arms and leans down to embrace his master.

Erol immediately lifts his arms in return and holds onto the prince tightly. "Prince Takashi," he replies.

The two of them stay like that for a moment more.

Satoru leans back. "Master Kinali," he says again.

Despite his torso and arms being wrapped with bandages, Master Kinali's muscular frame is still evident through the layers and his body exudes an aura of strength. The tops of a few scars peek out from beneath the bandages. He has a strong facial structure, violet eyes, and a trimmed beard.

"My son," Erol says.

"I am absolutely overjoyed to see you," Satoru replies.

"As am I." Erol beams.

"Where is Mrs Kinali?" Satoru asks. "I must see her too, before I go."

"She is in the ward next door." Master Kinali leans back onto the pillows of his bed and winces. He squints his eyes shut as he waits for the pain to pass, then shuffles into a more comfortable position.

The loud, muffled chatter of excited patients outside their side room seeps through the gaps of the side room door. They must be in disbelief that the royal leader is here.

Satoru sits down on the chair by Erol's bed and leans towards his master, his face full of seriousness. "Please, tell me everything."

"Where do I even begin?" Erol says. He takes a breath.

Satoru tenses in his seat as he prepares to hear what his master has to say.

"Aiyla was unwell," Erol begins. "My wife was at

home with her whilst I went out to buy some more Sadore—in case she spiked another fever. I was in the queue when suddenly, a vast troop of soldiers on horses came rushing into the square. They were wearing black armour and had red cloths over their faces."

Satoru bites his tongue to keep from interjecting.

"It was horrifying. Any unlucky villager who happened to be in their way was killed on the spot. The soldiers carried long lances and started going on a rampage. I noticed that children were being taken and carried away."

Satoru nods, his eyes wide.

"My first instinct told me to find my wife and my daughter. I immediately began making my way back home, trying to cut through back alleyways to avoid the chaos. As if something above was watching over us, I bumped into Yasmina, who was looking for me using the exact same route. She had hidden Aiyla in the cellar in our back garden."

Satoru gestures for him to continue.

"We managed to make it close to home. However, a few soldiers came charging towards us. There were a few empty canoes on the river which flows behind our houses. I urged Yasmina to jump onto one, hoping the soldiers would be unable to reach her."

Satoru listens on, his hands in tight fists.

"A soldier charged towards me, but I managed to disarm him. I got hold of his lance right before five others charged at me. One of them had a bow and arrow. He was about to shoot it at my wife just as I managed to knock him down, but a dozen more soldiers were coming. I ran to Yasmina, and we flipped the canoe over."

Satoru pictures this and wishes he had not.

"I do not know how long we were in the water for. But we managed to stay there until the rampage ended. The soldiers must have thought we died, and they left. The water was absolutely freezing, and I could see Yasmina was becoming unwell." Erol shook his head. "We managed to swim down the river towards our home. However, by the time we got there, Aiyla was gone."

"We then journeyed on foot to the nearest Infirmary we could find."

Satoru's heart is thumping. "You both walked all the way from Hinoki to Akamatsu?"

"It was the nearest one. Hinoki was absolutely ransacked," Erol replies. "By the time we got to the entrance, my wife had collapsed and I wasn't feeling too well either. It appears I lost consciousness. Next thing I knew, I woke up in the infirmary. I am just glad that my wife is alive."

"This is absolutely terrible," Satoru says, shaking his head.

"It was a disaster I never thought I would witness in my lifetime. The number of dead bodies and screams would haunt anyone's sleep." Erol's gaze goes distant as he continues to speak. "My wife developed hypothermia and then pneumonia, and I had quite a few broken bits here and there. Fractured ribs, lacerated kidney, I can't remember what else." He manages a small chuckle.

"Master Kinali, I launched an investigation into this," Satoru says, frowning, "and it appears the children are being traded off the shores of Neril. However, since our soldiers began to patrol the area, there have been no more sightings."

"Typical," Erol replies, closing his eyes and sighing. "Whoever started this must have gone into hiding."

"I still do not know where the children have been taken . . . and I have not heard from Akalin in quite a while."

Erol raises his eyebrows. "My son went to look for them?" he asks, his silver eyebrows raising with concern. "We were wondering why we hadn't heard from him."

"He sent me a Ketu to explain, Master Kinali," Satoru discloses. "He explained that on the day he journeyed back home, he ended up witnessing the remnants of the Hinoki disaster."

Erol leans towards the prince, the fine lines around his eyes deepening with worry.

"I believe he decided to go on a journey to look for Aiyla," Satoru continues. "The last time I heard from him was when he brought me news that the children were being traded off the shores of Neril. He witnessed boats with cages containing the children."

"My silly son." Erol shakes his head. "No wonder every Ketu I've sent him has returned with the message undelivered."

"The same happened to me, Master Kinali," Satoru replies. "I believe this means he is no longer in Shinrin."

Erol sighs. "Both my son and daughter are missing." He squeezes his eyes shut and takes a breath. He gulps. There is a pause.

"I know," Satoru acknowledges. A wave of sadness sweeps over him. "However, Akalin is extremely smart. Not to mention, he is one of the best fighters out there—" Satoru manages a small smile. "—after you, of course."

Erol laughs quietly. "My silly son is as headstrong as always." Erol sighs again. "I guess I will have to trust whichever being is watching over us." He looks up towards the ceiling and blinks a few tears back.

"I believe both your children are alive," Satoru says firmly, looking into his master's eyes.

"I do, too," Erol replies.

The prince and his martial arts master look at each other with a mixture of sorrow, sincerity, and hope.

CHAPTER FOUR

A Kaidara

SOMETHING BRIGHT HITS ALBERT'S FACE, causing him to stir and open his eyes. A harsh, rough surface grazes his skin. Slowly, he realises that he is lying on the floor and that something bright and rectangular is in front of him.

Is that light coming through a door?

Someone is standing by the entrance. They are covered from head to toe in white fabric.

It looks like a ghost. If Albert was not feeling so weak,

he may have jumped at the sight.

The 'ghost' holds out a bowl of some sort and places it onto the ground. The light then disappears, and Albert is back in complete darkness.

Albert uses all his strength to push himself up. Pain stabs at his muscles and his head spins as he slowly sits up. He is awfully dizzy. The room keeps spinning round and round, intensifying the nausea in his stomach. He drags himself towards where the light was and reaches out. His hand touches the edge of a bowl.

Is this food? Albert wonders. He tries to lift the bowl up, but his grip falters and he spills some of the contents onto the floor. With effort, he steadies the bowl back on the ground, before crouching in front of it. He trembles as he attempts to take a sip.

Soup, Albert thinks. This must be his first taste of food in . . . he is not sure how long. The warmth of the liquid flows into his mouth, bringing him some comfort. He cherishes the refreshing taste for a second longer before swallowing. His throat, however, is tight and dry; his gulp is sharp and painful as he swallows.

Tomato soup, he confirms once his throat stops protesting and he guzzles the rest down. He rolls onto his back and his eyes drift upwards. There it is—the small square window. Moonlight is pouring through it once again.

Suddenly, a small azure bird appears. She chirps, before swooping down to land on the patch of moonlight on the ground.

Is that a Kaidara? Albert thinks. His eyes widen. He uses all his strength to drag himself towards the bird.

The small creature blinks at Albert before hopping around on the patch of moonlight. Her movements are light and energetic—a complete opposite to Albert's condition right now.

Her feet are dipped in an ink of some sort; she stamps out a small message:

Are you in Qieta? Satoru.

Albert inhales. How is he supposed to send a message back? Before he left, Prince Takashi had told him that Kaidaras do not carry messages. Instead, they read and transcribe them, and they can only do so with short, limited messages.

Albert neither has a calligraphy brush, nor a piece of parchment.

"Please, don't go," Albert says to the bird. It feels odd hearing his own voice. It sounds tired and raspy.

The bird cocks her head to one side and blinks at him again.

Ssssst. Ssssst. Ssssst.

Again? What is that sound?

Albert cannot focus on it. He desperately needs to inform Prince Takashi of what is happening, but he has no idea where he is nor how to get out. He thinks quickly.

Spontaneity flows over Albert, and he immediately brings his right thumb towards his lips before biting it. The pain causes him to wince. The warmth of his blood flows as a thick trickle towards his wrist.

Albert uses this to smear a desperate response on the ground, just under the prince's message: *YES. HELP.*

The Kaidara peers at the red smears before giving a simple chirp. She then takes off with speed and disappears into the night sky.

But wait, Albert suddenly realises, *it is dangerous here.* His gulps with horror. He does not want Prince Takashi to come.

But his mind is not working properly. He squints his eyes shut, shakes his head, and sighs.

It is too late.

CHAPTER FIVE

A New Feeling

SATORU LIGHTLY KNOCKS ON THE door of the guest chamber room before the guard pushes it open gently.

A young lady with braided, butterscotch-coloured hair stands up briskly from her chair and bows deeply. "Prince Takashi," she says.

"Good evening, Healer Harlande," the prince greets her. He takes a few steps forward. "How is she?"

"She is recovering," Eirlys reassures. "Her body is

fighting hard."

Satoru peers at Sana, who is lying on the bed. Her black hair is splayed out over her pillow and her shoulders. Her eyes are closed and her chest rises and falls. A grey cat nudges her face against Sana's arm before curling up next to her.

"Your parents, are they still here?" Satoru asks. He had offered for the family to stay in the palace if they wished.

"I told them to go home," Eirlys replies. "I feel it would be better for them to be at home—somewhere comfortable that they are used to—rather than to stay here and constantly worry over Sana."

Satoru nods. "So, it really was sidium poisoning?"

Eirlys nods. "Yes." she replies. "I was absolutely horrified when I found out, but the purple tinge on her lips was unmistakable."

"Mm," Satoru acknowledges. "I knew something was not right, so I called for the palace healer immediately."

"Thank goodness you did, Your Majesty." Eirlys takes a breath. "If he had been any later, I worry—" She stops abruptly. Some tears well up in her eyes. She blinks hard and manages a small laugh. "You would think that I'd be used to emergency situations like this,"

Eirlys whispers. "Yet when it is someone you love, it hits differently."

Satoru looks at her. Her honey-coloured eyes glisten from a watery film. His mind flashes back to the moment when he saw his handkerchief covered in blood. Something tore inside him that day. The feeling had been so intense that it shocked even himself.

Eirlys draws a clear solution into a syringe and injects it into a vein on Sana's arm. Satoru walks by the nearby side table and picks up a chair before placing it next to Sana's sister and sitting down next to her.

"I have read about the classic purple-tinged lips associated with sidium poisoning," the prince says. "However, how long should we expect her to be in this state?"

"Sidium is one of the deadliest poisons out there," Eirlys begins as she carefully removes the needle from the syringe before placing it inside a wooden box. "It causes a severe reaction inside the lungs. The inflammation leads to fluid formation and also causes the blood vessels to rupture. Sana must have felt like she was drowning."

Satoru glances at Sana as concern seeps into his eyes.

"The reaction is rapid," Eirlys continues. "But what makes it all the more terrifying is that one could seem perfectly fine, yet the next thing you know, they absolutely are not." She sighs. "Thankfully, Sana received the antidote promptly. Still, I expect her to be in this semi-unconscious state for the next few days while her body fights hard to recover."

"I am still trying to figure out how this could have happened," Satoru says, holding his chin in his hand.

"Has my sister been out of the palace much, Your Majesty?" Eirlys asks.

"Not to my knowledge," Satoru answers.

Eirlys sighs. "The thing with Sana is that she is like a cat."

The sudden statement comes as a surprise.

"Why do you say that?" Satoru asks.

"She's been like this since she was young. She will disappear and then come back at random times. She likes to explore—it used to worry our parents ever so much."

Satoru glances over at Sana once again. "I see."

Eirlys holds onto Sana's hand, lacing her fingers between her sister's. She squeezes them tightly. "She is a fighter, though. Soon enough, she will be up and running again. I know it."

Satoru wonders if the lady in front of him is aware that her sister is the Mutoren. These small glimpses of

Sana's past that her sister is disclosing are . . . intriguing. After all, Satoru has not learned much about her—if anything at all—since her unmasking. He wonders if he can obtain some more information from this young healer.

"So, how were things going with her as the temporary first-hand guard?" Eirlys pipes up.

"She is a good fighter," Satoru replies, "and now she is training our soldiers."

"We are so proud of her." Eirlys beams. "Just like Father said, she will excel in whatever she chooses to do."

There is a small pause.

"However, I am glad that the palace didn't announce her name to the kingdom," she adds. "She would not have liked that."

"Is that so?" Satoru asks, although he knows that already.

"Yes, Your Majesty," Eirlys replies. "She is quite private."

"And what was she like as a child?" Satoru tries. He wonders if this question is too sudden, but he cannot diminish his increasing curiosity.

To Satoru's relief, Eirlys does not seem to think anything of it. "She is a hard worker, Your Majesty," she replies. "She appears indifferent on the surface, but deep down, she has a big heart. I only wish I had more years with her."

Satoru raises his eyebrows. "What do you mean by that?"

"I was four years old when Sana first came into my life. I loved her from the moment I saw her. I still remember."

Satoru nods. He listens intently, wanting to know more.

"But when I was six, she disappeared. I was eighteen by the time Sana returned."

Does this mean they are not blood-related? Perhaps she really is *Qietian*, he ponders.

"Anyway, I must go," Eirlys says as she stands. "I have a few visits to make tomorrow in the early hours. I shall try to be back in the evening if things allow."

Suddenly, an inaudible sound floats into the air. Satoru's ears perk and his eyes snap towards Sana's face.

Eirlys peers at her sister, then smiles. "She is such a loud sleeper." Eirlys laughs. "Do not be surprised if she starts talking."

"Right," Satoru says, slightly amused.

"In her sleep, she once confessed to me that she'd eaten the last dessert Mother brought from a famous bakery in Ajisai," Eirlys says, laughing some more.

Satoru bites his lip. There is something very amusing about learning these sides to the Mutoren.

"I shall get going then, Prince Takashi." Eirlys bows as she makes her way out.

Satoru gives a nod in return. "Thank you, Healer Harlande."

After the Mutoren's sister leaves the room, Satoru sits back in the chair and watches the girl lying before him. He gazes at her intently before heading to the bathroom to refill the bowl of water which sits by her bedside.

Satoru dips a cloth inside as he remembers the day the Mutoren burnt herself. He thinks of her delicate hand on his lap as he carefully wrapped it with a bandage, then wonders why this thought is crossing his mind.

The prince wrings the water from the cloth before folding it into a neat rectangle and placing it on the girl's forehead. He then sits back and sighs.

Satoru's eyes linger on the window. It is dark outside. His mind drifts towards the case of the killings and he wonders if dead bodies are still appearing in the Kingdom of Rheahldere. He had advised Queen Saeya to stay in her land for the time being—with everything, it seemed unsafe to visit Shinrin at this time.

He glances at the girl in front of him and wonders why he is so fascinated by her. Why had something torn so hard at his heart that day when she had coughed up blood? The sight was frightening, yes, but something much deeper had clenched inside him at that very moment. He had felt almost suffocated.

The more he looks at her face, the faster his heart begins to beat. Something in him seems to have changed since the day on the rooftop.

A small mumble comes from the girl's lips. Satoru looks at her. He wonders if she said something. He waits but hears nothing.

A small mumble again.

Is she saying something? Satoru wonders. He peers at her curiously. Perhaps he is imagining things?

Sana whispers, "Please—"

Satoru leans close to her, his eyes full of curiosity.

"Don't—"

Satoru blinks and cocks his head. *Her sister is right. She really does talk in her sleep.*

"Don't—" The girl's eyebrows are furrowed, and her eyes are scrunched. She turns a little, as if she is struggling against something. Although she is asleep, the pain of whatever she is experiencing is evident. Her breaths become rapid and shallow. Beads of perspiration form on her forehead. It is strange, seeing her so vulnerable and defenceless.

Satoru looks at her. Something cracks inside him once more. He almost feels he should not be here witnessing this.

"Please—" Sana whispers.

"What is it, Harlande?" Satoru manages a whisper.

She doesn't respond. There is a silence.

"Come back—" she finishes. She starts to shake as her vulnerability overspills.

Satoru grasps onto Sana's hand in an attempt to calm her down. To his surprise, her hand immediately tightens around his and her tremors vibrate through their grip. His heart thumps hard against his chest. He looks at the Mutoren, wide-eyed.

"Calm down, Harlande," Satoru whispers. He wonders what she is seeing. Perhaps it is a memory? Or a nightmare?

"I am here," Satoru continues. "You are safe."

He wonders if she can hear anything at all.

After a short while, Sana's grip loosens. Her breathing slows, and the muscles on her face relax. Her chest continues to rise and fall in rhythm, just like earlier.

If he had not witnessed it, he never would have

guessed at her unconscious struggles.

Satoru's fingers linger on hers for a second longer, before he withdraws his hand. He looks at her face and wonders again about her past. The girl in front of him has always been nothing short of mysterious, but in this moment, he realises there is so much more he would like to know about her.

CHAPTER SIX

Memories

A SEVEN-YEAR-OLD SANA enters her home. It is a small, wooden hut situated in Sugi, a very quiet and sparsely populated village. She pushes open the front door and quietly steps inside.

A woman is sprawled on the cushions by the dining table with a trail of saliva oozing out of her parted mouth. There are unwashed plates and bowls scattered across the table and used chopsticks which have left greasy marks on the surface. A few grains of rice lay next to them. There are remnants of liquid spillages on the floor. The stains are rather unsightly.

Sana creeps towards the woman and gently pokes her shoulder. "Mother," Sana whispers.

The woman does not respond.

"Mother," Sana tries again.

The woman stirs.

Sana shakes the woman's shoulder a little more firmly this time. "Mother, I am hungry."

The woman frowns and tuts. She then slowly opens her eyes. They are brown and friendly, but Sana finds this look to be deceiving.

"What is it, Kudon?" the woman snaps. Her speech is slurred and unclear. She sits up and wipes the drool from her mouth with her sleeve before looking at Sana and raising an eyebrow. Suddenly, she bursts into manic laughter.

Sana jumps.

"Did you—did you just call me *mother*?" she exclaims. She takes a moment to catch her breath before leaning close to Sana and glaring. "I am *not* your mother."

The stench of alcohol makes its way through to Sana's nostrils. Sana takes a step back but is not fast enough to dodge the harsh nudge to her shoulder.

The woman continues to glower at her. "Don't you

ever call me that again."

Sana blinks back tears. *Don't cry. Don't cry.*

The woman suddenly laughs loudly once more. "Darling, if you are hungry . . . learn to cook, you pathetic *child*."

Something slices through Sana's heart.

The woman leans onto the surface of the table. Her clumsy arm knocks some of the bowls onto the ground. They land on the floor, creating a racket. Soon enough, the woman joins them on the ground and begins to snore once more.

Little Sana stands there, exasperated.

✤

A tall boy shoves Sana to the ground. She falls onto the gravel on her bottom and crosses her arms over her head, bracing herself for the fists and kicks that are about to come. Soon enough, the harsh punches and throws from various boys and girls land on her.

Sana squeezes her eyes shut as she prays for it to end.

"Stupid Kudon!" the tall boy shouts as he continues to lead Sana's torment.

"Stupid Kudon!" the rest of the boys and girls chime in as Sana endures more hard blows.

"What type of stupid name is that?" The tall boy snickers. "Why are you called Kudon when you are clearly so poor and battered?"

Sana's anger swells. She braces against the punches and manages to stand up before attempting to lunge at the boy. He steps to the side and she misses completely. A girl behind her shoves her and Sana falls back down.

"Your clothes are so ugly!" the girl shouts before pulling a face at Sana.

Another boy follows with, "You stink! Don't you ever wash?"

"Let's beat her up!" the tall boy announces.

The rest of the children laugh as they continue to hit Sana and pull at her hair.

Suddenly, a few drops of rain land on Sana's head. Soon enough, the dry ground becomes saturated with water, and it turns into sloshy, wet mud.

"Let's go, guys! Leave her to rot!" the tall boy shouts over the rain.

The children put their hands over their heads as they try to keep themselves dry. The crowd disperses and Sana is left in the middle, her already stained clothes now drenched from rain and mud.

✾

Sana trudges across the wet, sloshing mud and plops down. She has no idea how long she has been walking for. Her stomach growls with hunger, and every inch of her body aches. Her hair is absolutely drenched from the rain.

Suddenly, a shadow flashes past the corner of Sana's eye. She turns quickly to catch sight of it, but before she has time to react, a hand covers her face, and she immediately falls unconscious.

✾

Sana wakes up. The room is dark, and she has no idea where she is. The scent of delicious food wafts towards her nostrils. She sits up immediately and her eyes widen at the sight in front of her.

Is this a dream?

Although pain is aching through every corner of her body, Sana is distracted by the vastly adorned table in front of her. Amongst the candlelight are numerous bowls and plates of absolutely delightful-looking food. Her mouth waters at the sight.

Kneeling next to the table on a cushion is a person wearing a black-and-maroon robe. He wears a wooden mask which has a black circle with black flames radiating out from it—it is a symbol of a black sun.

"Eat up, my child," the man says from underneath his mask.

Sana has no idea who he is, but she immediately dives for the food in front of her with her bare hands. She eats like a starved, wild animal, barely chewing before swallowing. She practically inhales the food each time she stuffs as much as she can into her mouth.

Afterwards, her belly is big and satisfied. She had no idea what most of the food was, but it, for sure, tasted heavenly.

She glances at the masked man.

"Filled your stomach, my child?" he asks.

Sana nods ferociously. *Who is he?* She will have to thank him.

"Follow me, my child," he says. He rises from the cushion and strides across the tatami floor before sliding a wooden, parchment-lined door open.

Sana stumbles behind him down a few dark corridors. Her feet create sounds of little footsteps on the wooden floorboards. Soon, she is led outside to a clearing, one where there are many other children standing around—fifteen, perhaps. The area is large. There are various obstacles laid out across it. It is dark. Perhaps it is nighttime.

"Join them," the masked man says, gesturing to the

crowd.

Sana wonders who these children are but follows obediently. The children are all looking around. They appear just as confused as she is.

The masked man walks towards them. “My children,” he announces, his voice louder and firmer than before. “I am sure you have all enjoyed your meals. Have you all filled your stomachs?”

“Yes!” various voices respond.

“Well, if you would like to have abundant food like this for the rest of your lives, it is very simple. You see that big symbol in the distance?” He gestures to the tall wall opposite the children that stands right at the end of the obstacles. Painted on it is a large, black circle with flames radiating outwards. “Be amongst the first to get through the course and to touch the circle,” the man finishes.

Sana recognises this as the same symbol that is on the man’s mask. The children gaze on, wide-eyed as they begin to whisper amongst themselves.

“Stand behind the line, my children.” The man points to a thick, black line that is painted horizontally across the ground.

The children follow obediently. Sana shuffles herself so that her feet are just behind the line. She eyes the symbol in the distance. Her right foot slides backwards into a stance as she readies herself. She will do anything to never feel the pain of hunger again.

"On my count," the man shouts. "Three. Two. One. Go!"

The children scramble like wild animals. Sana sprints as fast as she can, even as every ache in her body from where she was hit earlier intensifies and gnaws away at her bones. She pumps her arms and makes her strides as wide as her little legs can manage.

Soon, Sana reaches some bars—the first obstacle. She leaps over them, only to run straight into dangling ropes. There are harsh, spikey-looking things below them, which tells her that she does not want to fall. She jumps onto the first rope and swings herself forward before leaping onto the next. She uses every muscle in her body and every last bit of strength she has to get past each hurdle.

Sana now faces a wall. She grips onto the lumpy parts protruding from this wall and using all her might, she begins to climb.

Several beams, bars, ropes, and walls later, the symbol is finally nearing. Sana is out of breath and her lungs are about to burst. Her heart is pounding inside her ribcage so hard that she forgets the rest of the pain aching through her body. She has new scratches and grazes all over her hands and knees.

Sana leaps towards the symbol and stretches out her hand to touch it. Two boys make it a few seconds before her. The three of them brace one hand on their thighs, panting, but all make sure to keep their other hand glued to the symbol. Their desperation to never feel the pain of hunger again is clear.

Another masked man appears by the wall. "Well done, children," he says.

Out of nowhere, another hand covers Sana's face. Once again, she falls unconscious.

✾

"Wake up, my children." A new voice of a young man drifts into Sana's ears.

She stirs and slowly opens her eyes. As she sits up, her senses slowly fade back into focus. She is in another dark room, one dimly lit by a few candles. There are three other children—boys—who are slowly waking up just like her.

"Come." The man gestures to the four plump, purple cushions in front of him. He himself is kneeling on one. There are black and maroon fabrics folded neatly in front of each one.

The children obediently get up and kneel on the cushions. Sana looks around. The other boys are around her age—perhaps some are a few years older.

"Let us go around and introduce ourselves using our full names," the masked man says.

Sana realises she is the first one. "Kudon Ozaki," she says.

One boy bursts into laughter and then immediately covers his mouth. Sana is used to this reaction. She turns to see that it was the young boy next to her, the one with short, lilac hair. His fringe, however, is long and falls sideways over his face, covering one of his amber eyes. He is thin and pale.

"Izumi Kido," the lilac-haired boy whispers. He blinks at Sana a few times, as if to say that he did not mean to laugh.

"Yuka Kawano," the third boy follows. He has sharp, sunset eyes and sleek, black hair that falls to his shoulders.

"Eric Rayes," the fourth boy finishes. His eyes are green and piercing. His nose is pointy, and his jaw is angular. His chestnut-coloured hair is tied into a tight bun.

"Splendid," the masked man says. "Now, your new uniforms are in front of you all. It is a privilege for all of you to be here. From today onwards, you will undergo rigorous training to become elite assassins. Welcome to the Kurai Clan."

CHAPTER SEVEN

The Kurai Clan

YOUNG SANA BRACES HERSELF AS the intense pain of burning metal is pressed into her skin. A masked man holds a scalding, hot piece of metal—shaped into the black sun of the Kurai Clan—into a special ink before pressing it between Sana's shoulder blades.

Sana squeezes her eyes shut and tells herself not to cry. The pain is absolutely excruciating. It is raw, painful, and blistering.

The masked man removes the metal to reveal the

black sun now branded onto her skin. He hovers his hand just above the symbol and mumbles something beneath his mask. Soon enough, the symbol disappears.

"You now have the official symbol of the Kurai Clan branded onto you," the masked man says to seven-year-old Sana.

She is struggling to take in all of this information. Too much has happened over the past few days, and she does not really understand what is happening.

"This will stay with you for the rest of your life. Anyone from the Kurai Clan will be able to reveal this symbol from you with the Kurai Code I just said," he continues. "Now, please make your way to the next room."

Sana slowly stands and steps out of the room. Her mind swirls with uncertainty and the pits of her stomach seep ice into her core. What is happening? What has she stumbled into?

She gently slides open the door of the next room and finds that the three boys from earlier are already there. There is also another masked man sitting at the front, awaiting her. There are so many of these masked men, and they all look the same.

Sana sits down next to the boys. They also appear unsettled, and their facial expressions reflect each other's discomfort. Izumi shuffles to sit closer next to Sana.

"Children," the masked man says. He adjusts his position before continuing. "Now that you have all been branded, I will run through the rules of the Kurai Clan."

Sana gulps. Eric wipes his nose.

"Number one: if one attempts to leave the Kurai Clan, they will be punished and then executed. Number two: No one in the Kurai Clan will be called by their birth name. Only their Kurai names shall be used. You will be rewarded with this name once we find your fighting style. Prior to that, you will be identified by numbers."

Sana listens on, her eyes wide. Her little hands are balled into tight fists which rest on her thighs.

"Three: One shall always obey the orders of the Kurai Clan. If they do not, they will be punished."

Izumi hugs his knees. He peers around the room before eyeing the masked man again.

"Four: One shall never miss an appointment with their assigned Healer. This will take place every fortnight."

Yuka blinks.

"Those are the four clauses of the Kurai Clan, which we follow under Master Kurai's orders," the masked man finishes. "You must understand that it is an absolute privilege that you have all been selected. It means that you are the strongest amongst your peers, and here, you will become even stronger. You will work for us and be rewarded for it. Now please, make your way to the next room where you will meet your assigned Healer."

✾

Sana sits on the examination couch, waiting for someone to come inside the room. This room is different from the others she has been in. Unlike the rest—which were lined with tatami and lit by only a few candles—this room is spacious, has stone walls and floors, and emits a blue glow.

Exhaustion sweeps over her. Her little mind is tired and confused from everything that is happening, and her heavy eyelids threaten to close.

Soon, the stone door slides open. A young man and a young boy enter. They both wear wheat-coloured robes.

The young man approaches her. "Hello, my child," he says. "My name is Healer Renge." He then gestures to the young boy next to him. "This is Healer Reishi. He is still in training."

Sana looks at the young boy. For the first time since coming here, a small bit of warmth flows into Sana's heart. The boy has olive skin, soft ivory hair which falls to just above his shoulders, and gentle, honey-coloured eyes. He looks at Sana and cocks his head to one side. He smiles.

Healer Renge puts a small case on the surface next to the examination couch before he opens it up. Inside, are various vials and syringes. He begins to set up his equipment.

"My child, I am afraid we need to give you a few injections," Healer Renge says to Sana.

Sana's eyebrows furrow as she shuffles backwards on the couch. Her worry appears in her round eyes. She wants to go home, but the image of Mother sprawled out on the cushions crosses her mind. She squeezes her eyes shut and exhales.

"We will need your arm first, my child," Healer Renge says gently.

Sana reluctantly holds out her left arm and looks down at the floor. Her eyes and lips turn downwards.

"Reishi," Healer Renge says. "Every two weeks, these children will need to be injected with Soltair. Do you remember what that is?"

"Yes, Healer Renge," Reishi replies. His voice is soft

and reflects his kind face. "It heightens one's body and enhances not only their senses but also their agility, strength, and intelligence."

"Well done, Reishi," his trainer replies. He gently takes Sana's arm and injects a cyan solution into her vein.

Sana winces and holds back tears.

"And what will you expect to see, Reishi?" Healer Renge asks.

"The patient will experience a high fever for the next forty-eight hours whilst their body changes and adapts. In the long term, the patient's lifespan will be rapidly shortened—to be exact, their lives are shortened to just under a quarter of their original life expectancy."

"Well done again, Reishi," Healer Renge compliments. "I can see they truly meant it when they said they recruited a prodigy in Healing." Healer Renge reaches back into his case and takes out a thicker needle attached to a metal cylinder. The needle is frighteningly large.

Sana takes one look at it and immediately feels like she is about to faint.

"My child, we have one more injection to do," the young man says to Sana.

She cannot hold back her tears anymore and they well up behind her eyes.

"Reishi, this cylinder contains the Hoseki," Healer Renge says to the young boy. "Do you remember what it is?"

"Yes, Healer Renge," the boy replies. "This tiny stone contains Kurai magic, which not only enables it to sense one's location at any given time, but it has also been mixed with a certain poison that will cause one's death if they try to remove the Hoseki from their body."

Healer Renge nods, impressed. He turns to face Sana. "My child," he says, "this Hoseki will bind you to the Kurai Clan forever."

He lifts the side of Sana's shirt just enough to expose the side of her abdomen, then holds the instrument taut on her skin.

Sana's breathing quickens.

The healer presses down with his thumb and there is a loud click before an overwhelming stab slices through her. The pain is absolutely excruciating.

She bursts into tears.

"I am sorry, my child," Healer Renge says as he puts his instruments back into his case.

Reishi looks at Sana. He is not that much older than her. His eyes reflect some empathy as he leans towards her and gently clasps her hand. "Don't cry," he whispers.

Sana looks at the young boy with soft, ivory hair

and kind, honey-coloured eyes and wonders what is going to happen to her from now on.

CHAPTER EIGHT

Healer Reishi

DESPITE BECOMING CLOSER WITH HER three peers, Sana has had to get used to the harsh and unforgiving training environment around her since becoming a part of the Kurai Clan.

However, if there is one thing which she has learned so far, it is: Do not be last.

The first time she came last was in endurance training. Her punishment was three days without food. Another time, she came last in an examination that tested them on the ancient tongue of Shinrin. Her punishment was to be immersed in a tub of ice-cold water for three hours.

Amidst the punishments, the training, and the years that went by, the fighting style she developed was compared to a spider's movements. She earned the name *Kumo*.

Now, thirteen-year-old Sana and her fellow members kneel in front of Master Komori, their teacher of fighting and defence. He too, like the rest of the Masters of the Kurai Clan, wears a wooden mask with the Kurai symbol over his face.

"Kumo, Okami, Tora, Hebi," he says, nodding at each of them as he calls them by their Kurai names. "I have gathered you all today, because I have an important announcement to make." Master Komori eyes each of his students. He has a large black cloth bag next to him. "Okami—" The Master turns to face Izumi, whose eyes widen as he is singled out. "—please, tell me what is clause one of the Kurai Conduct?"

"If one attempts to leave the Kurai Clan, they are to be punished and then executed, Master Komori," Izumi replies. He bows deeply. His lilac fringe falls in front of him.

"Well done, Okami," the Master replies.

He takes the black cloth bag from next to him and turns it upside down. There is a thump when the object inside lands on the floor. It rolls out onto the tatami. The lifeless head of a young girl rolls towards Yuka before stopping. It leaves a trail of blood stains.

Yuka gasps. A small scream escapes Izumi's lips before he covers his mouth. Eric slaps his hands over his eyes. The unexpected, gruesome sight causes Sana to catch a breath before she immediately looks away. A sickness rises inside her stomach and a pulse of fear releases inside her. Her heart begins to thump rapidly.

"Look at it, students," Master Komori commands, "do not turn away. I repeat, look."

Yuka's eyes wobble, and he shakes as he stares at the lifeless head. Izumi looks on and appears to be about to burst into tears. Eric struggles to maintain eye contact, and Sana tries to stare straight through the head.

"We invest an unimaginable amount of kudon to train you children," Master Komori tuts. "But you still get little idiots like this. It is a privilege to be selected by the Kurai Clan, as we take on only the very best." Master Komori places a finger on the tatami, just shy of the trail of blood. "This little rascal attempted to climb over the outer walls of the Kurai infrastructure. I should think that, after so much teaching and training, one should be smart enough to know that this would not work."

Staring through the head is not working, Sana finds. She picks a space slightly above the head's left ear.

"This was an extremely selfish thing to do," Master Komori continues. "Especially as the punishment not only applies to the perpetrator, but also to their team members as well. This girl was made to endure torture by her fellow teammates before she was executed and dismembered."

Sana is about to vomit. Her back is dripping with perspiration as the fear inside her intensifies. Her mouth is filling up with saliva and her stomach muscles are urging to retch. She uses everything in her power to keep it down, for if she vomits, she is sure she will receive some sort of punishment.

"So, my students," Master Komori says, "this is to remind you to never disobey the Kurai, and to understand that the Kurai eyes are always on you. Is that clear?"

"Yes, Master Komori!" The four children shout in unison and in fear before they bow down completely until their foreheads touch the floor.

✾

Sana sits on the examination couch. This is something

she is very used to, for she is here every fortnight. She has started to feel that, every two weeks, coming into this room is the only time she can feel somewhat at ease. Whenever her mind starts to cloud over with the darkness that surrounds her, Healer Reishi will arrive to make her heart feel at peace.

The stone door slides open and Healer Reishi steps inside, wearing his usual wheat-coloured robe.

Sana looks at the young man. He must be around seventeen or eighteen years old, now. Three years ago—which is six years after she had started with the Kurai Clan—Healer Reishi had begun practising without a trainer. As a young, gentle prodigy in Healing, he has become extremely well-respected within the Kurai Clan, and is well-liked by her fellow team members.

Healer Reishi greets Sana. "Kumo."

"Healer Reishi." She smiles back at him.

"You know the drill," he says softly as he opens up his case and draws up the cyan-coloured fluid in his syringe.

Sana holds out an arm like she does every fortnight. The sharpness of the needle prick barely fazes her as Reishi injects the fluid into her vein.

"As usual, you will expect to have a high temperature over the next forty-eight hours," Reishi explains.

Sana nods. She looks into his kind, warm, honey eyes, and her heart thumps. This new, strange feeling seems to have begun a few weeks ago. This warmth continues to expand inside her.

Reishi proceeds to do his usual medical examination. He gestures for Sana's hand and presses gently onto her wrist, feeling for her pulse.

Sana gazes at his soft facial features and notes how his eyes stare at the floor with concentration as he counts.

Something flutters inside her chest.

"Your heart rate is a little fast today," Reishi says.

Sana blinks at him but remains silent.

"Look straight ahead," he says to Sana before holding up a glass lens to peer inside each of her eyes.

Each time he does this, his face closes in on hers so much that Sana can almost feel his breath on her skin. She has been going through this for the past three years, yet for some reason, she is starting to notice things she didn't notice before. The fluttering inside her heart is going out of control.

As Reishi continues with the rest of the examination, Sana is absolutely dazed. She continues to admire his gentleness, his kind manner, and his expertise. For some reason, each time Sana comes for her Soltair injection, Healer Reishi's face grows more and more . . . attractive?

"Kumo?" Reishi repeats.

Sana snaps back into the present. She looks at him. "Yes?" she asks.

"Your hand," he says. He points to the palm of her left hand which is raw and painful, full of grazes and broken skin.

"Oh." Sana is not sure what to say.

"I need to bandage it," Reishi says. He looks at her with sincerity.

Sana is suddenly out of breath.

"They sure do train you children hard," he says as he places Sana's hand on a cushion and begins to bandage her hand. The golden flecks in his eyes exude an aura of sadness. Healer Reishi rolls out the white bandage. His hands skilfully wrap it around hers, layer by layer.

Sana has watched him bandage things so many times, to the point where she can picture every line and angle of his hands from back to front. Something about his gentle, skilful-yet-delicate hands makes him so attractive.

She wonders how it would feel to lace her fingers with his. Immediately, the colour of roses blooms onto her cheeks.

"So, what have you been learning over the past two weeks?" Reishi says as he secures a knot on the bandage, snapping Sana back into reality.

"Oh, um—" Why is she so dazed today? "—More agility . . . and the ancient tongue."

"I see," Reishi replies. He sighs and the sadness appears in his eyes once more.

"Healer Reishi—" Sana suddenly says out of nowhere. Her heart beats wildly inside her chest.

"Yes?"

"What is your real name?" Sana asks. Her eyes are round and big as she gazes at Healer Reishi.

The question comes as a surprise to the young healer. He blinks at the young girl. "Why do you ask?"

Is it appropriate of me to ask? Sana wonders in a panic. She is aware of clause two of the Kurai Conduct, but she thought perhaps it only applied to the trainees and not the healers. She has always wanted to know his real name.

"Sorry—" Sana apologises.

"Seiji Hayashi," he says, without another thought. He smiles. "And yourself, Kumo?"

Sana's heart throbs once more. *What a beautiful name.*

"I'm. . .I'm—uh—well—" A surge of embarrassment

rises inside her. She does not want to say her name.

But Reishi is looking at her with his round, kind eyes.

"Uh . . . Kudon Ozaki," Sana manages to finish. She looks at Reishi and braces herself for his laughter.

"Kudon?" Reishi asks. His eyebrows raise up with genuine surprise. "That is interesting." He holds his hand to his chin. "I've never heard of Kudon as a name before."

"I got made fun for it a lot," Sana admits.

"Bullying is never acceptable, Kudon," Reishi replies. Hearing his soft voice call out her name causes Sana's breath to catch.

"If you were not a healer, what do you think you would have become?" Sana asks out of nowhere once again.

The young girl's spontaneity makes him smile. "You are always full of questions, are you not?" Reishi laughs.

Sana looks to the floor shyly, the roses blooming in her cheeks once more. She is always eager to know more about him.

"A musician, perhaps," Reishi replies after some time.

Sana looks at him curiously. "A musician? You play?"

"I wish I had the opportunity to. But, I have always been fond of music. It is something very beautiful. It speaks out one's heart and one's thoughts."

Sana nods, enjoying every minute of his presence.

Healer Reishi pauses, before he looks at Sana once more. "You know, you remind me of my little sister," he reveals.

"I do?"

"Yes. Quite a lot, in fact. She had dark hair and dark eyes. She was small and had a rather adorable face, just like you," he replies.

Adorable? The warmth in Sana's cheeks increases. Her ears heat up. "You—you had?"

"Unfortunately, she passed away," Reishi says. "Her heart had been weak since she was born."

Sana is taken aback. "I am sorry," she whispers.

"That is all right. She was six and I was ten. When I met you for the first time six years ago, I almost thought it was her sitting on the examination couch."

Sana listens on, holding onto her bandaged hand.

"If only I had the knowledge back then that I have now." He sighs. "Little Ayame may still be alive." He pauses and looks at Sana. "This isn't a place for a child to be," he says quietly.

This statement comes as another surprise to Sana.

Before she can stop herself, the words escape her. "This isn't a place for a smart young man to be, either." Something unthinkable crosses Sana's mind. "Perhaps we can escape," she whispers.

Reishi stiffens. He does not breathe a word, but looks at the young girl in front of him. He can tell by her eyes that she has unspeakable determination. However, if they are to take any action on what she had just suggested, they would most definitely be treading on extremely thin ice.

"Kumo, it is time for you to return," he whispers back, not wanting the young girl to dwell on this thought. He will need to think things through. "The medical examination is complete."

CHAPTER NINE

The Hoseki

A FOURTEEN-YEAR-OLD SANA sits with her peers on the tatami floor just a corridor from the medical room as they await their fortnightly injection and check-up.

"I cannot believe that soon we will be assigned our first mission," Eric says. "I'm scared."

"Me too," Yuka replies. "I am not sure I want to turn fifteen yet."

"Thankfully, I still have two more years to go,"

Izumi joins in.

"How did we all come to be here anyway?" Eric whispers. He peers at each of his friends. "I don't think we ever talked about it."

"I was sitting in the rain after I was beaten up by some bullies," Sana says. "Next thing I know, I was here."

Izumi gasps. "That's horrible!" he says.

"I ran away from the orphanage I was at," Yuka says quietly. "The staff there were nasty. Next thing I knew, I was here, too."

"I was out in the forest picking mushrooms," Izumi whispers. "I didn't have anywhere to go. I think I was five."

"I was at an orphanage, too," Eric adds. "We were actually on a trip to the local park. I lost my way and when I woke up, I was here."

The four children look at each other curiously. For the last seven years, they have gone through unimaginable pain together, yet they hardly know a thing about each other.

"I guess none of us have a family, huh?" Yuka comments.

Sana thinks of Mother. She sighs.

"You know, I've always wondered. . .what happened to the rest of the children who didn't make it to the wall?"

Izumi whispers.

"What do you mean?" Eric asks.

"Remember the first day when we ran across that yard?" Izumi continues. "Only four of us made it. What happened to the rest?"

"Oh, I heard they go through other tests, too," Yuka replies. "Like, for intelligence for example. I think ours was physical endurance and agility."

"Really?" Izumi asks.

"Yes, I've heard from other members through whispers here and there. I'm guessing that is how Healer Reishi came here too. But the ones who didn't make it through anything . . . I'm not sure," Yuka answers.

Sana's ears perk up at the mention of Reishi's name.

"I like Healer Reishi," Eric says. "He is the kindest person ever. I wonder how come he is so smart? Isn't he only like, eighteen?"

"He has been practising as an independent healer since he was fifteen," Izumi says. "If that doesn't prove that he's a true prodigy, I don't know what does!"

"I like Healer Reishi, too," Sana joins in before she can stop herself.

"I think you *fancy* him," Yuka teases.

Sana immediately blushes. "Wha-What? No—I don't!"

"Look, you're blushing," Yuka probes further.

Sana attempts to swat at him and Yuka leaps backwards, dodging out of the way.

The wooden door slides open, and a masked man enters.

"Tora," he commands. "Please make your way to the medical room."

Yuka immediately stands straight and bows deeply. Seriousness returns to each of the children's eyes. Sana kneels with the rest.

"Yes, Master," Yuka replies. The rest of the children bow after him.

✾

Sana almost skips along the corridor as she makes her way to the medical room. There are already butterflies fluttering inside her stomach. By now, it is undeniable that meeting Healer Reishi once every two weeks is the one thing that keeps her going through all the hardship.

Sana slides open the stone door. Healer Reishi is already there in his wheat-coloured robe. He immediately smiles at her. "Azuki," he calls.

Sana blushes. Over the past year, Sana and Healer Reishi have become rather close. He had even begun calling her *Azuki*, which he had explained was his pet name for his little sister—he claims she was small and adorable like a red bean.

Sana jumps onto the couch and holds out her arm like she does every time. Again, the sharp scratch barely fazes her as Reishi gives her the injection.

He proceeds to do the medical examination and Sana watches him intently. She admires his long, curly eyelashes and how his soft and attractive facial features exude both an aura of striking intelligence as well as overwhelming kindness.

Although Reishi has expressed his fondness for her numerous times, he has made it obvious that he cares for her like his own sister. Sana, however, has intense romantic feelings for him which are plummeting through the roof in his presence.

Reishi appears to be rather in a hurry today. Sana blinks at him.

"I am glad to see that, for once, you are not battered and bruised," Healer Reishi says to her. He puts his equipment back into his case and closes it. "All right, the medical examination is complete," he says.

Is that it? Sana thinks. *This has got to be the shortest slot ever.* She puffs out her cheeks.

"Azuki," Reishi says sternly. He has seriousness in his eyes. "I apologise for rushing through like that," he says, “but I needed time to talk to you.”

Sana immediately straightens. “Yes?”

“Do you remember what we spoke about that one time?”

“Of course,” Sana replies. Since she made the daring suggestion of escaping the Kurai Clan a year ago, Reishi has been working hard on obtaining as much information as he can to aid her escape.

“You need to get out of here,” Reishi whispers to her. His large eyes are almost burning into hers. “You need to live your life, Azuki. My sister did not get to, and I cannot see that happen to someone I care about ever again.” Reishi’s sincerity is radiating from him.

Sana gulps. “But Reishi,” Sana whispers, “won’t I die if we try to get rid of the Hoseki?”

“According to the principles of the Hoseki, yes,” Reishi replies. “Not only that, but I have come to find out that the poison will also be released if one turns the age of five-and-twenty. But there is a way to stop it.”

Sana’s eyes tremble. “But—But—what about the Soltair? Hasn’t that reduced my life span by a lot already?”

Reishi places his hands over Sana’s, causing her breathing to accelerate. “You will see,” he replies, not really answering her question. “The most important thing is that we get rid of the Hoseki first."

"Right," Sana answers.

"We will need to plan things meticulously." His hands are like brands on her skin. "Firstly, I need to find out how to deactivate whichever poison is embedded inside the Hoseki, so that it is neither released when we try to remove it, nor when you reach the age of five-and-twenty. Secondly, I need to deactivate the Hoseki's ability to know your location."

Sana listens on, gripping Reishi's hands.

"Thirdly, we need to find a way to actually get you *out* of the Kurai infrastructure."

"This is going to be difficult," Sana whispers, remembering the lifeless head of the girl. Fear sparks inside her. "Someone tried to climb it and they were executed."

"There must be a way, Azuki."

"How can you be so certain?"

"It appears that my brain has earned me some respect amongst the various Kurai Masters." Reishi manages a small laugh. "They have welcomed me into some of their meetings as they believe I can use my intellect to enhance the things they are working on."

"So—so what do we do, Reishi?" Sana asks.

"I am still working on it," he replies. "There are

many things I still need to find out. I do not have access to everything."

Sana swallows.

"Azuki, you often train in various parts inside the Kurai Clan, correct?"

Sana nods vigorously.

"Then you shall seek out the floor plan of this place as well as information about the wall of the infrastructure. Find out how things are. I know you have a good memory."

Sana nods vigorously once again.

"I know that one part of gaining access through the wall involves a keystone, which is something each of the Kurai Masters have. However, there is a lot left I do not know, and actually getting our hands on one is going to prove to be a challenge."

"Right," Sana whispers as she takes in all of this information. "Reishi—we are doing this together, right?" Sana asks as worry seeps inside her. She cannot shake off a feeling of fear.

"You are my main priority, Azuki."

"No—please. If we do this, please let us do it together," Sana pleads, her obsidian eyes wide with emotion. "I cannot go on in a world without you."

Reishi blinks for a moment, slightly taken aback. He

then leans in and looks into Sana's eyes. "First, let me finish up gathering information," Reishi replies. "The next time we meet, we shall share what information we have obtained."

"Do you have a Hoseki inside you too, Reishi?" Sana asks.

He nods. "But you are strong," Reishi says as he looks into her eyes once more. "You are a fighter. You are going to go on to do amazing things with your life. So, promise me one thing, Azuki."

Sana waits for what he is about to say.

"No matter what happens, you must do everything you can to stay alive and to live a long, healthy, and happy life. Can you promise me that?"

"Only—only if you promise me one thing back," Sana replies. Tears are welling up in her eyes.

Reishi did not expect this reply. He gives a small sigh and manages a slight smile. "Go on, then," he says.

"You need to promise me that *you* will do everything you can to escape with me. That we will do it together," Sana whispers.

Reishi thinks for a moment. "Very well," he replies. "I promise."

"Then I promise, too," Sana says.

The two of them look at each other. Their eyes

reflect an intense mix of emotions, all of which are embedded in fear. One thing they know is certain, however, is the deep bond they share and the true care they hold for one another.

CHAPTER TEN

Unfolding the Plan

REISHI SITS BY A TABLE inside the medical room. Unlike the blue glow that shines in the room where he usually examines his patients, this room glows an eerie red—the light reflects oddly on his open case, which is sitting on the table.

The stone door slides open and a masked man enters.

Reishi immediately stands and bows deeply. “Good evening,” he greets.

"Healer Reishi." The man nods. He takes out a small, glass vial containing a clear liquid and hands it over to the young man. "Please," the man says.

Reishi bows again before receiving the vial with both of his hands. He proceeds to draw the solution into a syringe and injects it into a vein in his own arm.

The man watches him behind his mask. After it is done, the man nods. "Well done, you may leave," the man says.

Reishi disposes of the equipment before closing his case and making his way out. As soon as the coast is clear, he hurries back to his allocated chamber.

As soon as Reishi steps inside, he immediately locks his door, puts his case on his bedside table, and opens it back up. In a haste, he attaches a new needle to a syringe and pierces the very vein he injected earlier, before drawing out the smallest amount of fluid as he can.

This has been his monthly ritual over the past year.

The colour of his blood is tinged orange. He proceeds to empty the syringe into a separate glass vial, takes a moment to sit on his bed, and then hurries back to his usual medical room with his case.

Once inside his familiar room, Reishi walks towards the smaller side room which contains his equipment, along with various herbs and medications. He opens his case once again and carefully empties his newly drawn blood into a larger vial—one containing the blood he had drawn previously and which he has carefully preserved.

He puts a few drops of the concentrated fluid onto a small piece of glass before peering closely at it through a pair of substance-analysing lenses.

Seiji, he thinks as he reminds himself of what has happened so far, *each month, I will inject myself with an antidote which is given to me by the Kurai masters, to prevent the release of whatever poison is embedded into the Hoseki inside me . . . the same poison inside the Hoseki in Azuki.*

So far, he has discovered that the poison in healers' Hoseki is manipulated to be constantly on the verge of release, unlike the young trainee assassins whose poison will only be released if one attempts to remove it or when they turn five-and-twenty.

The antidote which he is made to inject himself each month in the red room is weak and is only potent enough to keep the poison at bay. This antidote is given to him by the Kurai Masters each month, but only while they see the worth of keeping him alive. Even then, he is monitored when he does so, to ensure he does not have any other motives.

Reishi had been accumulating the contents of the

antidote over the past year in hopes of analysing its makeup enough to find out which poison is combined with the Hoseki and injected into them. If he can find this out, he will know how to neutralise the poison inside Azuki. However, he has only been able to remove the tiniest amount from himself each time, in order to keep himself alive. As such, this process has been an extremely long and troublesome one.

After peering through lens after lens for quite some time, Reishi inhales sharply. He takes a step back from the counter.

"This . . . This antidote means—" Reishi says to himself. He takes a breath.

This means the poison is sidium, he thinks in disbelief.

In a haste, he rips a small piece of parchment from the scrapbooks on the countertop and scribbles down a list of medicines and herbs with a calligraphy brush. He stuffs it into his case and goes on to get rid of any evidence that this investigation ever took place.

I can build this antidote from the medicines I have access to, he thinks, panting, *and concentrate it to five times of the antidote dosage that I usually receive. If I can inject this into Azuki, it should deactivate the sidium inside her Hoseki forever.*

✾

The four children sit on the tatami floor once again as they await their turn to go to the medical room.

"You know, I really look forward to these bi-monthly check-ups," Izumi pipes up. He lies down on the tatami and sprawls out like a starfish.

"I agree." Yuka nods as he tucks his black hair behind his ears. "I feel like we get to know each other better here and no one is around to tell us off. We can even use our real names here."

"And whatever we have wrong with us, soon Healer Reishi will see us to patch us up," Eric joins in.

Sana looks at the three boys around her. Their friendship has solidified more and more over the past few weeks.

"Yuka," Eric says suddenly, "how come you are so good with a bow and arrow?"

Yuka holds a hand behind his head as he smiles and attempts to shake off the compliment. "What are you on about?" Yuka replies. "Have you seen yourself during balancing training? I have no idea how you manage to stay on that rope for so long."

"What about Kudon?" Izumi sits up from the floor and looks at Sana. "Have you seen how she fights with her bare fists? I wish I could kick as high as her."

"Izumi, don't tell me this when you are the one who can swim for *a century* underwater. I don't know how you hold your breath for so long," Sana replies.

The four children laugh together as they share compliments. There is something endearing about this very moment. After a while, the wooden door slides open, and a masked man enters.

"Kumo, please make your way to the medical room," he says.

Sana immediately stands up and bows.

"Yes Master," the children say simultaneously.

Just as Sana is about to leave, Yuka whispers something rather loudly. "Enjoy your date with Healer Reishi!" he teases.

Sana turns to glare at him before she makes her way out. Eric nudges Yuka as if to tell him to stop, and Izumi sits on the side giggling.

As soon as Sana enters the medical room and sees Reishi, her mouth widens into a large smile. "Healer Reishi, I have news for you," she says excitedly.

"Tell me as soon as I finish our usual drill," Reishi replies, smiling in return.

As soon as he finishes, Sana leans in towards him and her eyes light up. "I found out some important information over the last two weeks," Sana says.

"Yes, tell me Azuki."

"The wall. I don't know much about the keystone, but I did find out that the guards who patrol the place have a changeover at a certain time each day."

Reishi nods, waiting to hear more.

"They must head back to the headquarters before the changeover can happen, which means that, every day, there are around three minutes where the wall is unguarded."

Reishi smiles.

"But—the changeover time changes every week," Sana finishes.

Reishi's smile widens. "This is very helpful," he says. "Thank you, Azuki. You really are a smart girl."

Sana's heart is warm and fuzzy from his compliment.

Reishi assembles something from inside his case. "And now, I have some news to tell you as well." Reishi's eyes are wide with excitement.

Sana has never seen such a bright glint in his eyes before. They are shining even more than usual. Sana smiles back. "Tell me."

"I believe this," he begins as he holds out a syringe containing a clear fluid, "is what will deactivate the poison inside your Hoseki."

Sana's eyes widen.

"Please give me your arm," Reishi says.

"N-Now?" Sana whispers. Reishi nods. "How—how did you—"

"May I?" Reishi asks, his needle hovering.

Sana nods, her eyes bulging.

"I pray that my work over the past year will not let us down," Reishi whispers. He proceeds to slowly inject the solution into Sana's vein. He then takes out a new syringe and, after a while, he pierces the same vein before drawing out the smallest amount of fluid.

A wave of relief sweeps over his face.

"Unmistakable," he whispers, as he looks at the newly drawn blood.

Sana peers at it. It is yellow, almost gold.

"We did it," Reishi whispers.

Sana covers her mouth. Did they really? Just like that?

"The poison has *actually* been deactivated?" Sana exclaims quietly, in disbelief.

Reishi nods. There are tears in his eyes. Before Sana has time to react, she finds that Reishi has flung his arms around her and is squeezing her in a tight embrace. Her whole body heats up and she blushes into a tomato.

"Rei-Reishi—" Sana whispers.

Reishi lets go of her and leans back. "Yes?"

"Have you done this for yourself, yet?"

"Not yet, Azuki," he replies. "My Hoseki is slightly different from yours. But now that I have done it once, I am certain I can do it again."

"Please do it as soon as you can," Sana urges. She looks into his eyes.

"You are my priority, Azuki," Reishi says. He notices the look on her face. "But I haven't forgotten my promise." He clears his throat and looks away. "With regards to the location tracking on your Hoseki," Reishi continues, "I have actually known how to deactivate it since the first day I came here."

"W-What?" Sana asks. There are too many surprises today.

"Yes. As healers, we also deal with bodies after death. So, for every young assassin who sadly passes away at the age of five-and-twenty, we are taught to deactivate the Hoseki remains and to remove and dispose of them. If we do not, they will explode after three days."

"My goodness," Sana replies.

"It is a safety feature. The Kurai Clan believe that, once an assassin has reached five-and-twenty, their abilities and bodies will start to decline. Usually, the bodies are disposed of inside the Kurai infrastructure but if, for some reason, the body was to be found outside, the explosion would get rid of any remains or evidence," Reishi explains.

"So that no one can know about the Kurai Clan," Sana follows.

"Correct."

"So . . . so what is it?" Sana asks, her eyes wide.

"As usual, it is Kurai magic. It is a spell—or a chant, if you so call it."

"So, we could do it right now?"

"Patience, Azuki. Think. If we do it right now, they will notice that you have suddenly disappeared and will come looking for you. We cannot do it until the very moment before you make it through that wall."

"Is it the same for you?" Sana asks.

Reishi smiles. "If only it were that easy," he replies. "I only know the chant for the bodies I have had to deal with, and as such, I have no information about how to remove the tracking for a Healer."

"Th-then we need to find out," Sana says, her eyebrows turning into a determined frown. "Be-because we need to do this together."

Reishi ruffles Sana's hair. "I still need some time to see how to get past the wall," he says. "Now that we know there is a changeover time and, coupled with our previous knowledge about the keystone, I hope it won't be long until we can tie up all the loose ends."

"When we get out of here," Sana asks quietly, "where would you want to go first?"

Reishi thinks for a moment. "Akamatsu, perhaps. That was home, for me."

"Do you have family there?"

"Not anymore," he replies. "My parents passed away in a boating accident when they were out collecting seaweed on the shores of Hafier. Ayame and I stayed with our grandmother for the most part, but as you know, Ayame passed away when she was six, and later my grandmother did too, due to old age."

"I—I'm sorry," Sana whispers.

"It is a common theme, is it not?" Reishi reassures her. "I think we are all orphans here."

Sana thinks about her mother. Although she has a mother, she is pretty much an orphan herself.

"There was a big, beautiful windmill," Reishi says quietly as he thinks back to his memories. "It was brown and white. Ayame used to love going there. We later buried her there when she was laid to rest."

Sana suddenly throws her arms around Reishi once more. She embraces him tightly and buries her face into his chest before inhaling deeply. His smell of sandalwood is a scent which has comforted her for as long as she can remember.

She leans back and looks into Reishi's eyes. She wants to know everything about the man in front of her. She wants to escape the Kurai Clan with him, hand in hand. She wants to see his every sight and breathe his every breath. A spark lights up inside her.

There is hope.

CHAPTER ELEVEN

The Keystone

AFTER DEACTIVATING THE SIDIUM INSIDE Azuki's Hoseki, Reishi taught her the Kurai spell—in the ancient tongue of Shinrin—to also deactivate its ability to sense one's location.

However, he is struggling to think of how to get hold of a keystone.

Only the elite Masters of the Kurai Clan have access to a keystone. How will he get hold of one? Not to mention, Reishi has since discovered that they will also need a master's unique fingerprint as well as the keystone in order to open the door of the walls.

He sighs as he lies on the bed inside his chamber, his mind working rapidly. He lays the back of his palm over his forehead.

Obtaining a fingerprint should be relatively doable, Reishi thinks. The material, papyrus, crosses his mind. When sliced to the thinnest fibres, it is often used in healing to obtain cell samples. The fibres are so thin that one usually cannot tell when it is laid on their skin.

Reishi decides that he will use this to obtain the fingerprint of one of his regular patients, one who is a Master. As for the keystone, he will need to think some more.

He sighs before drifting off to sleep.

✽

"Master Sasori." Reishi bows as he greets the master who enters his medical room. He is amongst one of the masters who teaches agility to the young trainee assassins.

"Good day, Healer Reishi," the master greets him back from behind his mask. He sits down on the examination couch.

"Please." Reishi gestures for his hand.

The master holds out his wrist.

Reishi had lined the inside of his right palm with the thinnest piece of papyrus—making sure to place its active part facing outwards. He holds onto Master Sasori's hand firmly with his right, simultaneously pressing the papyrus onto his index finger, while using his left to feel his pulse.

"You are what age now, Healer Reishi?" the master asks.

"Nineteen, Master Sasori," Reishi replies. He opens his box of examination lenses and takes one out. "Please, look straight ahead," he says, before peering into the master's right eye. He has the thin piece of papyrus scrunched up inside his palm.

He will need to be fast.

"We are lucky to have an asset like you," the master compliments. "Someone like you adds true value to the Kurai Clan."

"Thank you for your kind words," Reishi replies.

"In fact, I have a special request," the master continues.

"Yes, Master?"

"It appears that my son has fallen ill recently. He has come down with a fever and is complaining of abdominal pain."

"Is that so?"

"Yes," the master replies. "I thought it was a small bug and that it would resolve itself. However, he still hasn't improved, even though it has been a few days. Will you be able to come to our place to check him over?"

"Of course," Reishi replies.

"How about tonight, in the evening just after nightfall? This would allow me to finish my training so that I may be present."

"Certainly, Master Sasori."

"I thank you." The master smiles. "You are one of the best healers I have ever come across. I trust your expertise and have high regards for you. What you have been able to accomplish at such a young age is truly remarkable."

"I thank you again for your kind words." Reishi bows again. He proceeds to look back into the master's eyes through the lens. After a few moments, Reishi leans back, his eyebrows raising with confusion. He examines the lens he is holding and turns it around. "My apologies, Master Sasori, but this lens appears to not be functioning very well today."

"Is that so?" the master asks.

"It seems like it. May you bear with me whilst I go to the storeroom to find a lens of the same degree?"

"Very well."

Reishi strides towards the smaller side room. As soon as he enters and is out of sight, he hastily opens up his right palm before peeling off the papyrus ever-so-gently with his fingers. Quickly, he dips it inside a powder he keeps in one of the drawers before attaching the papyrus onto a piece of parchment, praying that the cells are still there.

To his relief, a dark red fingerprint immediately forms on the piece of parchment. Reishi's heart thumps inside his chest.

Master Sasori peers around the room whilst he waits. He glances at the various equipment around the room and hums to himself. He then turns to look at Reishi's case, which is left open on the table next to the examination couch. The master peers inside curiously, looking at the various needles and syringes.

Something catches his eye.

A small, brown piece of parchment pokes out from between the layers which hold the case together. Master Sasori leans forward and stretches out his hand. With a gentle tug, he pulls it out.

The master scans the writing quickly. His dark eyes enlarge with surprise before his eyebrows turn down into a frown of suspicion. In front of him is a list of various components of medicines and herbs. He recognises this as components of the antidote to sidium. He frowns and glances across at the side room.

Why has he got this? The master thinks. *That kid is a prodigy. He must have figured out which poison we use inside their Hoseki and is planning on creating a potent antidote to save himself. I must inform the higher-ups of this. This is treason. This is betrayal.* He briskly stuffs the piece of parchment into his robe.

Reishi reappears with a lens in his hand. He finds the master sitting there in the exact same position as earlier.

"My apologies for the wait," Reishi says. "Shall we continue?"

✾

Reishi is back inside his chamber. He ponders about his accomplishments this morning. He has managed to obtain Master Sasori's fingerprint and pass it off to Azuki, due to the lucky fact that the children's fortnightly injections had occurred later that day.

Now, the last step is to get hold of the keystone. But how?

Just as he is pondering, there is an urgent knock on his door. He stands up from the floor and opens it briskly. There is a man with the Kurai mask.

"Healer Reishi," he speaks with urgency in his voice. "Master Sasori's wife has summoned you. Please immediately make your way to their residence within the Kurai infrastructure. Their son's condition has greatly deteriorated."

Reishi bows and grabs his case before he follows the man out of his chamber in a haste.

✾

"Oh! Healer Reishi!" A young woman opens the door to Master Sasori's residence immediately, "I am so grateful you are here!"

Reishi bows quickly before removing his shoes and stepping inside.

"Mrs Sasori," he greets her, before striding down the corridors quickly behind her. He is led to the main chamber of the house. There is a young boy, perhaps around ten years old, lying on a mattress next to his parents' large bed.

"Healer Reishi," the lady pleads, "my son does not look well at all. He is pale and he suddenly became so drowsy. He is not responding to my voice. I had been trying to look after him in our chamber the past few days." There is fear in her eyes as her worry spills over.

Reishi crouches next to the boy. His heart is beating

hard inside his chest as a surge of adrenaline rushes through inside him. It is true that the boy does not look well at all.

Reishi quickly examines him, while the boy's mother watches with a hand covering her mouth.

"How long did you say he had been ill for?" Reishi asks as he checks over the boy in a haste. He remembers how the master had mentioned abdominal pain.

"Around four days," the lady replies, shaking.

After only a short moment, Reishi speaks. "The child has appendicitis," he confirms. "I believe it has perforated. His body is fighting hard, but he will need to have his appendix removed imminently."

The mother gasps.

"I need to administer some medicine into his veins first. Would that be all right with you, Mrs Sasori?"

"Please, do whatever you can to save him," the lady replies, holding back tears.

Reishi lifts his case up onto the bedside table of the main bed. He opens it up and just as he is about to reach for the powdered medication to mix into a solution, something catches his eye.

A sapphire stone is laid right next to his case. He blinks in disbelief. *The master's keystone?* He cannot believe it is lying there right in front of him.

But, if I take it, they will be sure to find out.

His mind works quickly. What should he do?

A bizarre idea crosses his mind. He looks at the scroll of papyrus inside his case. Normally, this papyrus would be sliced into the thinnest sheets for its purpose. They can extract cell samples, but can they also extract the contents of a keystone?

Reishi, being put on the spot so unexpectedly, cannot think of another way. He has no idea whether or not it will work, but it is worth a try.

While the child's mother is still worrying over her boy with her back turned, Reishi pulls out a length of the thick papyrus and wraps it around the keystone—he hopes that, by using such a thick segment, he might have the greatest chance of extracting the keystone's contents.

He holds it firmly in his grasp for as long as he can before he stuffs the papyrus back into his case and proceeds to prepare the medication for the master's son.

✾

Later in the evening, Master Sasori bursts through the door before rushing towards the main chamber.

"Elsie!" he exclaims to his wife. He soon finds himself looking at her, where she is seated next to their son.

She is relaxed. A soft smile spreads across her face. "My dear," she greets him warmly.

The master glances at his son, who looks to be sound asleep. His cheeks are pink and rosy. Master Sasori takes a moment to catch his breath.

"Healer Reishi saved him," his wife says to him quietly as she strokes their son's forehead, "It was appendicitis, and it had perforated. The surgery is already done, and our boy is doing so much better."

"Appendicitis?" the master asks, his eyes wide.

"Yes, my dear. I cannot be more grateful for that young healer."

"Elsie, you let him into our residence?" he asks before he turns his head immediately to the bedside table. But he is suddenly reassured by the fact that his keystone is still there, gleaming back at him.

"Of course. I know you said you called for him to come in the evening, but it would have been too late. He saved our boy, my dear."

"And so, he did," the master looks at his wife and his son softly.

He sighs deeply.

✾

Sana lies on the bed in her chamber, daydreaming about Healer Reishi.

"Seiji," she says to herself. "Seiji Hayashi." She then giggles and squeezes her eyes shut, allowing the warm and fuzzy feeling to sweep over her. The sound of his beautiful name is music to her ears. She clasps her hands over her cheeks as the warmth radiates outwards to her palms.

Sana thinks about the last time she met with him in the medical room. He had told her about how the doors on the Kurai wall would only open to the masters who had access to their own fingerprint and keystone. He mentioned something about how the keystones must be topped up every two months or so with the masters' biological material, in order for them to retain their usability as well as to stay personalised to their owners.

Sana rolls over onto her side as she lets her mind wander. She finds herself daydreaming about Seiji's handsome face. She imagines his sandalwood scent and pictures the glint in his bright, honey eyes. She thinks of his delicate, attractive hands and his soothing voice, and suddenly remembers when he sang for her for the first time.

Sana begins to hum a tune, envisioning the words in her mind as she remembers that very conversation.

✾

"Reishi, I don't think I can go on anymore," Sana says quietly. Her heart is heavy, and her mind clouds over. Existing in the Kurai Clan is eating away at any light she has left inside of her.

Reishi sits down next to her on the examination couch and pats her on the head. "Azuki," he says, his warm eyes looking into hers. "The Kurai Clan may be evil, twisted, harsh, and ruthless, but there is something they can never take away from us."

Sana looks back at him, tears welling up. She notices how the colours in his eyes are different hues of amber and gold; they swirl into a soft gleam which reflects his kind spirit.

"What have they not taken away?" Sana asks, sniffing through a runny nose.

"This," he whispers. He gently takes hold of her hand and places it in the centre of her chest. "In our hearts, we hold onto what matters to us. We hold onto what we call home," Reishi explains.

Sana blinks her tears back.

"Although I have no direct family left," Reishi continues, "and each day I, too, live a life in the Kurai Clan, I know that I am never alone, because of what I have here." He places his own palm in the centre of his chest. "No matter what the Kurai do, they will never be able to take away the memories of happiness I hold, nor the bonds I have created with people who matter the most," he comforts Sana.

"Who may that be?" Sana asks, her mind jumbled.

He looks at her and smiles. "You, silly." He pokes her in the shoulder.

Sana blushes, despite the sadness inside her. "Ri-Right," she whispers.

"There's a song I used to sing to Ayame, each time we went to the windmill," Reishi continues. "It's a song that reminds us of home."

Sana looks at Reishi, wide-eyed. Is he going to sing? Her heart begins to flutter.

Reishi takes a breath.

"O, watch how the windmill turns,
Each day as time goes by,
Our family's love will always shine,
Like the sun in our big blue sky."

"Taste the softness of freshly baked bread,
Hear the sweetness of mother's songs,
For us the windmill forever spins,

In this home where we belong."

Sana's soul lights up. Her mouth opens into a surprised O. The more she listens, the wider her eyes become.

Reishi's voice is gentle, soothing, and sweet. His melody seeps into her and touches her heart. Somehow, the weight inside her disperses. She is now a whole lot lighter.

Sana stares at Reishi after he finishes his song. Her eyes shake as she takes in every word and melody she hears. Before she can stop herself, her tears spill over and she leans against Reishi's chest, her tears dampening his robe.

A soft, delicate hand lands on Sana's head and he pats her gently. "That was supposed to lighten you up, not make you cry," he whispers.

Sana sniffs. "It did," she manages to say. After a while, she leans back. "Was . . . was that a song you were taught at school?" she asks curiously, wiping away some tears.

"It is a song I wrote," Reishi replies softly. "Just a little song to remind Ayame that we will always have a home." His gaze is distant. "The first time I sang this, Ayame was holding onto my hand like this," Reishi continues. He reaches out and touches Sana's fingertips with his own, before curling his fingers into hers, forming a tight grasp.

Sana takes a breath.

"Look," Reishi says, holding up her hand in that grasp. Their fingers have entwined into the shape of a spiral. "Ayame said it looked like the shell of a snail," Reishi explains, pointing at the shape. "So, from that day on, every time I sang for her, she would ask to form the special snail shell with me. The snail's home is a symbol that represents our home." He smiles and looks at Sana, his eyes soft. "Don't cry now," he says.

"It is—I-I love it," Sana manages to say. "You have a beautiful voice."

Reishi laughs. "Don't cry now, little Azuki," he repeats. He puts a warm, comforting arm around her and rubs her on the shoulder.

Although Sana is certain that it is not possible for her love for Reishi to increase any more, in that very moment, she is even more so head over heels for this truly wonderful angel who has fallen from the heavens.

✾

Sana continues to think about Reishi's beautiful voice. She knows the melody and the words of his song like the back of her hand. Each time she was feeling down,

Healer Reishi would sing this wonderful song for her, and each time, her soul would lighten up.

Sana's love for him bleeds through every vessel of her body, so much so that she suddenly sits upright with overwhelming determination and decides that, next time they meet, she is going to confess her love for him.

"Healer Reishi," Sana begins. "I love you."

She shakes her head after hearing this out loud. Is that cringeworthy?

She thinks of something else. "Healer Reishi," Sana tries again. "I want to be your wife. Let's get married after we escape."

A manic laughter escapes Sana's lips uncontrollably. She can imagine the look on Reishi's face. He will probably flick her on the forehead and tell her to stop being silly.

"Healer Reishi," Sana says in a more serious tone. "I want to be your lover." She blinks as her heart throbs inside her chest, then continues. "I believe we are destined to be together. You and I are bound by a connection so strong, I doubt anyone else has anything like it. Together, we will live a life of true happiness."

Sana takes a deep breath, her emotions suddenly overflowing.

"Your very presence is the epitome of my existence.

The sound of your voice is the song which keeps my heart beating. You light up the flames inside me that I never knew existed. I want us to experience our whole life's journey together, hand in hand. You were there for me when I needed you the most, and I vow to be the girl who you can count on for the rest of eternity. I want to see your smile every day for the rest of my life. I want to be the mother to your children, and I want to see the aging lines on your face and the greying hairs on your head as we grow old together."

For some reason, tears begin to well up around Sana's eyes.

"Seiji, I love you," she whispers, before she begins to sob.

The fear inside her lingers on. She prays that she will truly be able to escape the Kurai Clan with the love of her life. She falls face down back onto the bed as she lets go of her emotions.

✾

Reishi is back in his small, side room. He is absolutely exhausted from the day's back-to-back events. He struggles to keep his eyes open as he waits for the extraction from the material on the papyrus.

Please work, he prays as he rests his head on his arms

on the counter.

Soon enough, the extraction is complete. Reishi uses a type of salt to dissolve this new solution inside the glass dish in front of him and waits for the crystals to form. After a while, he finds himself looking at a small, sapphire keystone.

It gleams back at him.

Reishi picks it up, his hands shaking. He has no idea whether or not this has truly worked, but he guesses that when the day comes, they shall find out.

CHAPTER TWELVE

Seiji Hayashi

SANA'S HEART IS THUMPING INSIDE her chest. She leans against the wall of the dark tatami room with the other children, thinking about what is about to happen. Soon, she is going to confess her love to Healer Reishi.

The voices of her peers talking to each other go in one ear and straight out of the other.

"The wait is taking longer than usual today, is it not?" Izumi pipes up.

"It seems so," Yuka answers. "But that's okay. There's more time for us to chat!"

"I wonder what is taking so long?" Eric comments.

Suddenly, the door slides open. A masked man appears.

Sana's heartbeat speeds up. Is he going to call for her? Healer Reishi had better ready himself, for he is about to hear her ultimate declaration of love!

"My children," the masked man says, "you shall all come with me at once."

The children look at each other, their eyes wide. What is going on? They stand obediently and follow behind the man.

Sana blinks as she strides down the corridors after her peers. Why is it that on the very day she has decided to do something as important as this, something else has to happen? She puffs out her cheeks.

The children are led to a large, dark room lit by a few candles, one that uses the same theme as the rest of the rooms inside the Kurai house. There are four small, wooden tables laid out in front of them, each with a weapon placed on top.

The children recognise these as the weapons they excel with.

"My children," the masked man says, "please stand

before the weapon you specialise in."

Yuka immediately makes his way towards the table with the bow and arrow. Izumi stands in front of one with a slingshot, and Eric walks towards the table with a small dagger. Sana strides towards the empty table. Her weapon of choice has always been her bare hands and feet.

She wonders what is happening. Why are they having a training session right now?

Suddenly, a door at the other end of the room opens. Someone—a young man—is carried out by two masked men. They slam the man against a beam that is wheeled in by a third masked man, before tying him against it with ropes around his wrists and his ankles.

His olive torso is bare and covered in wounds: whip marks, cuts, bruises, and burns. His beautiful soft, ivory hair is matted and stained with crimson blood, and there is a big, angry bruise swelling up over his left eye. Blood is trickling out of the side of his mouth.

Sana's heart rips apart.

Someone steps into the room. He has the Kurai mask over his face, but the black sun is outlined in red. A long, white beard protrudes from the bottom of his mask. It moves as he speaks.

"Good day, my children," the man with the beard

says. "My name is Master Kurai. Good to meet you all, at last."

The children are shaking. All of them stunned to their core, their eyes wide with terror. Izumi is struggling not to cry.

"Tora," Master Kurai commands, "who is the young man you see in front of you?"

"He-Healer Reish-shi," Yuka stammers.

"Very well. And do you know what he has done?"

The children are frozen. Sana's heart has stopped beating. What is happening right now?

Please, if this is some sort of twisted nightmare, make it end, she thinks. Her airway is closing up and this suffocation is threatening to consume her. Her insides have been completely torn into two.

"Let me explain," Master Kurai continues, as he walks towards the children. "Despite being a highly respected young man and an absolute prodigy whose intelligence anyone would envy," he says, "Healer Reishi has succumbed to unethical temptations." Master Kurai sighs, as if he is in pain. "He has been found guilty of attempting to construct an antidote for the poison inside his Hoseki, knowing fully well that this is against the Kurai laws. He has confessed that he has used his intelligence for his own personal gain, as he wished to deactivate his Hoseki in order to leave the Kurai Clan." The master is close enough now to whisper, "Now tell me, Hebi, what is clause one of the Kurai Conduct?"

"I-if one attempts t-to leave the—" Eric struggles to speak as he stammers uncontrollably. "—Ku-Kurai Clan, th-they are to be pu-punished and then exe-executed."

"Well done," Master Kurai compliments the child. "Remember," he continues, "one's selfishness leads to the punishment of others. As such, before we execute him, you are all to practice your weapons of specialisation on him. What a waste, really, of a young genius."

Sana is about to vomit.

"Children, you are to watch this fully. If any of you look away, I shall punish you," Master Kurai warns. "If any of you show any signs of weakness, I shall punish you also," he continues. "I want you to practice your precision."

Sana is about to strangle the blasted bearded man.

"You are to keep him alive during this punishment, as only the Kurai Masters deserve the pleasure of the final execution. If any of you accidentally kill him . . . again, I shall punish you."

Sana stares at him, her blood absolutely boiling over.

"Come, Tora." Master Kurai beckons Yuka to come forward. "Use your bow and arrow and remember what you were taught. I want you to be precise. So, do not aim for the heart, as that will kill him. Shoot him somewhere which will cause pain but will keep him alive."

Yuka is shaking to the core. He can barely pick up his bow and arrow. He drops it onto the floor but immediately tries to pick it back up, in fear of being punished. The master's eyes are on him, and fear is absolutely dripping through every inch of his body.

He struggles to keep his bow and arrow straight. After he lets go of the string, his arrow falls limply and hits the floor only a few paces in front of him.

"My, my, that was not very good, was it?" Master Kurai shakes his head. "Again, my child."

Yuka hoists his bow once again. He does everything in his power to keep from shaking.

Sana can hear what he is saying through his sunset eyes, which are screaming, *I am sorry, Healer Reishi.*

The arrow shoots through the air and pierces Seiji's right shoulder. Seiji barely reacts outside a tiny flinch that tells her that he is holding back his pain. Even in a time like this, Seiji still spills kindness—he does not want to cause any more agony for the children.

Sana's heart shatters.

"Good. Now five more, at least," Master Kurai demands.

Sana has stopped breathing. She looks at the love of her life. The torment is so intense that strangely, she has suddenly gone completely numb.

"Okami," Master Kurai summons, "I want you to aim your slingshot at his right eye."

Sana looks on, the numbness now spreading through her entire body. The room suddenly feels empty. There is nothing but her love, Seiji Hayashi, in front of her.

There is a peaceful silence. Sana is sure that Seiji almost smiles at her; beneath the swelling, the glint in his warm honey eyes is still there.

"Kumo," Master Kurai commands.

Sana blinks. How much time has just passed?

"Kumo, do not make me repeat myself. Come forward."

Sana walks forwards slowly, her mind completely blank. Each step takes an extreme effort. She cannot breathe. She is about to faint.

"Now Kumo, you are interesting. The weapon you specialise in is, in fact, no weapon at all," Master Kurai comments. "So, use your strong kicks to break his shin."

Sana continues to walk towards Seiji. How long has

it been since her heart stopped beating? As she suddenly snaps back into reality, she notices the excruciating, overwhelming new injuries that have appeared all over Seiji's body.

In her mind, she begs for this to end.

Sana stands right in front of him. She reaches out and holds him tightly. She wants to howl and scream, but the pain is so intense that she no longer knows how to feel. The room once again falls silent, and she sees nothing but Seiji.

His warm heartbeat thumps through to her chest. The smallest rumble and an airy vibration come from his lips. He is, right now, still alive. Here, in her arms.

Sana looks through tear-filmed eyes to see there are various bruises and agonising marks around his neck: remnants of repeated strangulation. Seiji must have been subjected to so much damage that he can no longer speak.

She will never hear his sweet voice again.

Despite this, through the airy vibrations, Sana can still hear what he is trying to say: "Live on, Little Azuki."

Seiji looks at her with his warm, sweet eyes, which are almost not visible underneath the copious amounts of swelling and bruising. He still manages a small wink.

Sana breathes in his scent of sandalwood. She holds

his head tightly, cherishing this painful, last moment they have with each other.

"Seiji," Sana stammers. She really cannot breathe.

Using the last of his strength, Seiji manages to lift his hand, just enough to grasp onto Sana's. He is trembling as he curls his fingers into hers, forming their snail shell. His hand then slips, and he knocks the back of her hand before his arm drops back down.

Sana cannot bear to see him go through any more pain. She squeezes her eyes shut as her hands tighten around his head. A tear drops from her eye and trickles down to her chin.

I love you, Seiji.

"I'm sorry," she whispers.

With one swift movement she breaks his neck. She then collapses to the floor and faints.

✾

Sana wakes up. She is sprawled out on the cold, hard floor. She slowly sits up, but she cannot breathe. Heaviness weighs down on her chest and her lungs are struggling to expand. As she scans the room, she begins to realise that this is where she was locked up the last time she was punished—made to starve for three days.

Suddenly, something clinks and clanks. Someone

unlocks the bars of the door and slides it open. Sana looks up to see a masked man standing there.

"Kumo," he says.

Sana does not have any energy to respond.

"You killed Healer Reishi," he says. Those words poke sharp daggers at her. "So, this is your punishment. You have one more day of confinement in here without food or water."

Sana has no idea how many days have passed.

"I hear you were rather fond of Healer Reishi," the man comments. "As such, I have a gift for you." Something lands in front of her with a thump. "Enjoy your little souvenir," the man says as he slides the bars back shut and locks it once again.

A segment of a forearm—lifeless, dead—lays in front of her. Sana instantly recognises it as Seiji's. The delicate hand she knows so well is unmistakable. She howls internally as she reaches out to it, her fingers trembling. This absolutely inhumane torment will never end.

Sana sits cross-legged on the cold ground and wonders how her life has come to this. Is this really happening? Is this some sick, twisted nightmare? Her eyes drift to the arm on her lap. Suddenly, something hits her.

There is a slight change in angle on the back of Seiji's hand, between the base of the thumb and the index finger. It is unmistakable. She knows the contours of his hands too well, and this is not what it normally looked like. Her mind suddenly flashes back to her last moment with Seiji, when his arm slipped and he knocked the back of her hand.

Was that on purpose?

"Sei-Seiji," Sana stammers as she feels for the part in question. She cannot feel anything. However, something relights ever so slightly inside her.

Live on, little Azuki, Sana hears Seiji say inside her mind.

"Get yourself together," Sana says to herself. Now is not the time to cry. She must be brave, for Seiji. The determination she once had crosses her eyes once more, cutting through the agonising pain within her.

✤

As soon as Sana is released, she makes a dive for her chamber room as discretely as possible. She immediately reaches for a small hand blade tucked inside her training equipment set.

"I am sorry, Seiji," Sana whispers as she slices the blade through his hand.

Sure enough, it hits something hard. Heartache continues to gnaw away at her as she probes open the wound and digs her fingers inside. She feels something.

Moments later, Sana drops a sharp, sapphire stone onto the surface of the table. She gasps.

"The . . . the keystone?" Sana says to herself. She bends double and allows herself to cry quietly. She has no idea how Seiji did it, but he somehow managed to suture the stone inside his own hand with such meticulous skill that it left no single recognisable sign on the external surface.

"Seiji," Sana whispers as the tears roll down her face. "How could I ever—" She sobs. "How could you—"

She does not manage to finish her words.

✾

Sana's eyes are wide as she sits bolt upright in the middle of her chamber room. She is repeating the spell inside her head again and again. She pictures the time when she and Seiji sat inside the medical room, and he taught her how to deactivate the location-sensing ability inside her Hoseki.

Sana tries to clear her mind. She is doing this for Seiji. She will only have a few minutes between deactivating her Hoseki, reaching the Kurai wall during the guard changeover, and trying to get through it before someone realises that she is gone.

She briefly thinks of her fellow teammates and wonders where they are. However, she does not have time to think about them further.

She must do this. For Seiji.

Sana gathers her things: the parchment with the thumbprint. The keystone. A small blade. All the kudon she has left. Seiji's forearm. She packs everything inside a black cloth bag and throws the strap over her shoulder before she manages a small laugh.

Seiji, this is the craziest thing I have ever done. I am doing this for you.

She waits for the clock on her wall to strike the hour.

Now, she thinks. As quickly as possible, Sana places her hand over the side of her abdomen as she concentrates with all her might and mumbles the spell in the ancient tongue of Shinrin over and over again. She does so until heat rises from her stomach to her head.

I feel it, Sana thinks, as she thinks back to what Seiji had explained to her.

She stands and breaks into a run.

✾

Sana reaches the wall. She cannot believe that she is really here. Just like she had observed, the wall is currently completely unguarded. She has no idea how much time she has left before someone comes after her.

She holds out the parchment with the thumb print and the keystone to one of the doors. She has no idea where to put it. This is something they had not yet found out.

Please, please, Sana begs. Urgency is rising and cold sweat forms around her temples. More perspiration gathers and drips down her neck.

She is sure she will be caught any moment now.

Seiji, I'm trying, Sana thinks. She continues to hold the objects in her hands near the door, wondering if she is about to die. Her heart is beating so hard that she is sure she will vomit it up her throat.

In that very moment, the large, heavy door clicks open. Sana stares at it, panting, before stepping outside. The door immediately shuts behind her.

She runs for her life.

CHAPTER THIRTEEN

The Price of Escape

SANA HAS NO IDEA HOW long she has been running. Her shoes have fallen apart, and she is now barefoot—there are cuts and grazes all over the soles of her feet. She ran past the point that her lungs are about to burst. The intense fear permeates her even though she has physically made it out of the Kurai Clan. The thought of capture haunts her to the core.

Every corner she turns, she is sure that someone with the Kurai symbol on their mask will appear and find her. Her heart beats wildly inside her chest, each thump a painful reminder of who she lost.

The more she runs, the more her hatred for the Kurai grows.

She finds herself nearing a town of some sort. The sight of normal people walking around is something she has not seen for the last seven years. The brightness of the sun is blinding and the noise of so many people in one place makes her want to flee. Being so exposed in the daylight is nothing short of unsettling.

"Excuse me, sir," Sana manages to say as she pants to catch her breath. She has stopped next to an old man with a friendly face. "Are we far from Akamatsu?"

The old man smiles at her. His eyebrows spring up with surprise as he notices the cuts and grazes all over her feet. "My goodness, my child! What happened?"

"Not a worry, sir. Please—are we near Akamatsu?"

"In fact, we are, my child," he replies. "It is a few minutes by cart from here." He points to a row of carts in front of them. "You can take them from here."

Sana bows and thanks him before dashing towards the carts. There is a young man perched on top of a horse; she flags him down as she nears.

"Excuse me, sir," Sana says to him, "can you please take me to Akamatsu? There is a windmill there."

"Certainly, my child," the man responds. "That will be two kudon, please."

Sana flings the coins into his hands as she leaps onto the cart. She shuts the door immediately and holds her face in her hands as she trembles, praying that the Kurai will not find her.

It is not long before they come to a stop.

"Akamatsu, my child," the man says from his horse. He hops down and opens the cart door. "The windmill is a further walk from here," he explains as he points to it, visible in the distance. "The carts cannot get through. But you can reach it by foot."

Sana thanks the man before making a run for it. She uses all of her remaining strength to get there.

✾

Sana looks up in awe at the windmill. It is tall—standing proudly in the middle of a lush and secluded green field—and walnut coloured, with white spinning blades. There is no one around.

"Seiji, I'm here," Sana says, watching the white blades as they go round and round. She stares for a few moments longer, then drags her gaze away. She looks around and finds a spot with some delicate bluebells swaying in the breeze. She kneels down and, with her bare hands, she begins to dig.

The more Sana digs, the more her contained emotions begin to spill over. She howls loudly as—for the first time since everything unfolded—she allows herself to scream out the pain and torment she endured. She cries her heart out and tears stream down from her eyes and nose. She yells, the excruciating pain of her own voice deafening her ears.

"Seiji!" she screams.

Her hands are raw, and they sting as she keeps digging. She lets go of everything inside her and mourns the loss of the one person who mattered the most in her life.

Sana gently places Seiji's forearm in the newly dug hole and covers it up with the soil. The flowers sway peacefully in the breeze.

"Please, rest in peace now," Sana whispers, wiping her nose with her sleeve. She can barely breathe, and each time she inhales, her breaths are short and difficult. "Rest in peace with little Ayame."

She kneels in front of the small grave and howls some more.

✾

After some time, Sana makes her way from the windmill.

She finds a small stream and follows it, wandering aimlessly. She then sits down by a rock and reaches for the blade inside her bag.

Despite making it out of the Kurai Clan, Sana cannot shake her fear. She constantly feels like there are eyes on her and that, any minute now, someone will appear. She wonders if the Hoseki inside her has really been deactivated.

Sana rolls up her shirt near her abdomen and sinks the blade into her side. Blood immediately drips down her skin, but her heartache has numbed her to the point where she barely feels any pain. She has no idea where, exactly, her Hoseki is; she probes further, creating an unsightly wound.

Soon, her hands touch something. She plucks it out and looks at the tiny, thin, grey pellet on her blood-covered palm. She gazes at it some more—thinking about how their whole lives revolved around this tiny, little object—before crushing it in her palm and letting the fragments drop into the stream.

She sits there for a while longer, wondering if she will die. They were told that, if one attempts to remove their Hoseki, they will be immediately poisoned.

However, after a while, nothing seems to happen. Sana thinks back to the excitement in Seiji's eyes when he first told her he had managed to create the antidote.

Sana peers at the stream, catching her own reflection. It wobbles along with the water. She looks at her own face—at her dark eyes and raven hair. Her solemn reflection looks back at her.

A rather adorable face, just like you, Sana hears Seiji's voice in her head.

She begins to cry once more as she thinks of him. "Even if I made it out," she sobs to her reflection, "they will find me, Seiji." Her tears hit the water and warp her image. "It is only a matter of time before someone recognises me and kills me," she cries.

Live on, little Azuki, Seiji's voice says inside her mind once more.

Suddenly, Sana reaches for her blade. Her breathing quickens and she begins to tremble. *I need to destroy my face*, she suddenly realises. *Now that the Hoseki is gone, if they don't recognise me, they won't know it is me.* She holds onto the blade, her hands trembling out of control.

"I will not need this face anymore," Sana says to her own reflection as some more tears trickle down her cheeks. "I shall bury my appearance along with Seiji and put an end to this chapter."

Sana looks at her own reflection one last time. She

takes a moment to be grateful for her rather adorable facial features.

She bids herself goodbye.

Sana slices herself across the face; the pain is unimaginable. She does it again and is unable to hold back further tears. She cries hard but keeps going and continues through with shaking hands.

She cannot breathe.

I will never love again, Sana thinks through the pain. *A girl may care about her appearance, but if my face means that I might lose everything Seiji sacrificed for, I must destroy it.*

Soon, Sana collapses on the grass behind her as she struggles to breathe. Her blade falls into the stream and drifts away in the water. The grass surrounding her is a comforting embrace, and the scent of the earth is rich, even mixed with the iron smell of blood.

Despite the agonising pain, a strange sense of serenity sweeps over Sana. The surrounding nature gives her a sense of tranquillity, and now that her face is unrecognisable, her heart feels oddly at peace.

O, watch how the windmill turns . . .

Is that Seiji's sweet voice?

She falls unconscious.

The fourteen-year-old girl lies in the middle of the

Akamatsu field with a large, gaping wound in her abdomen and an adorable, youthful face—one that has been absolutely ravaged.

It is truly a harrowing, terrifying, and bloody sight.

CHAPTER FOURTEEN

A Stolen Miracle

A SIX-YEAR-OLD EIRLYS sits a two-year-old Sana on her lap and jiggles the lovable toddler on her thighs. Sana giggles and makes sounds of delight, enjoying the moment with her sister. Her round, obsidian eyes are bright and wide.

"You are sweet, little Sana," Eirlys coos to the toddler, booping her on the nose with her own. "Sweet little Sana, sweet little Sana," Eirlys sings. She strokes the soft, raven strands of Sana's hair.

There is a knock on their front door.

"My dear, someone is at the door!" Elian calls for her husband from the kitchen. Her hands are covered in flour; she is baking treats for the children. "Would you mind getting the door?"

Delwyn stumbles into the front room, his eyes adjusting to the brightness of the day. He was busy analysing various nocturnal plants inside his study. He is still rubbing his eyes as he pulls the front door open.

A woman—who appears around the age of thirty—is on their doorstep. She has chestnut skin and dark brown eyes. Her black hair is pulled into a neat, tight bun.

"Good day," Delwyn greets her.

"Good day, sir. Am I speaking to Mr Harlande?" she asks. She has a firm tone to her voice and appears somewhat strict.

"Correct," Delwyn replies, wondering where this is going.

"My name is Ms James. I am from the Shinrin Child Protection and Adoption Agency. We have been notified that there is a child in this residence who does not have an official registration document."

Delwyn blinks at her. He is tempted to shut the door.

"Unfortunately, according to Shirinese laws, this is

not legal, sir," the lady continues. "We have the authority to come inside the property to conduct an inspection." She takes off her shoes and, just as she is about to enter, she asks, "May I?"

Delwyn peers at her uniform. She is wearing a smart, dark green robe that has a wooden badge etched with her name on the front. It seems very official. Perhaps he will not be able to shut the door on her so easily.

"Very well," he says. He turns to look at his wife, who is patting her hands on her apron and peering back at him, her hazel eyes wide.

As Ms James steps inside their home, Elian sneaks over to her husband. "What is going on?" she whispers.

"Child Protection or something," he mouths back at her.

The lady in the smart, green robe walks around, peering into each room. She pulls out a hard, wooden board with a few pieces of parchment clipped on top and starts to scribble away with a calligraphy brush. "I must say, the property is very well kept," Ms James comments.

The couple look at her, wondering when she will leave.

The lady reaches the cosy chamber where there is a young girl with butterscotch hair tied into two braids holding a tiny toddler on her lap. Her stern frown immediately softens. "Hello there," she says.

Eirlys looks at the lady suspiciously, her small eyebrows turning downwards. She holds Sana tightly and notices her parents standing behind the lady.

"May I?" Ms James asks the couple, who look at her with uncertainty.

They eventually nod.

"Please follow me, my child," Ms James says to Eirlys.

The six-year-old lays Sana gently onto the floor before she hops down from her bed. Eirlys eyes the lady carefully, holding out a hand to Sana as they both walk towards the main room.

"What are the names of your children, please?" Ms James asks Delwyn.

"Eirlys and Sana Harlande," he replies.

"May I see the official birth registration documents for them both, please?" she inquires.

Delwyn looks at his wife, his expression looking a bit concerned. Elian walks to a wooden chest in one of the side rooms and flicks through some piles of parchment. Once she finds the one, she reluctantly brings it to the lady and places it onto the countertop.

Ms James flicks open the pieces of parchment and

scans the script. She peers at the official stamp and even holds it up to the light, checking for how the colours reflect. "Very well," she says. "I can see little Eirlys Harlande was born at Akamatsu Infirmary. And this little one?" she asks, pointing to Sana.

"I'm afraid we do not have one for Sana," Elian admits reluctantly.

Delwyn's heart thuds inside his chest.

"Where did you acquire this child?" Ms James enquires.

"Someone abandoned the poor child on the riverbanks," Delwyn replies. "This is now her home."

"I am afraid this is not legal, sir," the lady replies. "Any child who is not related by blood requires official adoption documentation. This can be received after an official agency has assessed the potential caregiver's personal and home circumstances."

"We were not aware of that," Delwyn says truthfully.

"That is all right, but I am afraid this child will have to be removed from this property."

"Excuse me?" Elian asks, a tinge of annoyance sparking in her voice.

"Yes, ma'am. The child will have to be taken to an official adoption agency and be rehomed."

"Surely, now that you are here, we can just sign

whichever documents we need so that we can adopt her officially?" Delwyn asks.

"I'm afraid, Mr Harlande, your family would not be considered eligible caretakers for adoption. You and Ms Harlande already have a child. Adoption is reserved for those who are unable to bear children, sir."

"This is ridiculous," Delwyn replies, the annoyance in his voice now mirroring his wife's.

Eirlys's little eyebrows slant with concern. She grasps onto Sana's hand tightly. "Is the green lady going to take Sana away?" she asks.

"I'm afraid we will have to take her imminently," Ms James states. She bends down and scoops little Sana up under her armpits, pulling her away from Eirlys.

Sana grunts with disapproval and soon begins to cry louder.

Ms James attempts to calm her down by cradling her and making soft, annoying noises, but it does not work.

"Ms James," Delwyn tries again, "can't you see how loved and cared for she is here?" He takes a breath. "You cannot give a child a better home than this."

"I appreciate that, sir," Ms James replies, balancing the still-crying Sana in her arms. "But the law is the law." She strides towards the front door.

"No—" Elian reaches out her hand.

"Don't take Sana!" Eirlys pleads.

Ms James continues out the door, trying to speak over the unfolding protests. "Please be reassured that she will be rehomed to a place that is just as warm and as loving as here. Every caregiver's circumstances are thoroughly assessed before a child is rehomed."

"You can't do this!" Delwyn protests some more. He reaches out and attempts to grab Sana back.

Ms James holds out her palm, gesturing for him to stop. "Stop, sir," she warns. "My apologies, but we are the official Child Protection and Adoption Agency, and we have full authority to act in cases like these. If you so much as to lay a hand on me, you can be charged with attempted assault."

Delwyn looks at her with disbelief. The lady in green resumes her walk out of their front door.

"P-please at least let her keep her name," Elian pleads, blinking back tears.

"I'm afraid that is not something I can promise," Ms James replies. She puts on her shoes. "Good day, now." She nods before exiting the house and boarding a cart.

The Harlande family look at the little child in the lady's arms, bereaved as their miracle is stolen away.

✾

A young lady with a round face, kind doe-like eyes, and soft, chestnut hair stands by the Child Protection and Adoption Agency counter, waiting for her documents to be finalised. Her facial features give her a look of innocence and charm.

"This is the day!" she says with excitement.

"Good to see you, Ms Ozaki," Ms James says to her. "After a thorough assessment, we are pleased to say the adoption has been finalised."

"Oh, wonderful. How long I have waited for this!" Ms Ozaki replies.

"I thank you for your patience over the past few months, Ms Ozaki," Ms James replies. "But the time spent was very necessary. This will all be very worthwhile."

"Certainly," Ms Ozaki agrees. "There is nothing quite like having a child when one is unable to bear one."

"With such a loving mother like yourself, I am sure this young one will grow into a beautiful girl," Ms James compliments. "What a lovely and unusual name you have chosen for her, too."

Ms Ozaki smiles sweetly.

"You shall expect an extra two thousand kudon to

be delivered to you each month ma'am," Ms James says. "Please use it to aid you in bringing up this lovely girl."

"I thank you." Ms Ozaki bows.

✾

The young, three-and-twenty-year-old Marlene Ozaki enters her home, carrying her new child in her arms. She plops the toddler down on a cushion by her dining table.

"My goodness," she says, looking around her own house with amusement. "This is the longest my house has ever remained so well kept." She laughs.

The child looks around with wide, curious eyes.

"Now, you!" she says excitedly as she leans down towards her new daughter and taps her on her nose. "You are going to bring me lots of luck." She scoops her up and spins her around before plopping her back down on the cushion.

The child wobbles and falls over.

"Because of you, I shall become richer." She smiles. "And I shall live a life of abundance. Welcome to my abode, little Kudon."

CHAPTER FIFTEEN

Lost and Found

AN EIGHTEEN-YEAR-OLD EIRLYS strolls across the field, her light blue dress blowing in the breeze. She recently started studying Healing at Furukawa Academy and has reached the first Academy break. With her free time, she came home to her village of Akamatsu.

She shields her eyes from the bright sunlight as she enjoys the fresh scent of flowers and the warmth of sun on her skin. Blue butterflies flutter around the water and birds chirp happily in the sky.

From afar, something appears in Eirlys's vision. Someone is laying in the grass just next to the stream.

Eirlys does a double take. *Is that blood?* She thinks, her heart stopping. Her pace quickens. Her eyes widen in horror and shock as soon as she nears the person. *What in the world?*

A young, unconscious girl lays before her. Her face has been completely ravaged and there is a huge, gaping wound in her abdomen. Her black hair is matted and tangled with congealed blood, which has crusted all over her face and hands.

This is the most brutal wound Eirlys has ever seen. She immediately crouches down on the grass and shakes the girl gently by the shoulders. "Excuse me!" she calls, her heartbeat accelerating. "Excuse me!"

The child does not respond. Eirlys presses her fingers to her neck; there's a slight pulse. The young girl's chest is rising and falling.

She is alive.

Eirlys looks around desperately. There is not a single person in sight. The fields of Akamatsu are quite secluded, which is extremely unhelpful at a time like this.

In a haste, she fits her arms underneath the young girl in an attempt to carry her. It is a struggle at first, but after a moment, she manages to balance the girl on her back. She walks as fast as she can and eventually manages a small run as she heads towards the nearest Infirmary.

Eirlys bursts through the front door of Akamatsu Infirmary. "We need help!" she shouts.

The staff immediately surround her, their eyes wide. They panic as they approach and take the girl from her arms and rush her to the nearest emergency room.

Eirlys pants, catching her breath. She runs after the staff and follows them inside.

The healers immediately begin to check over the young girl and start to supply whatever they can to keep her alive. Eirlys watches, her blood pulsating, and thinks about the things she has learnt in her lessons. She is in disbelief that she is watching such skills be used in real time in front of her.

She wonders who could have done this to a young, innocent girl. A deep pain aches inside her heart.

✾

"Young Harlande." A gentle, middle-aged lady approaches Eirlys. She wears a cobalt-coloured robe, and her brown hair is tied up in a ponytail. Her deep, blue eyes are surrounded by a few graceful age lines.

Eirlys recognises her instantly as one of the professors in Healing at Furukawa Academy. She is one of the best and is *very* well known.

"Healer Wendell!" Eirlys greets her and bows instantly.

"My child, you have done well to carry the poor girl all this way. What a truly horrific event to occur!"

"Healer Wendell, is she doing all right?" Eirlys asks.

She gestures for Eirlys to follow. "Come. Let us go and see her together."

The two of them step into a side room where the young girl lies peacefully. It is quite dark outside, and the room is lit by a few warm candles. The young girl has been cleaned up and her wounds have been dressed. There are patches and bandages over her abdomen and her entire face; there is only a small gap for the eyes, nostrils, and mouth.

"Not only were her wounds horrific," Healer Wendell says to Eirlys, "but this has to be one of the most difficult cases I have worked on."

Eirlys looks at the girl with intense sadness. She must have endured an unspeakable amount of pain. She notices how her long, dark eyelashes curl up from her eyelids and how her lips are slightly rosy.

"For a young face to be ravaged like that . . ." Healer Wendell sighs. "It would be anyone's worst nightmare."

"How long do you think it will take for her to recover?" Eirlys asks.

"Months, at least," the Healer answers. "I have done my absolute best to restore her facial features using the strongest healing magic and the finest skills at my disposal. But her wounds are so severe that, without knowing what she looked like before, it is difficult to know if the restoration will be close to her original appearance. All I can say is that I have done my best."

"Certainly, Healer Wendell," Eirlys answers.

She reaches out to the young girl and gently tucks her raven hair behind her left ear. As the strands fall to the side, something catches Eirlys's attention—there is a slightly darkened crescent marking just behind the girl's ear.

Eirlys's eyes widen before she leans in and peers closely, inspecting the mark under the candlelight. Unmistakably, she is looking at a birthmark shaped like a crescent moon with jagged edges.

Something pulls at Eirlys's heart, and she immediately grasps onto the young girl's hand as she begins to tremble.

"Sa-Sana," Eirlys stammers. She is unable to hold

back her tears.

Healer Wendell looks at Eirlys curiously. "Are you all right, my child?" she asks softly.

Eirlys looks at the healer, her eyes watering with emotion. "Th-This girl—" Eirlys struggles to breathe as she stammers. "Is . . . my sister."

✾

Sana opens her eyes. The first person to appear in her sights is a young lady with braided, butterscotch hair. The woman has warm, kind, honey-coloured eyes. She leans in towards her and gazes at her softly.

Sana instantly thinks of Seiji. There is an overwhelming stab in her heart and tears immediately trickle down her cheeks, dampening the bandages wrapped around her face.

The young lady hugs her gently and kisses the top of her head. "Oh, Sana."

Sana stares emotionlessly, wondering who the young lady is and why she has kind, honey-coloured eyes just like Seiji. She cannot move any part of her face, but the tears continue to flow uncontrollably.

The young lady leans back, and Sana notices that a middle-aged man and woman are standing behind her—they also have very kind faces. They have the same butterscotch-coloured hair like the lady who just embraced her, and kind, brown eyes. They both have tears in their eyes.

Why does everyone look so sad?

Soon, they join the young lady in embracing her. Their emotions seep into Sana as they squeeze her tightly.

She has no idea where she is or who these people are. The only thing she can feel is an awful pain and emptiness that eats away at her core. The pain of never again being able to see the one person who matters the most to her is absolutely excruciating.

"Sana," the man whispers as he struggles to hold back his tears. He holds her tightly. "At last, we've found you again."

✾

"Good morning, my child." A young man approaches Sana, smiling. "My name is Healer Ergen."

Sana looks at him. Over the past few months, she has seen so many new faces that she cannot remember whether she has met this person before. From the moment she wakes up every day, there is only the pain of the unfillable void in her heart.

"How are you today, my child?" he asks gently as he

draws the curtains surrounding her bed. He sits down next to her.

Sana stares at her bedsheets, not looking the young man in the eye.

"My child, I need to check your wounds. May I unravel the bandages around your face?"

Sana looks at him briefly. He has gentle eyes, glossy bronze skin, and a gracious smile. He looks like he wants to help her. However, she cannot bring herself to smile back. She nods at him emotionlessly.

Healer Ergen begins to slowly take the bandages from her face with care. When he is done, he closely examines her from all directions. "I must say, Healer Wendell has done a remarkable job," he compliments. "The wounds are healing exceptionally. With wounds as severe as these, it is a miracle to see how well you are recovering."

Sana closes her eyes. Even the mention of the word healer brings an unexpected stab to her heart.

"May I check your abdomen?" Healer Ergen asks. Sana lifts the side of her gown so that the young man can peer at her healing wound. "Again, remarkable," he comments. "It is certainly healing very well." He covers her up and sits on the chair next to her. "My child, you are doing very well," he reassures. "You will need to eat and drink when you can and try to move around. But I am proud of how far you have come."

The kind words drift over Sana's head. She looks at Ergen with dull and lifeless eyes.

Healer Ergen rises from the chair and, just as he is about to pull open the curtains, another person pops their head inside. Sana peers at both men, wondering why she is receiving so many visitors today.

"Healer Ergen," the middle-aged man greets. "You may leave the curtains shut. I, too, need to check up on the child."

Healer Ergen nods and exits. The middle-aged gentleman steps inside. He looks a little familiar. She has been here for a few months now—perhaps Sana met him during her stay?

"Good morning my child," he greets. He has short, black hair and brown eyes. However, his skin is pale, and he wears round, silver spectacles. Gentle lines grace the skin of his face. "We have met a few times before," he explains softly, "but once again, my name is Healer Olea. I am here to check how you are feeling."

Sana blinks at him, before staring at the bedsheets in front of her.

Healer Olea sits on the chair next to her. "Tell me your name, my child," he prompts. He has a soft facial expression and gives off a gentle aura.

Sana does not respond.

"We are here to help you," Healer Olea reassures. "I understand you must have experienced an awful lot, but talking about it with us will help you work through it. Together, we can help you heal and get better." He smiles encouragingly. "So, my child, can you tell me what happened? Anything at all?"

Sana's mind is jumbled. The only thing she can think of is Seiji. She has no energy left and she cannot bring herself to utter even a single word.

Just like how the Kurai took away Seiji's voice, they must have stolen hers, too.

She looks at the man in front of her and the anguish eats at her heart once more. Her eyes scrunch up with sadness and pain as she blinks back tears.

Healer Olea's eyebrows raise with alarm, and he reaches out to gently pat her hand. "I am so sorry," he apologises, his eyes glowing with genuine sympathy. "Please, take your time."

They stay like that for a while longer. The healer looks at Sana with sadness in his eyes. Each time he has tried to work with her, she has refused to speak a single word.

"Would you like me to come back later?" he asks

gently.

Each time they ask her about what has happened, Sana feels like she is being suffocated as the events come back to terrorise her mind. She cannot bear to have anyone else try to talk to her. She nods at him to tell him that she wants him to leave.

After he makes his way out, Sana lies down and pulls the covers over her head.

"How is she?" she hears one of the carers whisper to Healer Olea.

"The poor child still does not speak," he replies.

"She must have gone through something awful," the carer answers, sympathy evident in her voice.

"It is going to take quite some time," Healer Olea explains.

"I've heard her speak before though," the carer whispers. "She spoke to the young student healer . . . Harlande, I think her name was. She comes to visit the child often. In fact, the family are working to adopt her. Apparently, they cared for her when she was a toddler."

"So, I have heard," Healer Olea replies. "Perhaps I can speak to young Healer Harlande to see if she can help us with talking to the child."

The whispers become more muffled, and Sana cannot hear what is said next. She closes her eyes and tries to empty her mind.

✾

"Knock knock," a kind and gentle voice says from beyond the curtains.

Sana wakes up and slowly opens her eyes. The newcomer is the young lady with braided butterscotch hair—Eirlys.

Eirlys sits on the chair next to Sana. "Good morning," she says and smiles. Her face is radiant and her eyes glisten.

Since the first time Sana saw this lady, she has felt like she can trust her. Perhaps it is her warm, honey eyes—which are similar enough to remind her of Seiji—or her loving and kind-hearted nature.

Eirlys told her many stories over the past few months. According to her, Sana was found and taken in by the Harlande family when she was a baby. However, she was soon removed from their home by an adoption agency and rehomed to someone who must have been her substance-abusing mother.

It turns out that her name was never Kudon Ozaki after all.

"You are doing so well." Eirlys smiles at her again, before leaning in and clasping onto her hands. "We are working hard on getting you back home," she says excitedly. Her eyes are bright, just like how Seiji's would be whenever he had exciting news to share with her. "And this time, it is going through legally so that they can never take you away from us again." Eirlys's smile stretches from cheek to cheek. "Due to the nature of what has happened and your circumstances, my status as a student healer has allowed us to officially take you in as our family."

Sana looks at her sister, feeling the warmth of her hands radiating onto her own. She nods.

"Your wounds have healed so well, Sana," Eirlys compliments. "It is a miracle. Nobody will be able to guess what happened before."

Sana's heart beats in sudden alarm. She has not yet seen her reflection after cutting herself apart by the stream.

Eirlys reaches into her bag and takes out a mirror. "Would you like to have a look?" she whispers excitedly, as if she just heard Sana's thoughts.

Sana gulps and her forehead creases with worry. She reaches out and slowly takes the hand mirror. She does not look at it and instead, stares at her bedsheets. Her hands tremble. She does not know what to expect, and an intense worry is beginning to spill inside her.

Eirlys's grasp tightens around Sana's hand. "It's all right," she reassures. "I am here."

Sana takes a deep breath and holds the mirror to her face. Her reflection is crystal clear, and she gasps. Something tears inside her heart.

The healers are correct—it is a true miracle that her face looks almost scar-free. But it is more miraculous that her new facial features have come together to form someone she has never seen before, turning her into a girl who is still well-proportioned but in a different way, Sana does not recognise the person staring back at her in the mirror at all.

Should she be reassured that the Kurai will never recognise her with this new appearance, or should she be upset that she has lost the face which Seiji complimented as rather adorable?

Immediately, tears overflow from Sana's eyes. She drops the mirror back onto her bed and cries.

Eirlys stands and wraps her arms around the young girl. "I'm here, I'm here," Eirlys whispers to her reassuringly.

Sana sobs into her sister's arms. Eirlys pats her head, instantly reminding Sana again of Seiji and when he used to sing to her about the windmill. She sobs harder. The tears keep coming and they cannot stop.

Eirlys stays standing, holding her younger sister tightly. There is an awful pain in her heart as she watches Sana cry. She does not know how to fix this, but she is going to try. "You are safe now," she whispers. "I will never let any harm come to you ever again."

She gently strokes Sana's hair. Sana takes in the warmth of her sister and allows herself to imagine the familial love that she lacked as a child.

Her emotions overspill and she continues to cry.

✻

That night, Sana stares up at the ceiling. She thinks about the day at the stream when she bid her own reflection goodbye. She told herself that she must survive, for Seiji's sake.

Sana closes her eyes and places her hand on her heart. She hums Seiji's song quietly and remembers the time when he said that, even in the hardest times, no one can ever take away one's happy memories or the strong bonds they created.

Sana opens her eyes once more and links her hands together. She rolls her fingers into a spiral and holds it above her face, looking at the shell of the snail she has created.

No one will be able to take away her memories of

Seiji or her love for him. For the first time in as long as she can remember, there is a small warmth in her heart and the void inside her shrinks just a bit.

Seiji's tune, although hummed through Sana's own voice, is extremely comforting to hear. She thinks about how her last words to Seiji were, 'I'm sorry,' rather than, 'I love you.'

She manages a smile and thinks about how Seiji would have flicked her on the forehead and told her to stop being silly, no matter what she said.

In that moment, Sana tells herself that she will not cry anymore. Seiji's words are extremely soothing, and she holds them dearly in her heart.

"Seiji," Sana whispers, "little Azuki will live on."

CHAPTER SIXTEEN

Remnants

BACK IN THE ROYAL PALACE of Shinrin, Sana opens her eyes. There is someone sitting on a chair next to her, resting on the side of her bed with his head on his arms. His long, raven-black hair glistens in the sunlight.

Is that Prince Takashi? she wonders.

Sana lifts a hand to shield her eyes from the sun pouring through the chamber window. Her bedsheets rustle as she stretches out her arms and legs.

Prince Takashi immediately stirs. He jolts awake and his eyes widen before he straightens up abruptly. "Harlande," he says in shock.

"Prince Takashi," she whispers, wondering why he is here.

Before she can react, the prince leans in and pulls her towards his chest. His strong arms hold her tightly in a warm embrace.

This sudden gesture takes Sana by surprise. She stares over the prince's shoulder at her door and blinks a few times, wondering what is happening.

There is a light knock, and the door edges open for Ryota to pop his head inside. "Your Majesty—" He immediately covers his mouth with his hand to hide his smile before pulling the door back shut. "My apologies," Ryota whispers as the door closes again.

Sana stays in the prince's arms for a few seconds longer. "Prince Takashi?" she eventually asks, wondering what is going on.

Satoru leans back. "You're awake," the prince says, his forest eyes still wide.

"Yes," Sana replies, wondering why he appears so worried. *What is going on? Why did Prince Takashi just embrace me?* She pinches her cheek to see if this is a weird dream.

"I must go and inform your family. They will be overjoyed," Satoru says, standing up abruptly. He turns to exit the room.

"Wait!" Sana says. Satoru stops and turns around. "Please, what is going on?" she asks.

Satoru steps back towards the chair and sits back down. "You have been unwell and in a semi-unconscious state for the past seven days," he explains.

"Right," Sana answers.

"You had sidium poisoning."

Something stops for a split second inside Sana's heart. "Right," she repeats, slightly softer.

There is another pause.

"Do you remember anything at all, Harlande?" Satoru asks gently.

Sana thinks back to the last thing she can remember. "I remember that day in the examination chambers," she replies. "I felt extremely unwell, in a way I cannot quite describe. The next thing I remember is waking up just now."

"We will need to find out how this could have happened," Satoru states firmly.

Sana leans back on the pillows and closes her eyes. *Sidium poisoning?* The idea of the Hoseki crosses her mind. She wonders if, even after all of Seiji's efforts, a slight remnant of the inactivated poison still remains inside her.

Although, why did it suddenly reactivate?

"Right," Sana whispers again. How many times has she escaped death from sidium? She suddenly thinks of the Soltair.

"I shall go and ensure your family is informed," Satoru says as he stands back up. "They will be eager to see you."

Sana gives a small nod as the prince makes his way out.

The guard by the door peers inside the room as he is about to close the door again. "Knight Lishuah!" Shou smiles. His eyes light up. "How wonderful to see you are awake."

Sana gives him a small smile and nods.

"The prince must be very pleased," he comments. "He has been looking after you over the past few days."

"He has?" she asks, surprised.

"Yes." He nods. "The palace healer and your sister have been coming to tend to you in turn, but in the gaps in between, Our Majesty has been checking over you."

"Oh."

Shou nods to her and smiles again before he closes the door.

Sana looks at the patch of sunlight on her bed before she turns to look out the window. There is a sudden sadness in her heart. *I wonder how much more time I have to live?*

According to the Soltair, her lifespan should have been reduced to around a quarter of its original length. Even if she has escaped the sidium, the effects of the Soltair linger on.

The Kurai memories enter straight back into her mind. There is a raw twinge in her heart as she thinks of Seiji.

She sighs and closes her eyes before leaning back into her bed.

CHAPTER SEVENTEEN

Into the Caves

AIYLA GLANCES AT CLAUS AS he finishes tying a knot in the rope around his waist.

He looks at her and Sako. "This is a special knot I learned how to tie after coming here," Claus explains. "It took a bit of trial and error, but this will not unravel, for sure." He walks towards Aiyla and ties the same knot around her. His hands twist the rope proficiently.

"How do we see down there?" Aiyla asks, her eyes large and full of worry.

His usual frown softens as he smiles at her. "I have my ways," he reassures. After he finishes tying the knot, he pulls open the small, cloth bag he has around his shoulder. "I've stolen quite a few candles. I do this on a regular basis." He scratches his chin, suddenly sheepish. "I guess I am lucky I haven't been caught yet, or I would have been hung by now."

Sako and Aiyla peer inside his brown cloth bag. Sure enough, there are quite a few white, waxy rods inside.

Claus closes the bag and ties a final knot around Sako.

"I guess you find places to put the candles?" Sako asks, drawing up knowledge from his experience of working as a cellar maker.

"Correct," Claus answers. "You will need to keep both of your hands completely free." He tightens the knot. "All good. Let's begin," Claus states.

He walks over to the entrance of the cave and finds a piece of rock that is protruding out from the rest. He ties his special knot around it before wrapping it around a thick metal ring.

"Where did you find that?" Sako asks.

"You learn to survive here," Claus replies. "I will go down first and light the way. Then you two can come after me."

Before Aiyla and Sako have a chance to respond, Claus leans back and lowers himself slowly into the caves. The two children peer down to see Claus bouncing his feet off the wall of the cave strategically. Soon, he disappears due to the lack of light.

Moments later, an orange glow appears. Then, a few more appear. Slowly, Claus ascends as he pulls on the other length of rope.

"Claus!" Aiyla exclaims. "You're back!"

"Right. Path is lit," he says. "Now feel this," he says before holding out a shiny black rock. It is glossy and sharp at the edges.

Aiyla and Sako both poke the rock.

"You see how it feels cold? Sometimes—" Claus pauses to knock the rock hard onto the ground, causing it to break in half. The inside glimmers like it has been dipped in stardust. "—You can see this glitter catch the light of the candles. If it does, you'll know the rock is sheen. But if you're not sure, the coldness of sheen will also help you tell it apart from the rest of the rocks."

Aiyla and Sako nod, committing the words to memory.

Claus pulls out a few more thick, metal rings from his bag and looks at the rocks in search for another suitable one to hold the tether. Once he finds one, he beckons to Aiyla.

"Here," he says. He helps her get set up, before doing the same for Sako. "Now, both of you, copy what I do," Claus says.

Aiyla peers into the terrifying dark cave below. She gulps. She peers at Sako, who is frowning with a determined look in his eyes.

Aiyla copies the platinum-haired boy as he descends again. She stretches her legs out so that her feet touch the walls of the cave. She slips at first and a burst of fear balloons inside her. She takes a deep breath and lowers herself down further.

It takes some time for her eyes to adjust to the darkness. She notices a few blobs of orange embedded into the walls of the cave—the candles Claus had set up. It is awfully quiet inside.

She lowers herself further and further until she reaches a large ledge of rock below. The further she goes, the colder the air around her becomes. She can just barely make out Claus's silhouette in the gloom when he stands next to her. Soon enough, Sako joins them.

"I am so grateful we have you, Claus," Aiyla whispers. She can feel him smile back at her in the darkness.

"Let's stick together, guys," Claus whispers. "One

day, the time for our revenge will come."

✽

The children scramble around, searching for sheen; their lives depend on this glittery rock. After being inside the cave for some time, a strange noise reaches Aiyla. Her ears perk up as she cocks her head to one side.

Is that someone crying?

"Guys," Aiyla whispers. "Do you hear that?" She looks at Claus and Sako, who both stop what they are doing and listen with concentration as they, too, strain their ears.

There is a very light, repetitive noise which sounds somewhat unsettling.

"I thought it was just me. I hear something too," Claus replies.

"There is definitely something there," Sako adds, pointing behind Aiyla. "I think it is coming from that way."

"Is it someone crying?" Aiyla asks.

Claus takes a few steps towards Aiyla, holding a hand against his right ear. "It sure sounds like it," he agrees. He tiptoes further in that direction.

A chill runs down Aiyla's spine. What could it be?

"Maybe someone else is down here too?" Sako

suggests. He follows behind Claus. "Shall we go and see what is making the noise?"

"Perhaps someone is lost," Claus says, holding his chin in his hand. "Perhaps they need help." He lights another candle and holds it in his right hand. "I'll go and see what it is. You guys can stay here."

"No, let's go together," Sako says. "We need to stick together. Let's not split up."

"I agree," Aiyla says, before shuffling to join the two boys.

"Very well," Claus replies. "But stay behind me, you guys."

Claus walks in the direction of the noise, stopping every so often to check if they can still hear it. He holds onto the candle tightly, and the flame wobbles as he moves.

As Aiyla follows, her heart thumps hard inside her chest. She can barely see a thing, except the flame of Claus's candle. Her steps are slow and careful, and she stretches out her arms in front of her, in case she might bump into anything.

"Hello?" Claus asks, raising his voice. It echoes through the caves. "Is someone there?"

After a short while, a voice responds. "Hello?"

Claus stops. "Hold this for me, Sako," he says as he

hands his candle over to him. He then lights another candle and waves it in front of him, peering around. "Ah!"

With Claus's exclamation, Aiyla can see what he saw. There is a young girl standing a few paces in front of them, wiping tears from her eyes.

"Oh guys, be careful," Sako says, gesturing to their side.

Aiyla looks up to see a reflection of the candle flames. There is a small body of water right in front of them. "There's a lake?" Aiyla asks.

"Looks like it," Claus answers. "Let's walk around this way."

The children walk towards the young, crying girl, manoeuvring carefully around the sides of the lake.

"Hey," Claus says, as soon as they reach the girl, "are you lost? How long have you been down here?"

The girl appears absolutely petrified. She is probably around six or seven years old. Her breathing is short and shallow, and she can barely speak. Her eyes are scrunched, and tears will not stop streaming down her cheeks.

"A long . . . time. M-My brother—" She gasps between breaths.

"What happened?" Sako asks as he approaches her

as well. He puts an arm around her shoulder in an attempt to comfort her.

"W-We were down here—looking for sheen—" The girl stammers. "A-And something came out—from here—" The girl points at the lake. "—a-and took my br-brother—" The girl is gasping through her tears.

"Something came out from here?" Claus asks, raising an eyebrow.

Sako looks at the girl, his eyes full of concern.

"What do you mean?" Aiyla asks her.

"Something horrible—it came out of nowhere! Now my brother . . . is g-gone—" The girl continues to stammer.

Claus frowns. He looks at Sako and Aiyla. "That's . . ." He pauses, clearly trying to find a word to describe it. "Disturbing," he finally says.

Aiyla wonders what in the world could have happened to the girl's brother. She steps towards the other children as fear sparks inside her. "Le-Let's all go," Aiyla says, suddenly wanting to get out of the caves. "Something doesn't seem right—"

Before Aiyla manages to finish her sentence, there is a deafening cry as something leaps out from the water of the lake and latches onto the young, sobbing girl.

The children scream.

Dark, claw-like hands cover the young girl's face, and she is dragged towards the water.

"No!" Claus exclaims. "Grab her!"

Sako drops his candle as he grasps onto the young girl's hand, using all his might to pull her back towards them.

Claus reaches towards the ground and scrambles for anything he can find. He throws a few rocks at the creature as hard as he can. The creature roars but the rocks do little save bounce off its terrifying form.

Aiyla screams once more. She has never seen anything so frightening in her life. It is difficult to make out exactly what is in front of them due to the lack of light, but one thing is clear—there is a horrifying monster that is about to drag the little girl into the lakes.

Aiyla reaches down and copies Claus, throwing rocks at the creature. Again, they do nothing.

The young girl continues to scream as she is dragged further towards the water. Her cries are deafening.

"Help!" Sako exclaims as he, too, is pulled towards the water by where he is holding onto the little girl's hand. The monster's strength is too strong, and he is struggling to hold on.

Aiyla runs behind Sako and throws her arms around

him, using all of her might to pull him back. Soon, she feels Claus's arms around her too. The children work together to do everything they can to pull the young girl back out of the monster's grasp.

But the monster is very strong. The three children slide on the wet, rocky ground towards the lake. They are struggling and all of them are absolutely terrorised, in disbelief about what is happening.

"Sako, I'm sorry—but you're going to have to let her go—" Claus stammers as he grips Aiyla tightly, not wanting to let his friends go.

"I can't," Sako replies. His hands are shaking, and he squeezes his eyes shut.

"I don't think I can hold on any longer," Aiyla whispers. There are tears forming in her eyes. Is this another nightmare? She would do anything to get out of whatever is happening right now.

Suddenly, Sako loses his grip and lets go. The three children fall to the ground, and the young girl is dragged away into the waters in an instant. Claus and Sako stare with frightened eyes, and Aiyla bursts into tears.

"Guys, we've got to run," Claus urges as he picks up Aiyla and settles her on her feet. "There is no time to panic. Whatever the hell that was, it might be back soon. We've got to get out of here."

He pulls on both Aiyla and Sako's arms and scrambles forwards. Aiyla is struggling to breathe as she stumbles behind them.

Using the light of only a single candle, the three children run for their lives, minds absolutely terrorised by what they just witnessed.

CHAPTER EIGHTEEN

The Cabin in the Woods

AKALIN LOOKS AT THE PRINCESS, exasperated. He steps down from the windowsill. *What does she want now?* All he wants is to escape this place.

"You must come with me at once," Princess Suyin Lore demands. Her crimson eyes light up and are filled with a level of determination that was not there before.

Akalin looks at her suspiciously.

"Do not make me repeat myself," she commands.

"You must come with me for your own safety."

Akalin sits on the windowsill, frowning. *For my safety?* He raises an eyebrow. The biggest danger to him right now is the woman standing before him.

"Every once in a while, my father will come and take away whichever soldier is with me," the princess states. "To this day, I do not know of their fate. I do not want this to happen to you, Sir Meness."

Akalin is not sure what to think. He holds his head in his hands and sighs before looking back at the princess. "And what happens if I come with you?" he asks. "You will eat me alive?"

"I will protect you," she answers simply.

Akalin frowns. He can either try to jump from this window and fall a thousand storeys to his doom, run out into the spears of the hundred guards outside, or follow this princess and risk getting eaten alive.

"Right," Akalin answers as he continues to frown. His increasing frustration is overpowering the intense fear he had felt earlier when he was alone with the princess in her chamber.

"So?" the princess asks, a hint of impatience in her voice. "Shall we make a move?"

"I guess I have no choice," Akalin answers. He rises slowly and walks towards her. She turns her back immediately and strides into the corridor.

The soldiers bow to the princess as Akalin follows behind her. He is led back into her chamber. As the door closes, Akalin stands by the wall uncomfortably. He tries to breathe through his mouth as the scent of perfume hits his senses once more and kicks his residual fear back into prominence.

"I am not going to do anything to you," the princess says when she sees Akalin's facial expression. "Go and sit down whilst I work out what to do." She points to the couch where they sat earlier.

Akalin blinks at her with suspicion before making his way to the couch. He plops down. Akalin wonders what is going on. He came all the way—to this land named Keska—in search of his sister. Not only has he not been able to find her, he is now completely trapped. He thinks of Samuel and wonders if he—at least—is doing all right.

Princess Lore opens her wardrobe and starts to rummage through her things. She opens various drawers, pulling out objects and stuffing them into a cloth bag. "Meness," she calls, before striding over and standing an inch from him.

Akalin stiffens.

"Tomorrow, in the early hours of the morning, we

shall try to leave the castle."

Akalin looks at her.

"I have always wanted to see the world, but my parents locked me inside this castle for the past fifteen years. They say the outside world is dangerous, but I now know that is not true."

"And how do you propose that we leave, then?" Akalin asks, wondering what she is on about and why she seems to be acting like a completely different person all of a sudden.

"There is a passageway right here in my room," the princess says, "but the door at the end is heavily locked and reinforced with strong magic."

She walks towards her bed, before bending down and pulling an extravagant rug to the side. There, in front of them, is a large wooden trap door.

"This leads outside of the castle," the princess says.

"Is that so?" Akalin replies, his eyebrows rising in surprise once more.

"Yes. I know the routes in the castle well, but I have never been able to make it past this door. I was hoping to find someone who could get us through it, but—" She sighs as she pulls the rug back over the hidden entrance, not finishing her sentence. "I believe you might be able to help," the princess says, "so let us try tomorrow." She then disappears into her bathroom.

Akalin wonders if the princess truly means what she says. How can he trust her?

However, in this moment, there is little else he can do.

✾

Akalin's ears perk up at the sound of the princess's footsteps. He is still on her couch but has not slept for a single second. His senses remain fully alert, his eyes wide and his ears straining for the slightest of sounds.

The princess has gotten up from her bed. She lights a candle before she disappears into her bathroom once again. Soon enough, she reappears and whispers from across the couch, "Meness."

Akalin sits up immediately and looks at her. Although Akalin believes that the princess is older than him, without her heavy layers of makeup, she appears rather youthful. She has pulled her black hair up into a simple ponytail and she wears a grey robe with plain grey trousers.

"Ready?" she whispers to Akalin.

He nods at her. Whether he is ready or not, there is nowhere else for him to go.

The princess throws a cloth bag over her shoulder

before handing a few candles to Akalin. She pulls the rug to the side to reveal the wooden door once again. She then curls her fingers under the flap and tries to pull it open. The stiff, wooden door does not budge.

"Here." Akalin gestures for her to let him try. The door seems to be cemented into the ground, but when he gives another hard pull, it suddenly creaks open.

Princess Lore's mouth drops open with surprise. As Akalin lifts the door further, they both peer into the darkness below. The smell is a mixture of dampness, earth, and mould. Cold air drifts up towards them.

"After you," the princess says, gesturing for Akalin to go first. "I need to close this behind us."

Akalin wonders if it is a good idea to go in front of her. However, once again, he does not have much choice. He stuffs all but one of the candles inside his robe, then watches as the princess strikes a match and lights the one he is holding. He then takes a step down onto the cold, stone stairs in the darkness.

Princess Lore reaches for the metal ring on the underside of the trap door, then tugs the rug back over and closes the door shut.

The two of them look at the stairs. They are rather steep, and the passageway is narrow. The candlelight does not reach very far, and the rest of what is in front of them exists in complete darkness.

"Let's go," Princess Lore whispers from behind Akalin.

The two of them begin to walk down into the depths of the castle. Akalin holds his hand out to the sides of the passageway, feeling out the stone walls as they begin to wind round and round. The stairs become narrower and narrower, and Akalin cannot shake the unsettled feeling which churns inside of him.

What will be at the end of these stairs? Akalin thinks. *Are we truly escaping, or is she leading me to my death?*

Despite his thoughts, Akalin continues on with constant vigilance, prepared for anything that may appear in front of him.

Stairs, stairs, and more stairs. The two of them sometimes cross levels of flat ground, before winding down even more stairs. At times, they pause to light another candle. They continue on in silence.

After what seems like a few hours, the sound of rain suddenly hits Akalin's ears and the smell of dampness increases. Sure enough, they soon find themselves standing behind a large, wooden door.

Akalin pulls on the metal ring. The door stays still.

"This is the door," Princess Lore says. "It is reinforced with heavy magic and has multiple locks."

"And you have never been able to get past it?" Akalin asks.

"No one has," she replies.

Akalin stares at the door, wondering if she is referencing the previous soldiers she had captured. The door appears large and heavy, but to him, it looks just like any other door. What sort of magic could it have been reinforced with?

Before the princess can react, Akalin leaps up and, using all his strength, he sends a side kick right at the door. In an instant, the wooden door flies open and falls to the ground.

They are immediately faced with freezing wind and very heavy rain. The skies are grey as the sun is yet to rise, and the weather is hostile. The cold bites at their skin. Akalin stares at the storm unfolding in front of them.

The princess stares wide-eyed at the outside world. Her jaw drops.

Akalin looks at her. "Sorry, but what? The door came down so easily." What sort of locks and magic had the princess been talking about? Why does it now seem that she does not really know much about this place?

He shakes his head as the princess continues to stare with her jaw open, like a child.

"I didn't even think to bring a cloak," the princess mutters behind him. She slaps her palm to her forehead. "How silly of me."

There is not a single person in sight. Only a large field and a deep forest looms ahead. The trees are swaying in the howling wind.

"There are no guards here?" Akalin asks, wincing as a gust blows through him. Having to walk through this weather is not going to be fun, but it will be even worse if they are trying to outrun guards, too.

"No," Princess Lore replies. "We are at the very west of the castle. The guards only patrol in this direction at certain times each day."

Akalin nods. "And what if someone sees us when we cross this field?"

"We will not have this chance again," Princess Lore says. "It is now or never."

"Very well," Akalin replies. He steps out the door. The cold wind immediately hits him harder. He blinks hard and struggles to keep his eyes open against the rain.

He squints against the storm. His long, silver ponytail flaps in the wind and is drenched immediately. It blows in all directions before slapping him in the face. This amusing sight causes the princess to burst into laughter.

Still laughing, she steps out after him. “Shall we run?”

Once he nods, the two begin to run across the field. As they go on, the rain drenches them both completely, and their feet slosh loudly through the wet mud in the field.

“This is crazy!” Suyin shouts through the rain.

Akalin slows down from time to time to allow her to catch up. He is unsure why he is looking out for someone who he thought was going to murder him earlier. Perhaps it is because she now seems so innocent.

Why is she so child-like? It is as if she has never seen the world.

After a while, when the sun is cresting in the sky, they reach the forests. The leaves of the trees protect them from some of the rain. They look at each other, both drenched from head to toe.

Suyin laughs. “You look like a drowned rat.”

“You don’t look much better,” Akalin comments, unamused. He wipes some rain from his eyes before the two of them continue on.

✾

After many hours of walking, the skies begin to darken. The temperatures drop even lower, and the wind is unforgiving. Thankfully however, the rain stops.

Akalin trudges behind Suyin. The cold, wet fabric of his clothing clings to his skin uncomfortably.

As they continue walking, he frowns. He is certain they have walked along this path already. Were they not here just a few moments earlier? Even if they are in a forest, Akalin can tell that they have already walked down this way before.

Akalin breaks the silence. "Where are you going, exactly?"

"I, uh—" the princess replies. She looks at him and then back ahead, taking a few more confident steps forwards.

Akalin sighs in disbelief. "I thought you said you knew the area well?"

"I know the *castle* well," she corrects. "Whereas these forests—"

"Great." Akalin sighs again. "So, all this time, you've had no idea where we were going? You could have just said." Akalin tuts and shakes his head. This so-called princess is just a child in disguise. Akalin strides forward and decides to take the lead, although he, too, does not have any idea where they are.

As they walk on, they come across a small clearing in the forests. There is a wooden cabin in the centre of it.

"Oh, look." The princess points at the cabin. "Perhaps we could use hide out there?"

Akalin sniffs. The cold is making his nose run. He desperately wants to find somewhere warm and to dry himself off.

The duo slowly makes their way towards the cabin, squelching with each step; their shoes are soaked from the wet mud.

Akalin peers through a small glass on the door, but it is too dark to see anything inside. Night is falling quickly. He pulls on the door gently and it opens with ease.

"It's open," Akalin says quietly. He steps inside.

Princess Lore lights a candle behind him. "Is there anyone here?" she whispers.

They look around. The inside is lined with wooden floorboards. There is a simple fireplace and a few shelves to the side. A tiny, stone cookery set stands in the corner. Next to it is a small side room.

"Does anyone live here?" Suyin asks.

"No idea," Akalin replies. He takes the candle from Princess Lore and tiptoes around the place before peering into the small side room. Inside, there is a simple bed and a shelf placed next to it. On the shelf, there are a few folded fabrics—perhaps they are clothes or sheets. There is a tiny bathroom further inside the bedroom.

"I don't think anyone is here," Akalin says as he steps back out towards the fireplace.

"Right," Suyin says.

"We need to light a fire." Akalin crouches down under the stone cookery and opens the cupboards. Sure enough, he finds some dry wood and a few jars of pickles. "Light a match, please," Akalin says as he carries some wood over to the fireplace. He gestures for the princess to throw the match into the fire.

As soon the princess does, warm, brilliant orange flames burst brightly into life. Akalin returns to the bedroom and takes out a few of the folded fabrics. He opens them up to find that they are thin rugs.

"Here," he says to Princess Lore as he drapes one over her. He sits down cross legged and leans in towards the fireplace, enjoying the comforting warmth of the flames.

He closes his eyes. Now that he is out of the castle, he is a little more at ease. Although he is still unsure of the princess' motives, now that there are no soldiers around, he is a lot more confident that, if anything is to happen, he will be able to defend himself.

But first, he must dry off. Akalin begins to towel his

hair with one of the rugs.

Suyin sits down next to him and holds her hands in front of the fireplace. "Thank goodness we found this place," she says quietly. She turns to see Akalin peeling off the top half of his robe, which is drenched with water. Her round eyes widen at the unexpected sight of his bare torso. She stares at his muscular frame and his smooth, bronze skin. Her mouth opens into a small O.

The hairs on the back of Akalin's neck stiffen up. Why is she staring at him like that? It is making him extremely uncomfortable.

The princess shuffles towards him and reaches out her hand. She touches Akalin's muscular arm curiously, then looks at him softly and smiles.

Akalin flinches and moves back. "Please, can you not?" he snaps. He looks at the princess with annoyance.

Princess Lore drops her arm and is taken aback once again. She sighs, as if she does not understand what she is doing wrong.

Truly, it is rather annoying.

Akalin tuts. His freezing, wet robe was clinging to his skin, and there is a chill all throughout his body. He feels like he is going to become ill. He lays the robe open near the fire, hoping that it will dry soon.

Akalin wonders if he should take off the bottom half

of his robe as well. The wet fabrics are attached to his legs uncomfortably . . . but the princess is staring at him too much. He decides against it.

"Your name is not actually Meness, is it?" Princess Lore asks quietly.

Akalin ignores her.

"Will you tell me your name?" Suyin tries.

Akalin looks at her. *Will she ever stop talking?* He sighs. "What if Meness is not my name?" Akalin asks.

"I am curious, that is all." She shuffles next to him again.

Akalin backs away from her a little. He thinks. Whether or not she knows his name, it probably will not make a difference. There is not much left he can do at this point, anyway. Perhaps if he answers her, she will stop talking.

"Akalin," he mutters. "Akalin Kinali."

Suyin smiles with her eyes. "That is lovely," she replies. "You are not from here, are you?"

Akalin shakes his head.

"Whereabouts?" she asks.

Akalin sighs again. "Shinrin."

Suyin's mouth opens in surprise once more. Her eyes light up, but then she sighs and turns back towards the fire. "I loved a man from Shinrin once," the princess says quietly. There is a change to her tone of voice. Her eyes soften and a little vulnerability seeps out from her. "It was Prince Takashi," Suyin says, her volume lowering even more, until it is barely a whisper. A watery film forms over her eyes.

Akalin inhales in surprise. "Satoru?"

"Satoshi," she whispers.

"Ah."

There is a silence.

"Your eyes remind me of him a lot," Suyin says after a while. She looks at him. "You are from the kingdom?"

"Mm." Akalin nods.

"Th-then you know how he is? Prince Takashi?" Suyin asks, leaning towards Akalin, eagerness overflowing.

Akalin is taken aback. He leans away from her, increasing the distance between them. "I'm afraid not," he answers.

"Oh," Suyin replies, her eyes looking to the floor with disappointment. She does not mention the prince anymore. Instead, she remains silent for a few minutes before asking, "So, what brings you to Keska?"

"I am looking for my sister," Akalin answers flatly. "Your people massacred my village and abducted our children."

"Oh," Suyin replies. She looks at him apologetically. "I do not agree with what my parents are doing. The Keskan empire is going to fall one day."

Akalin raises an eyebrow at her. "So, you are fully aware of what has been going on?"

"To an extent." Suyin sighs. "But there is not much I can do. It is out of my hands."

Akalin looks back towards the fire and does not say anything else.

✾

Princess Lore lies curled up on the floorboards, asleep next to the fire. Akalin remains sitting. He puts his robe back on, relaxing into the comforting warmth of the now-dry fabrics that flow snugly over his arms.

He holds his head in his hands as he squeezes his eyes shut, soreness thrumming in his temples. His eyes are dry and gritty. He is mentally exhausted, but something tells him he should not let his guard down.

Suddenly, Akalin's ears perk up. Something is moving. There is sounds of footsteps. He turns around briskly to see three people just as they burst through the front door of the cabin.

A young girl wearing grey and teal fabrics step towards them. Akalin immediately stands up and holds his arms out, ready to defend himself. Princess Lore wakes up and bolts upright, alarmed.

The young girl in front of them has black hair tied into two braids. She has some red markings painted on her face and wooden beads and feathers tied around her head. She looks at them with cold, icy blue eyes.

"Oh look," she says. Her voice is light and remarkably confident. She smirks as she draws an arrow from her quiver and nocks it on her bow. She points it straight at Princess Lore. "It's Princess Lore and her handsome companion!"

Princess Lore starts to tremble. Akalin's eyes are fixated on the the newcomers.

The girl closes one eye, as if aiming for her target. "Move," she orders, gesturing to the princess with her arrow.

Princess Lore stands up slowly, her eyes wide. Her trembling increases.

The young girl smirks again. "Good. Now follow me and don't try anything funny."

CHAPTER NINETEEN

New Beginnings

SEVENTEEN-YEAR-OLD SANA MAKES her way up the lush green hills of the Akamatsu fields. It is another beautiful, warm, and sunny day. She holds onto a fresh bunch of white carnations in one hand and her cloth bag in another.

The chestnut windmill stands tall and proud in front of her, its white blades spinning round and round. Sana takes a moment to admire the serenity of the sight.

She then finds the cluster of bluebells and sits on the

grass. "Good morning, Seiji." She smiles. "I have a lot of news to share with you today."

She lays the carnations in front of the bluebells and holds her palms together to say a small prayer.

"These carnations remind me of your soft, ivory hair," Sana says as she opens her eyes. She can almost see Seiji sitting here too, enjoying the warm breeze with her.

Azuki, you look excited, the image of Seiji says as he tucks some ivory strands behind his ear.

"I got accepted into Hida Academy," Sana says, her eyes bright, "and I am starting a semester early. They said they were impressed with my application and audition. I am going to become a musician, Seiji!"

Is that so? The image of Seiji replies. *I am so proud of you! I knew you were capable of anything. The world is in your hands, Azuki.* A delicate hand ruffles through her hair.

She closes her eyes and cherishes this moment. "I played your song, Seiji," Sana continues. "I realised you never told me the name of it, so I named it 'Our Home.' I played it on my harp."

The harp? Sana pictures Seiji's honey eyes widening in surprise. *That is your chosen instrument, is it?* He looks at her proudly.

"I've been playing it since I got out of the Kurai,"

Sana replies. "It is a wonderful instrument. I shall bring it here one day and play it for you."

I shall look forward to that, Sana thinks of Seiji saying.

"You know, Seiji," Sana says, watching the bluebells sway in the breeze, "you were right. This has always been our home." Sana looks up at the windmill again. "It turns out I am from Akamatsu too, and that I always had a loving family. My name was never Kudon Ozaki." Sana laughs. "It is Sana Harlande."

The imagined expression on Seiji's face turns into one of shock and amusement. *Is that so?*

"If I wasn't taken away by the woman who I thought was my mother," Sana continues, "I would probably never have ended up in the Kurai. But I would never change anything, Seiji. Because if I didn't go there, I would never have met you. And you are the greatest blessing in my life."

And you were mine, he says.

"Although I do not know who my birth parents are," Sana says as she holds her palm to her chest, "just like you said, no one can take away what we have here." Sana smiles up at the windmill. Her heart throbs painfully inside her but she manages to keep her tears back. "And that brings me to my next point, Seiji," Sana says excitedly, as she opens up her cloth bag and takes an object out. She holds it up to face the bluebells. "What do you think of this?"

What in the world is that? Sana imagines Seiji asking. He stares at the wooden mask with an odd-looking facial expression.

"I am not sure if you will approve of this, but I've given myself a new mission," Sana says. She holds the wooden mask proudly in her hands. "I designed this myself," she explains. "Look at the green spiral eyes. They are the spirals of our snail shell home on Akamatsu field. And the straight mouth is you trying to keep a straight face when I first told you my name is Kudon."

Sana can almost hear Seiji's immediate protest. *I never found your name funny!*

"It's all right. Looking back, I think it is quite funny." She grins. "To be named 'money' is odd enough to be humorous."

If you say so, Seiji says, not protesting. *But what mischief will you get up to, Azuki?*

"This shall be my disguise for my missions, Seiji. I am going to hunt down all the most powerful treasures in Shinrin."

Sana can see Seiji shaking his head. *Why?*

"I cannot bear to lose anyone I love ever again,"

Sana says, her tone becoming serious. "I do not know if the Kurai will ever find me, but I cannot risk my family being harmed. I need the powers from these treasures to be able to protect them as much as I can."

Azuki, the Kurai are something of the past. Do not let them control your future.

"I cannot risk it." Sana sighs. "I need to protect them. And it is for my own peace of mind."

Sana closes her eyes and imagines Seiji's warm embrace as if he is putting his arms around her to comfort her. Her heart twinges as the scent of sandalwood hits her.

"I miss you, Seiji," Sana whispers.

She hears nothing but the rustling of the breeze in the trees and the chirping of the birds in the sky.

CHAPTER TWENTY

The Cerus

EMIKO CLOSES THE BACK COVER of the navy-coloured book on her lap. She lies on her dormitory bed and traces her hands over the golden embossed writing that reads: *ANIMAL STUDIES: AN INTRODUCTION*. She has already read it through three times since receiving it in class.

It has been a few months since she started studying at Furukawa Academy. Most of the time, she is still in disbelief that she is really here.

As she leans back onto her pillow, her book suddenly slips from her grip, and she loses her position. The pages flip onto a different one—that of *THE HORSE*. The sketch of a stallion looks back at her.

"Erwin," she finds herself saying. An image of Sir Leon immediately pops into her mind. A memory of her preparing his bath follows. She then thinks of the moment when she sat huddled next to him under his cloak as they waited for the rain to pass.

Her heart begins to thump. *I wonder how you are doing, Sir Leon.* She then remembers how he would always tell her to call him by his first name. "Albert," she says out loud. Immediately, redness blushes onto her cheeks and she squeals before she rolls onto her side in her bed.

Putting those warm and fuzzy thoughts aside, Emiko decides that she should take the chance of a rest day to explore the outskirts of Ajisai.

She briskly hops to her feet and packs her things before making her way out.

✾

Emiko has been strolling through the grassy paths of the mountains for some time. She enjoys the warmth of the sun on her skin and the gentle breeze. Being so far out in the countryside reminds her of home. She wonders how her grandparents are doing.

From afar, Emiko notices that there is a young man perched on top of a rock, facing away from her. He looks into the distance, then down at his lap. His hair is of the palest blue, and it is tied loosely into a single, thin braid.

Is that Sair? she thinks.

"He-Hello," Emiko says, not wanting to give him a fright.

The young man's head pops upright as his back straightens. He turns around briskly, and his silver eyes enlarge into a look of surprise. "Oh, great," he says flatly.

Emiko realises it is indeed Sair. She recognises him as one of her fellow course-mates; he is a man of few words whom she met briefly during one of the lectures on Ornithology. She had found him somewhat arrogant, intimidating, and difficult to approach.

Emiko takes a few steps forwards. On the young man's lap is a sketchbook with a watercolour painting of the mountains in front of them. Sair puts down his paint brush.

"Wow, you painted that?" Emiko asks. She gazes at his art with astonishment as she admires his talent. The watercolour strokes are elegant and soft, and the colours bleed together into a beautiful piece of work.

Sair shuffles on the rock, turning away from her and trying to hide his work. He sighs and looks at her. "Who are you again, red head?"

Excuse me? Emiko thinks, offended. *What sort of attitude is that?*

He may be talented, but his rudeness further confirms his unapproachable nature.

"Emiko," she replies, frowning. "We met during one of the lectures. You are Sair, are you not?"

"Mm," he grumbles. He starts to pack up his things. "How annoying. I was content and enjoying my space, until you arrived," he mutters.

What is wrong with this guy? Emiko thinks, frowning deeper. He sure has a nerve to treat her like this. "Well, I was about to compliment your talent until you opened your mouth. You are rather rude," Emiko says, the annoyance inside her increasing.

"Rude?" Sair stops in his tracks and looks at her, his silver eyes cold and piercing. "I should think you should reconsider your words, red head. One who intrudes into another's private space would be considered the rude one, in my opinion," he mutters. His mouth turns down into a frown that reflects his annoyance. "Also, I do not need you to inform me of my talent. I know it very well already."

"First of all, not the sun nor the moon cares about your opinion," Emiko states bitterly, her nostrils flaring. "And second of all, a space in the mountains is open to the general public. You sure have some nerve." Something ticks inside Emiko. This man's rudeness sure is something, and she is not going to let him talk to her like that.

Sair tuts. He shakes his head and continues to pack his things. Once he is done, he pushes himself off the rock and steps onto the ground. "Later, red head." He salutes to Emiko and does not give her so much as a second glance before he strides off in the opposite direction.

Out of nowhere, a loud boom rattles through the sky. Emiko peers up to see dark, grey clouds looming over above them. It does not take more than a few seconds before the rain pours down over them both.

In a panic, Emiko pulls the hood of her cloak over her head. She turns to stride back the way she came, towards the academy. Immediately, she notices Sair shove his sketchbook into his robe. The young man looks about as he holds a hand above his head, which does nothing to help keep him dry. He is drenched instantly.

That little fool, Emiko thinks, shaking her head. She loosens her cloak and strides towards him. "Put this over us both, you little nerve," Emiko shouts at him over the rain. She gestures to her cloak. Sair eyes her, annoyance still evident on his face. "This is what you get for being rude," Emiko says, satisfaction flowing through her.

He should thank her for being nice enough to help him, even after he had treated her with such a poor attitude.

Sair reaches over and covers his head with Emiko's cloak, his other hand hovering over his sketchbook, trying to keep it dry. Emiko shuffles in next to him. The two of them walk on, trying to hide from the rain.

This moment reminds Emiko very much of when Sir Leon held her close with his cloak over their heads. She shakes her head. Right now, the man next to her is the furthest thing possible from Sir Leon. If only it were Albert next to her right now, instead of this rude fool.

As they walk on, the rain gushes down even faster. At this point, there is pretty much a waterfall above their heads.

Emiko has not been in such heavy rain in a long time, if ever. She tries to make out what is in front of them, but a dense fog is blurring everything into a smudge of grey. The ground is turning extremely slippery with wet mud and the more they trudge on, the more dangerous things are becoming.

"There are some caves around here," Sair says out of nowhere. "We should go to them."

"I agree," Emiko says reluctantly. It is almost impossible to go on in weather like this. She walks next to Sair as he takes off in a direction. Soon, large rocky boulders begin to appear out of the fog.

They head inside and immediately, Sair steps away from her. "What a day." Sair stares out at the rain from inside the caves. "Thank God I know my way around here."

Emiko's cloak falls in a heavy heap on the ground. She briskly picks it up and begins to wrench it, trying to remove as much water as she can. It is absolutely saturated with rain. She sighs as she sits down on one of the rocks. It is cold and some moss is growing along its sides.

Sair too, sits down on a rock further away. The two of them sit in silence as they stare miserably at the storm unfolding in front of them.

✽

After what seems like a few hours, the rain starts to lessen. Soon enough, it stops almost completely. The clouds part slightly, allowing a ray of sunlight to shine onto the ground.

"Ah, great." Sair jumps down from his rock as he strides towards the cave entrance. "Sun is out. Later, red head."

Emiko grumbles. "Can you stop calling me that?" Her frustration is increasing once again. "Do you want me to call you blue head, or something?"

Sair shrugs. He continues on his way out.

"Sorry, but how old are you?" Emiko continues. She has an urge to throw a punch at the man in front of her. "You're acting like an immature little child. Grow up."

Sair turns around and stares at Emiko. "You little—"

His sentence is cut off by a strange noise. There is something chirping. Or crying? It is something high-pitched. Emiko stares at Sair and he stares back. He must have heard it too.

"What was that?" Emiko whispers.

Sair puts a finger to his lips and turns towards where the sound was coming from. He listens, staring into the distance with concentration.

The sound appears again. It most definitely is coming from somewhere to the left. Is it the sound of an animal?

Emiko takes a few steps toward the noise and slowly

makes her way out of the cave.

"Are you crazy?" Sair asks out of nowhere.

"What?" Emiko turns back to stare at him.

"Why are you following the noise?"

"To see what it is. What do you think?" Emiko asks, frowning again.

"It could be something dangerous," he replies. He stands firmly in the same position, just inside the entrance to the cave.

Something inside Emiko tells her that she should go and see where this noise is coming from. She continues on, leaving Sair behind.

Sair tuts and shakes his head. After a while, he follows Emiko.

Emiko climbs over boulders and boulders, balancing herself and using her hands and feet to keep steady. She nearly slips at times, but she keeps on going. Soon, she approaches a different cave. There is something large, furry, and white laid on the floor.

Emiko's heartbeat quickens inside her chest. She tiptoes slowly towards the creature. As she nears it, the large, ivory wings protruding from its back are unmistakable.

Emiko gasps. *A Cerus!* She is in disbelief. It is her first time seeing one of the large, magical wolf-like creatures with wings.

"Hey!" a loud whisper comes from behind Emiko. Sair follows on behind her, tiptoeing carefully. "Be careful!"

Emiko ignores him. She wonders why he is following her. Did he not want to leave earlier? This moment would be so much better without someone as annoying as him around.

Emiko frowns. The large creature lies completely still. Its chest lays as stiff as stone. She creeps closer until she can see better.

She gasps. There, sitting by the Cerus's paws, is a tiny white creature. He is nudging and nudging at his mother. He cries once more as he pokes his head into his mother's fur.

"Oh." Emiko clasps her hand to her mouth as she realises that it is a baby Cerus. His mother appears to be dead; she is not moving, and there is blood smeared over her fur. "Oh, poor thing," Emiko says once more. She peers at the helpless baby creature.

His amber eyes are large, round, and distraught. The wings on his back are tiny.

"The mother is dead?" Sair whispers.

Emiko almost forgot he was still there. "I think so," she whispers back. She looks at the creature. Something aches in her heart. She cannot just leave the poor creature by himself.

"What could have happened?" Sair asks, his annoying and rude tone of voice changing into something softer.

"I'm not sure," Emiko says back.

Sair hops down next to her and starts to check over the mother Cerus. Emiko watches as he looks around, examining her from the left and then the right.

"Weird," he comments. "There is some blood, but I cannot see an obvious injury."

"Could it be from illegal poachers?" Emiko suggests. She has read that Cerusae are still hunted illegally to this day—their claws and teeth are used to create illegal medicinal substances.

"Possibly," Sair replies.

"What should we do with the baby?" Emiko asks. "We can't just leave him here."

The baby Cerus looks up at them both, his large amber eyes taking in what is in front of him. He steps out and starts to sniff at Emiko's ankles.

"Perhaps we can inform the Academy," Sair comments. He pauses. "Actually, better not. You know about the animal sanctuaries at the Academy, right?" Sair asks.

"Oh," Emiko realises.

There are very strict rules there. Due to the fear of diseases and wild animals being too ferocious, if a creature is considered to have too high of a risk towards humans, it will be put down instead of taken into care.

"He's a Cerus. He's never going to make it there. They are too ferocious," Sair says.

"I agree," Emiko replies.

"Not to mention . . . did you hear the talk about how some professor was linked with illegal trading and had networks with poaching back in the day?"

"Oh, the one that was taken to prison?" Emiko replies, thinking about the whispers she had heard from here and there. It seems that, even at a prestigious Academy like Furukawa, there can be dark things going on behind the scenes.

"Mm," Sair answers.

The two of them stare at the helpless baby creature.

"Then . . . then, we are going to have to take care of him," Emiko eventually says.

"Sorry, *we*?" Sair exclaims.

"Who else? Without his mother, he will die here," Emiko states.

Sair looks at her in disbelief. However, Emiko can tell that, deep down, he agrees with her. She is determined to help the creature, and she shall do everything she can to look after this helpless baby.

She picks up the Cerus and an overwhelming wave of love flows into her heart. Something tells her that she must protect this creature with all that she can.

"You are honestly crazy," Sair comments unhelpfully. The annoying tone has returned to his voice.

"If you are so against this idea, why are you doing animal studies again?" Emiko comments. "You know as much as I do that he won't survive. We should take responsibility."

Sair shakes his head. "And how are *we* supposed to look after him? You are in the girls' dorm. Obviously, I do not live there."

"We will find a way," Emiko replies, hugging the baby Cerus to her chest.

Sair shakes his head again. The two of them look at the small white furball, who continues to squirm and cry. He is truly helpless.

Sair sighs and closes his eyes. The sun is to beginning set.

"Let's go, then," Sair says quietly, as they both step out into the sunset.

CHAPTER TWENTY-ONE

King Rheinallt

SATOSHI GETS UP FROM HIS grand, ornate throne and strides out of his chamber. His haven is dark, extravagant, and luxurious. The floors are carpeted in the softest maroon fabrics, and each room is adorned with the finest dark, marble furniture. There are gold patterns painted tastefully along the corridor walls, and the orange glow of candles lights up the paths in every direction.

He ascends some stairs and reaches a large, wooden door. He opens it and steps out into the Qietian night.

The stars glimmer brightly in the night sky and the waters of the sea lap gently at the ivory staircases in front of him. He steps into the water. It soaks into the raven fabrics of his robe, but he continues on until he is mostly submerged.

As Satoshi continues to walk, an orange, glowing rectangle appears in front of him. Despite being nearly swallowed by the water, the wetness does not seem to reach him. He arrives, steps through the glowing entrance, and is immediately met by a few guards. They wear dark grey armour and bow frantically as soon as they see him.

"Lord Azrael!" they shout in unison as they bend forward.

Satoshi nods at them, barely giving them a second glance. He strides onwards.

"Lord Azrael, what brings such a great lord as yourself to Incarae today?" one of the guards asks.

"I am here to see Rheinallt," Satoshi states. "Take me to him."

"Certainly, my lord!" The guard bows frantically once again. He moves in front of Satoshi and leads the way.

After walking through several dark candlelit corridors, Satoshi is led to another grand wooden door. It is shaped like a circle, and there are various carvings on it, all depicting people trying to escape onto the land. But before they can, monsters drag them into the waters.

Two guards stand on either side of the door—they are wearing the same dark grey armour as the other guards. They each have a spear in their hands.

"Lord Azrael," they say as they bow forward.

Satoshi nods. "Make way," he orders.

The guards bow again frantically and immediately open the door. Satoshi steps inside. He is in a very large and almost empty room. The ceilings are extraordinarily high and are covered in paintings of terrorised angels. They have their hands over their faces and their eyes are turned up at a frightening angle. Horrifying, dark red blood drips out from their eyes and onto their chins. Their mouths are open wide, as if they are screaming out the depths of their terror. A single large, black chandelier hangs from the centre of the ceiling, and the flames from its candles flicker back and forth.

In the middle of the room is the back of a large maroon-and-golden throne.

A low, raspy voice comes from the throne. "I hear

the doors have opened," the voice says. The seat turns slowly until the person in it is facing Satoshi.

"King Rheinallt," Satoshi acknowledges as he steps towards him.

The king in front of him lies in a heap, as if he has melted into the chair. His skin is maroon, and thick, dark liquid drips from him onto the floor. It is nearly impossible to recognise where his face is, as the features dissolve together and trickle down onto what might be his chest. He gasps and wheezes as he talks, and every movement seems to take extensive effort.

"Good Lord Azrael," King Rheinallt begins, gasping as he speaks. "You have not stepped into the waters of Incarae in quite some time. What good news have you brought me?" His speech is slow, and it takes quite some time for him to finish his sentences.

"How do you fare?" Satoshi asks flatly. There is no sign of care or actual concern in his voice. He looks at the melting man in front of him, uninterested.

"Good of you to ask, Lord Azrael," the king wheezes. "We are still in search for the one."

"We have released the Katek into the waters," Satoshi says.

"Ah," the king replies. "I am still waiting on the first feed. I am grateful, Lord Azrael."

"Mm," Satoshi says. He looks at the man in front of him and shakes his head. Such a pity, to be in a state like that. Such a poor, helpless soul.

"You are very kind, Lord Azrael," the king says as he gasps for some more air and burbles on his chair. "And you are also a very intelligent lord. Not to mention . . . your face is as attractive as always."

Suddenly, there is a light knock at the door and a voice calls out, "King Rheinallt!"

"Come in," Satoshi answers for the king.

One half of the round, wooden door eases open, and a guard comes through, holding a tray with a large, marble bowl. He bows before stepping forward. "King Rheinallt," he says, "this is for you. Freshly prepared."

He places the bowl in front of the king. There are fresh organs inside, drenched in bright red blood. A kidney sits on the left, and some intestines are twisted up beside it. A single eyeball floats to the side, swimming amongst globules of blood clots.

"Ah, speak of the devil," Satoshi says.

"This must be the first kill by the Katek," King Rheinallt says, breathing heavily.

Satoshi can almost make out a gleam in what could be an eye on the king's face. Rheinallt drops a melting hand into the bowl, splattering blood all over himself and onto the floor. He digs out an intestine and yanks it up towards him. Some more blood splashes out of the bowl. An odd, dark, oval opening appears on his so-called face, and it widens as he pushes the organ straight into it. He devours the whole intestine in a single slurp. Immediately after, he stuffs the kidney into his mouth as well. The bloody mess is unsightly, and it is made even worse by how he gasps and groans as his face begins to twitch.

Soon, his unrecognisable, melted form starts to rearrange itself. Now, he almost definitely has facial features—two eyes, a pointy nose, and a mouth—and they look well proportioned. The gelatinous appearance of his skin tightens up. When he speaks, his voice is deep, clearer, and much younger. His wheezing and gasping stops.

"Lord Azrael," King Rheinallt says once the transformation finishes, "I thank you."

Satoshi nods, his facial expression indifferent. "As I said earlier, the Katek have been released into the waters. I believe what you are devouring right now is the first Shirinese citizen the Katek have collected."

"My, you have obtained bodies all the way from Shinrin?" the king asks. "You are good to me, Lord Azrael. I am touched." He pauses. "And how did you come to create these Katek creatures, so to speak?"

"Dark magic, Rheinallt," Satoshi replies indifferently.

"Lord Azrael, despite the number of beings I have devoured, I still cannot seem to find the one," the king mentions. "I require a child, I believe."

"The Katek have heard you. It will take time," Satoshi replies. "They are rare. Be patient."

"Rare, but we must find one."

"And we will," Satoshi answers. "For now, at least this will sustain your existence and halt your transformation into that lamentable visage."

"I am offended." The king almost laughs. His now-younger face turns towards Satoshi and his mouth curls up into a smirk. "You do know that your harsh, yet elegant, words make you all the more attractive, my lord?"

Satoshi ignores him.

"I am touched you have come to visit me," the king continues. "Is this proof that you care for me, Lord Azrael?"

Satoshi's lips flatten into a forced, crooked smile. Even then, he exudes his aura of elegance and indifference. "Only in the most fantastical depths of your imagination, Rheinallt," Satoshi says.

"I am offended, once again!" the king replies. He pauses before continuing to speak. "Your face is a gift, Lord Azrael," he compliments. "Even if you offend me like that, I could stare at you all day. Your presence is a blessing." He sighs and leans forwards towards Satoshi.

"My duty is done. I shall leave," Satoshi says, ignoring the king once more. He turns around to exit the large throne room.

"You are good to me, Lord Azrael," the king calls from behind Satoshi. "One day, you will realise what I am to you, and when that day comes, we shall rule Incarae together."

Satoshi does not give the king a second glance as he makes his way out.

CHAPTER TWENTY-TWO

An Unexpected Message

SANA PEERS AT THE LAKE from behind a tree. It glistens a bright, cyan colour, and the night air is still. There is barely a single sound to be heard around her.

Satoru stands behind her, peering in the same direction as well. The two of them are standing amongst the trees in the Oku Forests.

"Harlande," Satoru whispers, "I do not feel it is wise for you to be here. You have barely recovered."

Sana continues to stare ahead at the lake. Today, they both carry bows and arrows. Since she woke up from the sidium poisoning, her mind has been racing non-stop. Despite having survived it this time, she is sure the effects of the Soltair will cause her life to end soon.

Seiji, Sana thinks. *I promised you that I would live a long, healthy, and happy life, but it seems I cannot escape the effects of the Soltair. My mission was to protect my family from the Kurai, but these killings are getting out of hand. I need to think of something before I meet my end. I cannot let my family fall into this new danger.* Sana shakes her head to focus her thoughts.

Satoru whispers again. "Harlande—"

Sana turns, her mouth firming with determination. She puts a finger to her lips, telling him to not make a sound.

Satoru's mouth immediately shuts, and he blinks at her.

Since her waking from the sidium poisoning, the prince revealed to her that a creature was seen, right here in the Oku Forests. After that, two more Shirinese victims were discovered before the prince commanded for most of the large lakes in the kingdom to be drained. Even with the order, drying out the rivers is currently proving to be a challenge.

As it stands, the fresh kills are posing a new threat to the general citizens. Shinrin is becoming a land that is unsafe.

Sana fears what could happen to her family. She must try to help catch one of these creatures so that they can finally find out what is behind these killings and put an end to it. At this point, she will need to work together with the prince.

The Shirinese soldiers have been patrolling lakes and rivers, day and night. However, there has not been another sighting of a weird creature, nor has a crimson sky been seen since the patrols began.

Sana has a feeling that these creatures must have gone into hiding. She suggested that the prince ask the soldiers to stop patrolling this lake for one night, just to see if any of the creatures appear. The prince was going to come with only one or two soldiers, but she was determined to be present.

Now, hiding in the shadows, she continues to look at the lake.

Sure enough, something is now moving in the water. She turns to face the prince, before pointing at the ripples. "Something's there," she whispers.

She cannot believe that they really might see the

creature again tonight. Satoru steps forwards to stand next to her. He peers ahead, and his eyebrows frown with concentration.

The ripples of the water increase. Something pokes its head out from the surface and slowly heads to the line of shore nearest where they're hiding. It is now standing upright, looking around.

Sana does a double take. Her heart begins to beat hard inside her chest.

It is not a creature. It is a young man who now stands, not too far from her. His ivory hair flows gently in the night breeze. He turns around slowly and Sana gulps. She never thought she would see this face again in her lifetime. Something aches so hard in her heart that she has to take a moment to look away.

Her breathing becomes heavy and sweat starts to form on her face. The young man looks in her direction, and his facial expression holds the same softness she had learned to love during her childhood.

Don't be stupid, don't be stupid, she repeats to herself, squeezing her eyes shut. *Whatever is happening, this cannot be possible.* Fear sparks inside her. What is this? What, in truth, is she seeing in front of her?

The prince shuffles next to her, interrupting her thoughts.

Sana opens her eyes.

Seiji is looking back at her.

She breathes. In an instant, she draws an arrow from her quiver and aims it at him. In a flash, the arrow flies through the air and pierces into his chest. Sana winces, reliving the trauma of the last moments she had with him—trauma that has been haunting her for all these years.

Immediately, Seiji's image disappears. In its place is a terrifying, deranged creature. Its colour is one of a dusky grey. There are three triangular horns protruding its head—a head with eerie upturned crescent eyes. Its mouth is a black stretched void, widening at impossible angles as it screeches and screams. Disproportionate limbs flay out in all directions as its mouth continues to enlarge in agony. It falls onto the ground, lifeless.

"What in the world is that?" Satoru asks, in shock.

Sana is still breathing heavily. She braces herself on the tree trunk in front of her, catching her breath. After a while, both Sana and the prince step out from the trees. They walk slowly and carefully towards the creature. Sana crouches down next to it, her heart still beating heavily inside her chest, driven by longing, fear, and regret.

The creature's face is elongated. It has drooping,

lifeless eyes and a large mouth full of sharp pointy teeth that are bent at horrifying angles. She wonders what in the world she is looking at.

"Be careful," the prince warns as he catches up.

Just as he says this, the creature suddenly moves. It screeches deafeningly and leans towards Sana, its mouth impossibly wide. A sound of shock escapes Sana's lips as she falls back from the unexpected sight. The creature reaches out a claw and grasps onto her ankle.

Swiftly, another arrow pierces the centre of the creature's head and, in an instant, it explodes into a pile of grey ashes onto the ground.

"Are you all right?" the prince exclaims as he lowers his bow and crouches next to Sana. His eyes snap towards her right ankle, where the creature grasped onto her. The fabric of Sana's trousers has been completely eroded and there are angry, red sores blistered deep into her skin.

"Don't worry," Sana says, panting. She stares at the ashes.

"Harlande, your ankle," Satoru says.

"It is all right," Sana replies, turning to face the prince. "The more worrying thing right now is—" She takes a breath. "How do we get these ashes back to the palace for them to be analysed?"

"I will call for the guards," Satoru replies. "They are just a little outside these forests."

"Very well." Sana tries to get up from the ground but a sharp pain eats away at her ankle. It is a pain she has never felt before, like a combination of an intense burn from both ice and fire, as well as a deep-seated ache inside her bones. She stumbles.

"Harlande—" Satoru reaches out towards her, steadying her on her feet. "You are injured. Please, sit back down. I will carry you."

Sana sighs as she does as commanded. She is aware that she is not yet fully recovered from the poisoning, and now she has sustained a new injury on her ankle. She feels rather useless. She sighs again, wondering why Prince Takashi is so keen on helping her.

"I can walk," Sana states.

"No, allow me to carry you," Satoru replies.

Sana tries to get back up but stumbles again. A firm push from the prince on her shoulders keeps her sitting on the ground.

"These are the prince's orders," Satoru states firmly. With a simple scoop, the prince hoists her into his arms and strides through the forests. Sana's legs dangle from his arms as she remembers that day by the examination chamber when she became ill.

She closes her eyes and swallows a feeling of embarrassment. She does not like to appear vulnerable.

✽

Sana sits on a chair in her chamber as the prince crouches by her feet, bandaging her right ankle after applying some ointment. The palace healer had confirmed that, despite the pain, it is only a superficial injury that should not cause too much concern.

Her eyes stare into the distance as she wonders why things keep repeating themselves. Why does she keep getting hurt recently? Why has the prince become so insistent on helping her? Not to mention, it feels strange to have the great leader of Shinrin kneeling before her. She is unsure where to look.

"What did you see before the creature died?" Sana asks, frowning as she thinks back to the earlier encounter.

Satoru looks up as he finishes tying a knot. "What about you? What did you see?" He gets up and sits on one of the chairs across the room, facing her.

"I asked you first," Sana replies, wondering why the prince is bouncing the question back.

"Weirdly enough . . ." Satoru says slowly. "I saw

someone who reminded me of you."

Sana looks at him, wanting him to elaborate.

"It looked like you as the Mutoren. It had a wooden mask with the spiral eyes." Satoru keeps his eyes on her.

"Is that so?" Sana asks, wondering what this means.

"And yourself?" Satoru asks again.

"I saw someone I knew as a child," Sana says, looking into the distance.

"I see," Satoru replies, not pressing for more details. After a pause, he speaks again. "The palace substance analysers will look into the components of the ashes. Hopefully, this will give us more information. Perhaps afterwards, there will be an explanation for what we saw."

Sana nods. The fact that they actually saw something and obtained some evidence is a step forwards. She looks down at her bandaged ankle.

"Prince Takashi," Sana says. "I heard that you tended to me daily during my illness."

Satoru's eyes are round and questioning, as if he is wondering why she is bringing this up. "That is correct," he replies.

Sana cannot help but wonder why the prince is helping her so much so. Did he forget her crimes and how she has attacked him more than once?

"Why did you do that?" Sana asks.

Satoru frowns, as if wondering why this is even a question. “You are my new first-hand guard in Sir Leon’s absence, as well as one of the palace knights. You hold an important role here in the palace. It is my duty to ensure you are all right.”

“Hm,” Sana responds. Could he not have left her care to the palace healer and her sister? For some reason, her suspicion towards the prince has lessened since she fell ill. She thinks also of the night on the roof and the intense emotions which were in his eyes.

Perhaps the prince is truly only human after all.

“I believe I hold a possession of yours,” the prince suddenly says out of nowhere.

“And what may that be?” Sana asks, pretending not to know what he is talking about as she immediately pictures her emblem in her mind.

“Don’t pretend, Harlande,” Satoru says.

“Well, I too, hold a possession of yours,” Sana replies, now thinking of the treasures. “. . . If not more than one.”

Satoru sighs. “The emblem of Qieta. That is yours, correct?”

Sana does not respond.

“I’ve wondered what your ties are with the island. I thought perhaps you knew more about the killings. That is why I went out of my way to search for you," Satoru explains. He says this gently and there is sincerity in his eyes. "I wondered, too, if you are Qietian."

Sana ponders a bit before speaking. *Should I tell him about myself?* It seems like something so minor in a time like this when the land of Shinrin is truly in danger.

"That emblem is a part of a necklace that was around me when I was found as a baby," Sana says.

The prince nods. He gazes softly at her, prompting her to continue.

"In other words, I have had it all my life. It is the one thing that may explain where I came from," she continues. "So, in answer to your question, I do not know if I am Qietian, but I could be."

"Right," Satoru acknowledges.

"About the killings, I knew just as much as you did, if not less," Sana says. She is unsure why she is giving all of this information so voluntarily, but in this moment, it seems like there is no benefit to hiding it.

Satoru opens his mouth but then shuts it again. He looks at Sana and then down to the floor.

"What is it?" Sana asks quietly. The prince looked like he was about to ask something.

"Never mind."

"Tell me," Sana replies.

The prince waits a little while before speaking. "Since I first heard about you over three years ago, I have been wondering," Satoru starts, "why are you stealing all these treasures?" He gestures at her. "I mean, looking at you now, I doubt you have an evil reasoning behind all of this."

"Ah," Sana replies. This question again. She sighs. Even the very thought of the Kurai is enough to make her sweat and shiver. She does not dare mention the word. She looks at the floor.

Satoru waits for a response. After a while, he gathers that Sana is not going to speak. Again, he does not press any further for more information. Instead, he clears his throat. "It is late, Harlande," he says gently. "I shall leave you be." He rises from his chair and prepares to exit her chamber.

"Thank you for this," Sana whispers.

As the prince turns around to face her, she points at her bandaged ankle.

"Oh," Satoru says. He blinks a few too many times. "Not at all."

Sana smiles. "Good night, Prince Takashi."

"Night, Harlande," Satoru replies. He turns back to the door briskly and exits her room.

✾

After the prince exits her chamber, Sana gets up and slowly opens the front door. She decides that she needs to do something.

"Hello?" Sana whispers to her doorman guard through the open door.

"Knight Lishuah!" Shou replies. "How may I help you?"

"I wondered if you may ask the palace healer to pay me a visit. I hope that is not too much trouble?" Sana asks.

"Right now, Knight Lishuah?"

Sana nods.

"Certainly." Shou bows and strides off into the corridor.

Sana returns to her room and waits. Soon enough, there is a knock on her door. "Come in," she says.

Healer Aoki, the palace healer, enters. He is an elderly man and is dressed in the long, ivory-and-cyan robe he is usually seen in. He bows to her, holding onto a case with both of his hands. "Knight Lishuah," he says, "I am glad to see you are doing well. How may I help you?"

"Please, sit down." She gestures to the chair where

Prince Takashi sat earlier. "I want to thank you for tending to me during my illness," Sana says.

"That is not a problem," Healer Aoki replies. "It is what I am here for." He hobbles slowly towards the chair and plops himself down.

"I have a question too, if that is all right?" Sana asks.

"Ask away."

"Apologies for checking, but as a healer, have you heard of a substance named Soltair?" Sana asks. *I need to find this out.*

Healer Aoki leans in towards her and scratches his head. A few strands of white hairs are all that is left. "I have heard about it in my early days," Healer Aoki replies, "but it is a substance that is very much banned now. I have not come across it in many, many years."

"And as a healer, everything I disclose to you remains confidential, correct?" Sana checks.

"Of course," Healer Aoki replies. "That is one of our main principles."

"I wanted to ask . . . is there a way for you to check how much Soltair is left inside of me, to see how long I have left to live?"

The old man's eyes widen. "My child, what may have caused you to come into contact with something so dangerous?"

"It was injected into me every fortnight, from the ages of seven to fourteen. I understand this substance shortens one's original lifespan to about a quarter of its original length," Sana says. "Is that correct?"

"It is."

"I am one-and-twenty now. As such, I wonder if I am approaching the end of my life," Sana says. There is no fear in her eyes. She states this firmly. *I must find out.*

"My child, I suppose I could analyse your blood to see how much of it is left inside you," Healer Aoki replies. "And with some calculations, I should be able to answer your question."

"That would be extremely helpful," Sana replies. "When can we do this?"

"We could draw your blood right now, if you wish," the healer replies.

He gestures to his case. It reminds Sana so much of the case Seiji would bring every time she was with him in his examination chamber.

"Let us do this now then," Sana agrees. "How long will it take for you to get the results?"

"Oh, the analysis will take a while, I'm afraid," Healer Aoki replies. "Perhaps a few weeks."

"That is all right." *I* must *find out.*

She is glad that she will get an answer for this once

and for all. She readies her arm for blood to be drawn as Healer Aoki prepares his things. He approaches her and places his case by the side, then inserts the needle into a vein on Sana's arm.

✾

Satoru puts on his night clothes after he enters his chamber, then slowly sits down on his bed. His heart is thumping wildly inside his chest. He thinks about what he saw at the lake.

Why is it that he saw the Mutoren, whilst Harlande saw someone she once knew? Does this mean that this creature can disguise itself as someone one knows? Is it some sort of protective mechanism for it?

Satoru's mind drifts towards Harlande. Seeing her get hurt once again put a pain through his heart, and while carrying her out of the forest, Satoru felt the urge to protect her, with all that he has.

Why are these new, strange feelings stirring up inside me?

During their conversation downstairs, he very much wanted to find out more about her and was pleasantly surprised at the new information she gave. However, he did not want to press further or force her to say anything she did not want to. He wonders why he is getting new urges to be around her as much as possible, and why his heart sinks slightly every time he has to leave.

Satoru thinks about her bizarre—yet impressive—fighting style, her witty remarks, and how she always seems to surprise him. He thinks about how his heart cracked when she fell ill, and how each time he tended to her while she was unconscious he felt an overwhelming sadness seeing her in that state.

He has so many questions he wants to ask and so many things about her he wants to find out. *What is going on?*

An image of her sitting on the roof next to him that night appears in his mind. Her soft raven hair was flowing in the wind, and her round, obsidian eyes looked at him so softly. She seemed to see him for who he was, although she barely spoke a few words. The way she said his name pulled at his heart. Her face was beautiful.

Satoru's cheeks are burning. He is a little breathless and he holds the back of his palm to his forehead, then to his cheek.

He shakes his head and sighs. *What is wrong with you, Satoru?*

Just as he is about to flop backwards onto his bed, there is a *tap tap* on the window. Satoru's attention shifts as he gets up immediately and strides towards it. A small, azure bird is tapping its beak onto the glass.

A Kaidara? His heartbeat quickens. Albert must have replied. *It sure takes some time for these messages to be delivered.*

As soon as Satoru slides his window open, the small bird hops inside. She immediately swoops towards his desk, uses her beak to pull out a scrap piece of parchment from a pile on the side, and drops it onto the surface of his desk. She has red ink on her feet and, in an instant, she begins to hop around, stamping out some characters.

It only takes a few seconds for the message to be completed.

Satoru stares at the writing with wide eyes. The font is thick and red, as if the bird has smeared it with blood. A sickness rises in his stomach as his heart sinks right to the bottom of his core. He reads the message in disbelief.

YES. HELP.

The small bird hops back out of his window and disappears into the night sky.

"Al-Albert—" Satoru stammers. He picks up the piece of parchment and holds it in front of his face, willing the letters to change. He takes a big breath.

Albert, what is going on?

His hands shake as he reads the two-worded message over and over again.

His best friend is in trouble.

CHAPTER TWENTY-THREE

A Narrow Space

ALBERT SITS IN THE CORNER of his cell, eyeing the wall in front of him. Since the first time he managed to eat, he has slowly been able to build his strength back up. He now has enough energy to keep studying the interior of his surroundings and to try and find a way to escape.

He looks at the wall to his left. He has etched a total of twenty-one tally marks with a broken part of brick that came off the wall. This means, since that day he saw the 'ghost' who gave him a bowl of soup, twenty-one days have passed. The way the light of the moon moves across the small square of his window tells him that this 'ghost' appears once a day.

As Albert slowly recovered, he has been continuing to experience realistic dreams, just like Liuana Pharlos had warned him. Each time he woke from them, it took him some time to return to his reality.

Albert has been trying to work out how to get out of this place. Whenever the 'ghost' comes, a glowing, rectangular entrance appears on his cell wall, allowing that person to bring him his daily meal. After the 'ghost' leaves, Albert has tried and failed to find any trace of an opening on the wall.

Ssssst. Ssssst. Ssssst.

This sound again. Albert looks at the patch of moonlight—from the moon's position, it must be somewhere around midnight or the very early hours of the morning. Each day, at this time, this sound appears. It most definitely is coming from the wall adjacent to the window. Since hearing this sound, Albert has used the broken piece of brick to tap back on the wall, just to see if doing so elicits anything in response.

However, each time he does so, the sound

disappears.

Ssssst. Ssssst. Ssssst.

The sound comes back once more.

Albert picks up his piece of broken brick and, just as he is about to tap on the wall once more, he stops. *Should I try something different?* he wonders. Something tells him that he should try this one last time. Perhaps this time, there may be a response.

He taps on the wall hard, twice. Almost instantly, the sound stops once again.

Albert shakes his head. *Same thing again. What is creating that sound? Is there someone there, just like me, who has also been locked up?* Albert sighs. He sits on the ground, wondering what he can do. *If I can't get out, I am going to rot away in here.*

His mind wanders to Prince Takashi. Has he received his message? What will he do? Will he send the Shirinese soldiers to Qieta? And what is going on with the case of the killings back in Shinrin?

He is still in disbelief that brother Satoshi has been here all this time. There are too many questions spinning around in his mind. He sighs again and slowly lowers himself to the floor. He lies in a foetal position, staring at the wall of his cell once more.

The moonlight reflects off the bottom of the wall

on the left. Something catches his eye. Albert blinks, looking at the wall from his sideways position, and his eyes widen. There is something there. A marking of an arrow pointing to the floor in front of him.

How did I not see this before? He has been studying the interior of his cell for as long as he can remember. He does not recall seeing this marking previously at all. He briskly gets onto his hands and knees and crawls towards it.

Sure enough, the faint arrow shimmers, straight back at him.

The patch of moonlight edges along, and in an instant, the arrow disappears.

"No—" Albert stretches out a hand. The arrow is completely gone. He squeezes his eyes shut, picturing where it was pointing to, and takes a breath. He opens his eyes and puts his face close to the floor at the very edge of the room, where he believes the arrow was pointing.

He examines the area as hard as he can, using his hands to feel all over the space. After a few moments, his hand catches on a piece of ground that moves. Albert gulps. *I am certain it moved.* He wobbles that part again. Sure enough, it moves a little, once more.

What does this mean? he wonders. *Can the floor come*

apart? What was the arrow hinting at? Was it drawn by whoever was locked inside here before me?

Against the pads of his fingers, Albert makes out a very fine, jagged line, one that links together into the outline of a large piece of rock on the floor; it is the very piece that wobbled when he moved it.

He attempts to pick at the corners, but it is not possible to lift the stone. Albert tries a different approach.

He presses his hand on it.

Suddenly, the rock sinks into the floor, and the edges beside it crumble apart. Albert gasps with shock. Now that the rock has been lowered, he can grab it. He lifts it up using both of his hands and sets it beside him.

A very narrow and steep passageway stretches out in front of Albert. Rocks are crumbling at the edges and are sharp and rough to the touch. It is pitch black down there.

What could this be? Albert wonders. His heart thumps inside his chest. Could this be the first sign of hope?

He lowers himself down as carefully as he can, his heart continuing to beat hard. The passageway is so narrow and jagged that he is unsure if he can actually fit inside.

However, what choice do I have? This may be my only

chance of escaping this cell.

His eyes cannot make out a single thing, and his adrenaline is rushing out of control. Being in complete darkness is frightening. He touches all around him, trying to find where the passageway is. The roughness of the rocks is sharp and it does not take more than a few moments for them to scrape through his skin.

Albert winces. As his hands roam around in the gloom, he realises that he will need to crawl to get through the hole in front of him. As he kneels, the rocks scratch and scrape at his skin some more. Putting weight on his knees and shins is nothing short of painful after having not moved much over the last twenty-one days.

Slowly, he begins to make his way through the tunnel.

Please don't be a dead end, Albert prays with all of his might as he pulls himself forward with his hands. Not being able to see a single thing is terrifying enough, but the passageway is so extraordinarily narrow that, if he meets a dead end, he will not be able to turn to get back out the other way. He will be stuck in there forever until he dies.

Come on, Albert, he tries to encourage himself, *you need to survive. You cannot die here. You cannot do that to Prince Takashi. He has been like a brother for as long as you can remember, and he will not survive losing another brother. You need to find out what in the world is going on.*

Despite his own words of encouragement, the passageway in front of him becomes narrower and narrower. The fear inside him increases, flooding through every part of his body. He tries to picture a large, open field—a forest perhaps, one where he is riding Erwin through the wind. The brief thought of an open space distracts him from the looming claustrophobia for the briefest moment.

Thinking about himself riding in the forest reminds him of the young girl who he picked mushrooms with: Emiko, and her endearing grandparents.

Albert wonders how they are doing.

He reaches out again before he edges forward. This time, his hand hits some rock. He has come to a dead end.

Oh, no you don't, Albert thinks, panic rising inside him. Cold sweat is forming all over him, and he can hear his own panicked, heavy breathing. He closes his eyes in an attempt to calm himself down but realises that it is so dark that shutting his eyes does not make a difference. It is an awful feeling. Absolutely awful.

Albert touches all around him once more. He reaches to his sides, then above his head, and suddenly, his hand touches nothing. There is a space—open space, not a dead end—above him.

The tiniest bit of relief sweeps over him. However, the space is, once again, extremely narrow. He struggles for quite some time to straighten himself up and then squeeze through the space that is there. His tall frame is an absolute hindrance at a time like this.

After a long struggle, Albert finally manages to stand in an upright position, but he can barely breathe. The sides of the walls are right up against his chest and back, digging into his skin. He reaches above his head and his hand hits rock once more. Another dead end.

He pushes hard. *Please tell me this is an opening just like the one I entered through*, he prays.

He pushes some more, but it does not budge.

Albert knocks the piece of rock, hard. He balls his hand into a fist and strikes it. At the same time, he yells out, "Please! Please! There is someone in here!"

He wonders if anyone is there and, even if there is, will they kill him on the spot when they find him? He has no other options.

He knocks the rock some more, and soon the warm, thick wetness of his own blood oozes down his palms.

Albert pants and pants. He takes a moment to regain his strength. Just as he is about to strike the rock one more time, he hears it move above his head. Soon, the faintest light appears; someone has lifted the rock to the side.

Albert's eyes take some time to adjust to the moonlight. He finds himself staring at a middle-aged man. This man has fiery, copper hair laced with grey, and a matching, full beard. He holds out his hand and reaches towards Albert.

Albert grasps onto the man's hands, which are rough and calloused to the touch. With the man's help, Albert struggles up and out of the narrow passageway. The sharp edges dig into his back and his chest, drawing blood.

Albert finally climbs out of the tiny, cramped tunnel. He collapses forwards onto the hard ground in a heap, his breaths still loud and heavy.

The moonlight from a small square window allows Albert to see his surroundings as he slowly sits up. He is in a neighbouring cell. His right hand is stinging, and he catches sight of the blood all over his palm. The skin on his knuckles has torn off completely and there are angry, raw, open wounds as well as cuts and bruises all over his arms and legs.

The man crouches on the ground a few paces away from Albert. He is hunched over as he leans forward curiously. He appears extremely unkempt and has on a simple brown robe, although it is torn in many places. There is a dull grey film over both of his lifeless eyes but despite this, it is extremely comforting to finally be in the presence of another human being.

"Who stands before me?" the man asks slowly and carefully.

"I-I am . . . Albert Leon," Albert replies, still catching his breath.

"You sound young, my child," the man replies. "You were also imprisoned?"

"Yes," Albert pants. He wonders who this man is.

"How long for?" the man asks.

"At least . . . twenty-one days, sir," Albert replies. "And yourself, good sir?"

"Around twenty years, I should suspect," the man answers.

"My goodness," Albert says. Being in there for twenty-one days had caused him to nearly lose his mind. How did the man in front of him survive for twenty years?

"I-I have too many questions—" Albert stammers, his mind spinning.

"I am sure you do, my child."

"Please, good sir, who may you be? Why were you

locked up? Do you know someone named Azrael?" Albert asks one question after another.

"I—" the man begins. He pauses and then squeezes his eyes shut. He puts his hands on his head as if it is hurting, then leans forwards with a sigh. After a while, he speaks again. "I have trouble with my memory, my child." He opens his eyes. "I try to piece together bits and pieces of information, but there are many gaps. I do not know my name, and as for the name Azrael . . . I do not recall having heard of it."

Being locked up here for so long must have terrorised the poor man. Albert does not blame him for not being able to remember.

"I never thought I would meet another human being again," the man says.

"Good sir, I am absolutely relieved to stumble upon you, too," Albert replies. He is no longer alone. Perhaps there is hope.

The man nods and smiles through his bushy red beard. He gazes around him, his lifeless grey eyes rolling from left to right. He gestures for Albert to join him. "Come, my child."

Albert shuffles towards him obediently.

"In case you haven't yet noticed," the man says, "I am blind. I cannot tell what you look like, but I would like to get to know who it is before me." He reaches his hands towards Albert's face and pauses. "May I?"

Albert blinks at the man's hands. *Is he about to touch my face?* "All . . . All right," Albert replies.

The man lays his hands on Albert's face. The skin on his fingers is scruffy and rough, and he traces his fingers along Albert's eyebrows, his cheekbones, down his nose, and around his chin. He gently touches his hair and feels around his ears. He then lifts his hands away.

"Where are you from, my child?" the man asks, tucking his hands into his sleeves.

"Shinrin, good sir," Albert replies.

"Ah," the man acknowledges. "The land of forests. You have strong facial features, young Albert. You must be a man with important responsibilities, and I imagine you are also a skilled fighter."

How did he get that just by how my face feels like? Albert wonders in awe.

"As a blind man, I rely heavily on my touch and my hearing," the man answers Albert's question. The man turns away and shuffles to the corner of his cell.

Albert notices there are some metal tools where the man is standing. The man wipes one of them on his tattered robe and starts to mumble to himself. *"Mei dario, ke junge ci discoveri tono shuarda. Konen ci xiwang,"* he says.

My dear, a young man has discovered your passageway. There may be hope.

Albert does a double take. Did he hear that correctly? The familiar sound of the Cernese language brings him a sense of unexpected nostalgia and comfort. *"Esta, gut siensi? Ton laduer Cernisce?"* Albert asks quietly. *Excuse me, good sir? You speak Cernese?*

The man turns briskly and his bushy red eyebrows rise up in surprise. A slight gleam appears in the grey clouds over his eyes. *"Mei, hun ya istado supriomere!"* he exclaims. *My, what a pleasant surprise!*

"Ton ci Cernisce, gut siensi?" Albert asks. *You are Cernese, good Sir?*

"Nen, aber mei dario maleisa ci. Hun ya istado supriomere shide," the man replies. *No, but my dear wife was. What a pleasant surprise, indeed.*

Albert looks at the man and wonders what could have led him here. The unexpected bond they share *is* such a pleasant surprise. It puts his heart slightly at ease.

He exhales. Perhaps there is hope, indeed.

CHAPTER TWENTY-FOUR

The Maskaver

AKALIN'S ARMS AND LEGS ARE tied up. He eyes his surroundings carefully. Earlier, in the cabin, the young girl with a bow and arrow had appeared with two men. It did not take long for their whole army—a group of around twenty more of their people—to turn up.

He was not going to risk his life in a one-against-twenty fight, which meant he had to follow their orders. Now, he is in some sort of underground place, tied against a wooden pole, with a whole crowd of at least thirty people staring at him.

He shakes his head and sighs. *Honestly, escaping from one monster to another*. He has even less idea where he is now nor who these people are. He looks at the pole next to him—Princess Lore has been tied up, too.

She looks around, her eyes full of panic. She looks like she is about to hyperventilate or break down.

Akalin wriggles his hands. He can just about feel the knot of the ropes around his wrists. He tugs at the rope and touches the ties, trying to work out which knot was used. Despite everything, he is not panicking; he has a feeling that, if worst comes to worst, he will be able to get out of here.

The room is full of chatter and whispers as the people continue to stare at him and Princess Lore. He wonders where Aiyla and his parents might be. He wonders how Satoru is getting on in Shinrin and whether or not Samuel is all right.

The young girl who kidnapped them—who pointed her arrow at the princess and ordered her to move—walks towards him. She stops in front of Akalin and eyes him suspiciously.

How old is this girl? Akalin wonders while she stares at him. She must still be in her teens, perhaps only fifteen or sixteen. She is still a child. Why is she strutting around with such confidence?

The girl then steps towards the princess and smirks. "Princess Lore, high and mighty Princess of Keska. Now, tied up like this, you are nothing," the girl almost spits.

The princess looks back at her, eyes still wide with panic. "Wh-Who are you?" Suyin stammers.

"You stand before the great leader of The Maskaver. I am Lord Storm."

Lord Storm? Akalin thinks, staring at the child. *What is she on about?*

Princess Lore gulps. The young girl takes a dagger from her waist and pushes the back of it against Suyin's neck. Suyin gasps and leans as far away from the blade as she can.

"You evil witch," Lord Storm continues. "How many men have you fed to the devil?"

"I-I don't know what you are talking about—" Suyin stammers again.

"Don't lie." The girl pushes the blade harder and leans in towards the princess, her braided hair falling in front of her. "You enslave children in your mines and you feed men to the devil," Lord Storm states.

"Pl-Please—Let me explain—" the princess protests.

"Shh." The young girl puts a finger to her lips.

"There is no need to explain your crimes. Your royal, luxurious days are over, woman," she hisses. "Now, we shall bring justice."

A male voice comes out of nowhere. "Talia! Stop it!"

The young girl pulls back her blade and turns to the crowd, searching for the voice. She does not have to look for long—right at the back, a young man is pacing towards them.

Akalin wonders who this may be.

The young man, perhaps in his twenties, appears. He strides up towards the young girl. "Talia, stop it," he repeats.

The threatening look in the young girl's eyes vanishes in an instant. She looks at the young man and tuts. "What is it, brother?" she asks with annoyance.

Princess Lore gasps. The young man does not give Talia so much as a second look before he rushes towards Princess Lore.

"Suyin," he says as he flings his arms around her in tight embrace. His body shakes as he clutches her tightly.

"What the hell," Talia says from behind them, her face twisted in disgust.

"I didn't think I would ever see you again, Torin," Suyin is leaning as far forward as the restraints will allow, seemingly trying to press into the young man. Sadness sweeps into her eyes.

They stay like that for a moment.

"Brother, get out of my business," Talia states. She attempts to push her brother aside.

The young man turns and glares at her. "Talia, if you want justice, it isn't this. You have got the wrong person," he says. He frowns and leans in angrily towards his sister.

"You idiot," Talia replies. "This woman fed you to the devil."

"How many times do I have to tell you?" he asks impatiently, "I know Suyin. She would never do that."

"Ugh, I can't stand this," the young girl replies. She looks around, a muscle ticking at her jaw with annoyance. Her eyes roll back and her nostrils flare outwards. The crowd stares back at her.

"Torin," Suyin whispers, "where did you go? What in the world happened?"

"I will explain," he replies in a hurry. "But firstly, let's untie you." He scrambles at the ropes behind the princess.

"Oi—" Talia protests.

Akalin stares at the unfolding scene. He wants to get out. He is here to find his sister, not to watch some sort of drama unfold. He sighs again.

"And what are you sighing about?" Talia asks angrily, one of her eyebrows rising in frustration. "Mister princess's toy?"

"Quit talking, kid," Akalin replies, his own annoyance sparking. He is tired of this nonsense. He scrambles at his own ropes, trying to untie himself.

Princess Lore is untied, and Torin immediately grasps onto her hands. He looks her straight in the eyes. "Suyin, on the day your father captured me, I was taken to a boat by two guards. Your father told me that I was going to die. He said the devil would rip me apart and devour my organs and my soul. He sold me to some other men in exchange for ten thousand Vel."

Suyin gasps, looking at the young man in disbelief. "What?"

"He told me everything because, 'I was going to die anyway.' I was on a boat with the two guards and they were about to hand me over to someone else. But then, a bear came out of nowhere. It was on an absolute rampage and the guards fled in a flurry."

A bear? Akalin isn't sure what to think but continues to listen.

"I jumped into the waters and swam for my life. After I made it to the shores, I was discovered by the Maskaver organisation, who came to save me. Who knew that during all the time I was away as a soldier, my baby sister was leading and growing this underground organisation? I had no idea of the control your parents were imposing over our country."

"Torin—I cannot believe it."

"I didn't think I was going to make it, Suyin. And I didn't think I would ever see you again." His body is still shaking. He leans in and embraces her again.

Devour organs? Akalin thinks to himself, turning the story over in his head. That sounds a bit . . . suspicious. Why does it remind him so much of the case of the killings back in Shinrin? Was this the unfortunate fate that all the previous men mentioned by Princess Lore met? Akalin frowns.

"Brother, you escaped death, and we saved you," Talia states. "Now, we are here to bring justice. We are going to overthrow the Keskan Empire. This witch is the one who is behind all of this—"

Torin cuts her off. "That's nonsense—"

"Enough!" Talia shouts. The muffled whispers in the crowd diminish instantly. The young girl's icy blue eyes are blazing with rage. She leans in towards her brother, as a threatening aura grows over her. "In case you haven't noticed, Brother, I am the *lord* here, and people follow *my* orders. You should be grateful you are even alive." The more she speaks, the further in she leans towards him. "Take them away!" Talia commands the crowd.

However, the crowd remains silent, and no one dares to move an inch.

"I said, *take them away*!" Talia repeats, the anger in her voice rising further.

Two men briskly stand up. "Wh-Where to, Lord Storm?" one of them asks.

"Lock them in the cells," Talia grits through her teeth.

More men stand and gather around Princess Lore and Akalin. They take their hands, tie them with new ropes, and lead them further into the underground.

✾

Akalin sits cross-legged on the cold ground, his head hanging forward with concentration as he fiddles with his hands behind him, still trying to untie the rope. He stares out between the metal bars, his eyes darting left and right.

Princess Lore sits huddled in the corner of the same cell, her head on her knees.

After some time, Suyin breaks the silence, lifting her head. "So, this must be what my father was up to."

"Mm," Akalin responds, not moving from his position or turning to look at her. He continues to stare ahead. He is trying to work out how to get himself out of here. After a while, he turns to look at Princess Lore. "That young man—Torin—he was one of your soldiers?"

Suyin turns and her eyes rest on him softly. She nods and sighs. "He was the last one I picked, perhaps a few months before I met you," she says quietly.

"Mm," Akalin acknowledges her statement.

"To think my father would do something so horrific—" Suyin stops abruptly as she hears the sudden sound of footsteps.

Akalin turns back to peer out of the cell bars. He cranes his neck and tries to see where the sound is coming from.

Soon, the young girl appears once again. Lord Storm. Her facial expression is flat and the anger that was there earlier has diminished. She stops when she reaches Akalin's cell and turns to look down at him, her blue eyes stone cold. "You." She looks down at Akalin. "Who are you, please?"

Akalin blinks up at the young girl. He senses that, although she is young, she does hold the ability to command and lead. Clearly, she has built herself a modestly sized underground empire. She seems to want to bring justice for what has been happening to the people in this nation.

But Akalin senses no real threat from her. Perhaps he can gain her help to find his sister. "I'm Akalin Kinali of Shinrin," Akalin answers simply. "Add a 'sir' in front of my name, if you please." A mischievous edge returns in his voice.

Talia raises an eyebrow. Her facial expression does not change. "Shinrin?" she asks. She bends down and peers at Akalin, eyeing him suspiciously.

"Indeed, Lord Storm," Akalin replies, managing a smile. "Shinrin, the land of forests."

Talia straightens. Her expression softens a little, and she eyes him now with more curiosity than suspicion. "Thought you didn't look like you were from here," she comments. "What are you doing in Keska and how did you even get in?"

"That is the big question," Akalin replies. "I am on an important mission, but it appears things keep happening to stand in my way." Akalin sighs.

"And why are you with this witch?" Talia asks, glancing over at Princess Lore.

"I'm not a witch," Suyin grumbles in the background.

Before Akalin says anything else, Talia peers at him

once again and then takes something from her sleeve: a metal key. She inserts it into the lock and pushes the metal bars open. "You," she says to Akalin, "come out."

Akalin immediately stands before stepping outside. He wonders what this child is about to do.

As Talia closes the door and locks it once again, Akalin briefly glances at Princess Lore. She looks at him with tired eyes but does not even try to follow. She leans back and sighs.

Talia unties the ropes which are binding Akalin's wrists. Without a second glance, she walks ahead. As Akalin follows her down the dark corridors of the underground, he starts to raise his guard once again. *What if she is leading me to the soldiers?* He will need to be ready to fight.

They reach an empty, open area. There is a fire in the middle, its flames bright and orange. Sounds of crackles pop out now and then.

Talia gestures to the wooden benches surrounding the fire. "Sit," she says calmly. Akalin sits down slowly, and the young girl does the same. "I wanted to talk to you, alone," she says.

"Very well," Akalin acknowledges, wondering where this is going.

"You say you are from Shinrin?"

"Correct."

"Are you royalty then, Sir Akalin Kinali?" Talia asks.

"I reside amongst the palace, yes," Akalin replies.

"And tell me . . . what brought you to Keska?"

Akalin decides to be truthful. From his observations, he does not feel that this underground organisation poses any threat to him. This young girl appears to only hold hatred for the Keskan royalty.

"You are aware that children are being made to work in the mines, yes?" Akalin asks, and Talia nods. "My village was massacred. My little sister was stolen. I am here to look for her."

Talia's eyes widen. "They've gone all the way to Shinrin?"

"It appears so."

"I am sorry," she whispers. She shakes her head and looks down at the ground, frowning. "So why are you with the princess?"

"I was chosen by her from a line-up of soldiers. I was hiding in their camp."

"Right."

"There is a young soldier who helped me." Akalin thinks of Samuel. "Samuel Lorenz. I have been thinking of him since I was taken, as I fear he may be in danger. He went out of his way to help me."

Talia looks at Akalin, taking in what he is saying. "And did you find your sister?" she asks.

Akalin sighs. "I haven't had the slightest chance. I was taken before I could even step foot into the mines."

"These Keskan royals are really messing things up," Talia says bitterly. "What they are doing is extreme."

"This Maskaver organisation—tell me about it," Akalin says. He wants to know if this young girl may be able to help him. He leans in towards her, awaiting her response.

Talia blinks. "We—Well, I founded it," she replies. "We are an underground organisation. Maskaver means, 'The right to the truth.'" She tucks her hands under her thighs. "At first, people slowly began to discover what was going on and, day by day, those of us who wanted to come together to bring justice grew in number."

"And you built this yourself?" Akalin asks.

"Well, no one has been able to defeat me in a duel as of yet," Talia replies, looking proud of herself, "so I remain the strongest. That makes me the leader, yes."

"That is impressive, especially since you are so young," Akalin says, looking at her in awe.

The young girl's eyebrows spring upwards with surprise, and she suddenly blushes. She looks away and blinks at the ground. "Why were you with the princess in the cabin?" she asks after a moment.

"Princess Lore told me that, although she knew her father would take soldiers away, she never knew of their fate. She wanted to escape the palace, so we ended up getting out of there together," Akalin explains.

"Hm," Talia says, frowning. "I'm not sure what to think of this princess."

"Neither do I," Akalin answers.

"I guess we share that common ground," Talia says. She tucks a few strands of her raven hair behind her ear and fiddles with one of her braids.

"You mean that neither of us know what we think about the princess?" Akalin asks, stroking his chin.

Talia laughs. "Yes. That. But also that we both want to put a stop to what is happening," she says.

"Mm," Akalin agrees.

"What was his name? Samuel something?" she asks suddenly.

"Lorenz. Samuel Lorenz."

"And you believe your sister is in the mines," Talia says. She looks up at Akalin.

"I believe so."

"Then, let's see what we can do."

Something sparks inside Akalin and his eyes light up. There is hope and, perhaps this Maskaver organisation may be of help indeed.

The young girl seems to notice the sparkle in Akalin's eyes. She starts to fiddle with her braid once more. "You . . . You have pretty eyes," Talia says out of nowhere. She flicks her braid over her shoulder and smiles.

"Mm, I think the princess wanted to make my eyeballs into her rings," Akalin jokes, dodging the compliment. "Don't tell me you want an eyeball-ring too."

Talia laughs again. "You're funny. I like you."

"Do you have a bird here?" Akalin asks, changing the subject. He senses that the young girl is probably a bit hormonal. Earlier, her anger was blazing, and now, she looks like she is in love. His nostrils widen as he shuffles in his seat. *Please, not more trouble.*

Talia blinks at him. "A bird?"

"Yes, messenger birds," Akalin replies. "Since I was captured, Shinrin does not know my whereabouts. It is my duty to inform them."

"Oh," Talia replies, realising what he means. "I guess you don't know much about Keska."

"I do not. I was wondering why I cannot seem to picture the land on a map."

"The Keskan Empire has control over the whole

kingdom," Talia explains. "Meaning we have no such thing as messenger birds here. We have no way of transmitting messages, no rights, and no life." She sighs. "I guess you can say we are in hiding. If our organisation is ever found, we will be executed on the spot."

This takes Akalin by surprise. He wonders how come this girl seems to know so much if her world is so tightly controlled. There is no fear in her voice, even when she mentioned execution. "You seem to know a lot," Akalin says.

Talia smiles. "I've always been curious. I make friends with those at the borders. Gets you a lot of information."

"Brave," Akalin comments. "How long has this organisation been running for?"

"Since I was thirteen, so three years now," Talia replies.

"I see."

"About your message, I will see what I can do. I can probably find a way to transmit it via someone at the borders," Talia says.

"Oh," Akalin says. He wonders if this will put her or the organisation in danger. It seems that Keska is not a good place for someone to live.

"I've never met someone from Shinrin before,"

Talia says. She looks into the fire. "I'd love to go one day. I heard the forests are beautiful."

Akalin too, stares into the fire. He wonders if he is a step closer to finding his sister. He exhales as he thinks about his whole journey here—from discovering the massacre of his village, to not knowing whether his parents or his sister are alive, to coming to Keska and being taken by the princess. And now, he is here in the Maskaver organisation.

"I'll do what I can to help your friend," Talia says, turning to look at Akalin, "and to find your sister." She straightens and holds out her hand.

Akalin returns her handshake, giving her a nod.

"Let me introduce myself properly," the young girl says. "My name is Talia Jasmine Storm, leader of the underground empire. Welcome to the Maskaver organisation, Sir Akalin Kinali of Shinrin."

CHAPTER TWENTY-FIVE

A Bond Between Two Brothers

"COME ON! MORE, MORE!" A younger Satoshi shouts. He stands in the middle of the palace fields, holding a large pad stuffed with hay above an eight-year-old Satoru's head.

Satoru kicks again, high and with all his might. He wipes the sweat away from his forehead and pants. "Brother Satoshi—I can't—" Satoru protests as he catches his breath. "I'm so tired—"

"More," Satoshi commands. He takes another step backwards, waiting for Satoru to follow with another high kick.

Satoru protests again. "Brother Satoshi, I'm tired!"

"You said you want to become a big, strong fighter, did you not?" Satoshi asks. "Complaining will not turn you into one."

Satoru's face scrunches up with disapproval. His lungs are about to burst and his legs are aching to the core. Why is Brother Satoshi being so harsh with him?

"Keep in mind what Master Kinali taught you for this, Satoru. He said, 'Swing your knee as high as you can before you kick. Where your knee goes, your foot must follow,' remember?" Satoshi presses.

"I know, but—I can't lift my legs anymore—they're hurting—" The ache eating at his little muscles is too much for Satoru to handle.

"Don't exaggerate, brother!" Satoshi says.

"I'm not!" Satoru replies, the frustration inside him increasing.

"It is not enough to train only with the Master," Satoshi says. "You must practice in your free time, too. This is how you get better." He takes another step backwards and beckons for Satoru to follow. "Come on, one more," Satoshi presses.

Satoru groans. He concentrates all his energy into his left leg and swings another kick, wishing this would end right now.

"Well done," Satoshi says, his tone softening. He finally puts down the pad.

Satoru rests his hands on his thighs, gasping for air. "Why are you being so mean?" Satoru complains.

Satoshi laughs. "If you want to become a big, strong fighter, this is what you have to do." He puts a hand on Satoru's shoulder and looks into his eyes. "It takes dedication, effort, hard work, and perseverance."

"My legs are aching," Satoru protests again.

"Good. Now do fifty sit-ups," his brother replies.

"What?" Satoru's eyes contort into a look of shock. His brother must be joking, right?

"You heard me, brother. Fifty sit-ups. Come on, go, go, go!" Satoshi says, clapping away.

What has gotten into him today? Satoru wonders in frustration. He plops his bottom down onto the grass unwillingly and does a single sit-up. "Brother Satoshi, you are joking, right?"

"Do I look like I am?" Satoshi replies. There is a mischievous glint in his violet eyes.

Satoru flops backwards onto the grass, frowning. His arms and legs are flayed out like a starfish. "Hmph," he grumbles. He decides he does not want to do any more. He is tired and that is that.

"Someone doesn't want to become a big, strong fighter," Satoshi taunts.

Satoru's frustration grows even further. He hits his fists on the grass. "It's not fair!" he cries out.

Satoshi sits down next to him on the grass. "Come on," Satoshi says again, gently this time. He lies down next to his brother. "Let's do it together."

Satoru blinks up at the sky. Hearing his brother coming to join him causes some of his frustration to dissipate. He turns to look at Brother Satoshi, who is smiling. He is so carefree and content all the time. In fact, Satoru has never seen him angry. He watches as his brother does a single sit-up with ease.

"One," Satoshi says. His knees are slightly bent as he lies back down and sits up once more. "Two," he continues. He looks over at Satoru and raises an eyebrow. "I'm in the lead, brother."

"No! Wait!" Satoru shouts. He suddenly realises that his brother might continue on to fifty without him. He frantically lies back down and does one more.

Slowly, the Takashi brothers continue to fifty together.

Once they are done, they both flop backwards onto

the soft grass—one small starfish and one big starfish. The sky is bright and blue and there are a few fluffy white clouds drifting in the breeze.

"Well done, Satoru," Satoshi says as they both peer up at the sky.

Now, not only are Satoru's legs aching, his abdomen feels very sore as well. However, he is content, and is proud for completing the exercises.

"Feels good, right?" Satoshi asks, as if he heard what Satoru was thinking.

"Yeah," Satoru replies, smiling up at the sky.

"Training is hard, especially when you start feeling tired," Satoshi says. "Every part of your body is screaming for you to stop and to give up. But each time, pushing yourself that tiny inch further is what will help you improve. Not only that, doing so will help you feel great and proud of your achievements." Satoshi turns and smiles at his brother.

"Satoshi the Wise!" Satoru says, as he pumps a little fist into the air. He turns and smiles back at his older brother, who is laughing.

The sound and sight are radiant and heart-warming.

"How come little Albert didn't come to join us today?" Satoshi asks, as he crosses his arms behind his head.

"Oh, Mother and Father took him to see some ponies. He is going to start riding lessons soon," Satoru replies.

"Great news."

"Brother," Satoru says suddenly as he sits up, "I don't want you to leave." This thought has been plaguing Satoru's mind since his mother broke the news to him. He cannot stop thinking about it, and he does not understand why he is not allowed to know where his brother is going.

"Ah," Satoshi replies, as he too, sits up. "It's Little Satoru's worrying mind once again."

"I demand to know," Satoru states, his mouth turning into a frown. "I am your brother, so I have the right to know where you are going."

Satoshi laughs again. "You are something, Satoru," he says. "Come here." He opens his arms for an embrace.

Satoru grumbles and leans into his brother, still frowning.

"Our world is complex, Satoru," Satoshi says as he closes his arms around his brother, holding him close. "I know you have many questions, but many questions cannot be answered until the right time. Time is a special thing. And when the time is right, things will fall into place."

Satoru frowns further. His brother is going into one of his deep lectures again. He does not understand what he is saying. "I don't understand, Brother Satoshi," Satoru complains.

"That is because you are not old enough yet," Satoshi replies. His tone of voice then changes, and he laughs light-heartedly. "Now stop worrying your little mind over every little thing," he says as he ruffles Satoru's hair.

Satoru squirms and laughs. In this moment in time, the love he has for his brother grows even stronger. However, the ache inside his little heart lingers.

Satoru buries his face into his brother's chest, wondering why, out of all people, it is his brother who will leave his side.

CHAPTER TWENTY-SIX

Living in the Present

A YOUNG, SLIM MAN STANDS in the bright, green fields in the distance. He wears a simple, white shirt and black trousers. His arms are tucked behind him, and the knee of his left leg is bent as he leans against the old, grand windmill. His beautiful, soft ivory hair flows gently in the breeze.

Seiji? Sana thinks in disbelief. She rubs her eyes, but the vision does not disappear. In a flurry, Sana runs up the fields towards him. "Seiji!" Sana shouts.

The young man waves back.

Once Sana reaches him, she takes a moment to catch her breath.

"Azuki." Seiji smiles. His warm, honey eyes are soft. He holds his arms out towards her.

Sana immediately throws her arms around him in an embrace, burying her face into his chest. "Seiji," Sana whispers again in disbelief. She breathes in deeply and the nostalgic, comforting scent of sandalwood sweeps over her. In an instant, tears begin to form at the rims of her eyes.

"Azuki," Seiji repeats, patting her on the head. His sweet voice rings like music to her ears. He pulls away and looks at her, still smiling. "What a beautiful young lady you have grown into."

Sana blushes before the realisation hits her. Does Seiji still recognise her? Her face looks completely different from the last time he saw her. "Oh," Sana gasps as she touches her skin.

"You have been through something unimaginable," Seiji says quietly. "You are the strongest person I have ever known."

Sana stands still, her hands still covering the sides of her face. She looks at the man in front of her, wondering how this can be happening.

"You still have a rather adorable face," Seiji says, "so stop worrying." He smiles. "If anything, you have really grown into a beautiful young lady."

Sana blushes again, the heat pulsating through her cheeks. She blinks, not knowing what to say. After a moment, she speaks. "Seiji, how is this possible?"

"I should think the dead are allowed to visit, so visiting, I am." Seiji winks. "Now you have been up to some real mischief, haven't you?" he asks.

"I—I am just doing what I can to defend my family against the Kurai," Sana says defensively.

"You need to stop living in the past, Sana," Seiji replies.

Sana blushes again, for this is the first time she has ever heard him call her real name.

"Do not let the Kurai define your future," Seiji continues. "Start looking around you and start noticing what is going on."

"Shinrin is in danger," Sana replies, her eyes wide. "Is that what you mean?"

"Somewhat, although I know you are doing everything you can to help solve this case. I know Prince Takashi is working very hard, as well."

"How did you come to know all these things?" Sana

asks. She is still in disbelief that he is really here.

Seiji smiles. The glint in his warm eyes is brighter than ever. "What I mean to say, Sana, is that the prince is a good man."

"Huh?" *Why is Seiji saying this all of a sudden?*

"Stop living in the past and start noticing what is around you," Seiji repeats. "Prince Takashi cares for you, Azuki."

"What are you talking about?" Sana replies, her confusion increasing.

"What I mean is, you are the greatest girl I have ever known. And, a great girl deserves someone who can live up to her standards," Seiji says.

Sana laughs as she suddenly realises where this is going. "Don't tell me you are trying to set me up with the prince?" Sana scoffs. "You know I—" She stops mid-sentence.

Seiji looks at her softly, waiting for her to finish.

"I—" Sana struggles to say any more. The pain inside her heart intensifies and tears begin to trickle from her eyes. She takes a breath. "I said I would never love again, Seiji," Sana whispers as her wet, obsidian eyes drift towards his face. "My last words to you were, 'I'm sorry,' but all this time, what I wanted to say was—"

"Hey—"

"I love you," Sana finishes anyway. The pain inside her heart aches even further and more tears run down her cheeks.

"Hey," Seiji says again. "Come here." He beckons her with a finger.

Sana takes a few small steps towards him, her eyes darkened by sadness.

Seiji flicks her softly on the forehead, taking her by surprise. "Stop being silly," he whispers. "And stop crying now."

Sana gulps.

"You know I have always loved you too," Seiji continues. "I told you many times that you are like a sister to me."

Sana shakes her head. "I had a whole speech I wanted to recite to you, Seiji," Sana says. "A romantic confession of love."

"And I would have heard you out," Seiji says softly. "But look around you, Azuki. You got out of the Kurai, so go and live your life now."

Sana throws her arms around him once more, burying her face into his chest. She wants to feel his presence with her forever. She inhales and takes in every part of him that she can.

"Stop living in the past, little Azuki," Seiji whispers.

"Live on now. Live your life."

Sana grasps onto his shirt, clinging as tightly as she can. Suddenly, the softness of the fabric disappears from her hands. She looks up to see that he is gone.

There is nothing there.

Only the old, grand windmill remains, its blades turning round and round.

✾

Sana opens her eyes and sits up from her bed. *A dream?* She gazes ahead, staring at nothing in particular. She reaches a hand towards her cheek, touching it lightly. It is wet with tears.

She wipes it away with the bed sheets. The image of Seiji lingers in her mind.

The moon is shining brightly in the night sky. Sana gets up from her bed and peers at the window. There is a soft layer of snow already draped over the palace like a cotton blanket, and snow is still falling. It is truly winter in Shinrin.

Someone in a long, black cloak and holding onto an orange, glowing lantern, strides across the snow. His glossy, raven hair flows behind him under the moonlight.

Is that Prince Takashi? Sana wonders. *What is he doing*

up so late at night?

Sana edges the window open. “Prince Takashi!” she calls. Her voice is louder than she expected, amplified by the dead of the winter night.

The prince immediately stops and looks up at her. His eyes are wide with a sort of terror and urgency she has never seen before.

“Are you all right?” Sana asks, wondering what is going on.

“I—” Prince Takashi shakes his head and sighs. Something is clearly bothering him a lot. “I—” he tries again but stops once again. He holds a hand to his head.

Something is wrong.

“Wait, I’ll be right there,” Sana says, gripped by a sudden sense of urgency. She quickly makes her way to her wardrobe and pulls on a thick cloak and some shoes. She returns to the window and steps out onto the windowsill, which is about two floors up from the ground.

“Harlande, don’t—”

Before Prince Takashi is able to finish his sentence, Sana somersaults down from her window and lands onto the snow softly. She straightens up immediately and rushes towards him. “What is going on?” she asks once she nears.

"As if things cannot get any worse," Satoru sighs. "Albert is in danger." He looks around him, the worry in his eyes overflowing.

"And what makes you say that?" Sana asks.

"He returned my Kaidara," Satoru replies. "The message was . . . concerning. He asked for help."

"Were you on your way to somewhere?" Sana asks.

"I—" Satoru begins again. He is clearly getting worked up. He does not bother to hide his panic and fear.

Sana thinks of how she would feel if her family were in danger, and her own panic spikes. "Hey," Sana says. "Calm down, Prince Takashi."

Satoru exhales. "Things are getting bad, Harlande," he says, his eyebrows furrowing with concern. "Honestly, at this point—I don't know what to do—"

"Why don't we go inside and talk?" Sana suggests. The panic in the prince is absolutely consuming him. It appears that even the high and mighty leader of Shinrin has moments like this. He must carry an unimaginable weight of responsibilities over his shoulders.

Seeing him in this state, a small ache suddenly throbs in Sana's heart.

Satoru exhales again. "Good idea," he manages to say.

"All right," Sana replies. She begins to walk towards one of the entrances on the ground floor.

Satoru hurries behind her.

The guards bow immediately when they approach. "Prince Takashi! Knight Lishuah!" they say in unison as they bend forward into a bow. They then open the doors immediately.

"Where shall we go?" Sana asks. The prince stares at her, still wild-eyed. Sana does not think he is able to answer her. "We will go back to the guest chamber then," Sana decides. She is going to have to make decisions for him right now.

She strides up the staircase, and more guards bow as they pass. Soon, they reach her door. She nods and smiles at her night doorman who is guarding her room. She struggles to remember his name.

"Hikaru." Prince Takashi nods and greets the guard, answering Sana's question.

Hikaru pushes open the door and bows again, after which Sana and Prince Takashi both step inside.

"All right, sit," Sana says, gesturing to the chair where he sat before.

Satoru briskly takes his shoes off with his feet as Sana does the same. He shrugs off his cloak and hangs it on the wall before sitting down stiffly.

Sana strides across the room and picks up her furry grey cat. She returns to the prince a few seconds later and plops the cat into his lap. "Hold Luna," Sana orders. "She will help calm you down."

Satoru looks down at the grey cat in his lap. He blinks at the creature, clearly surprised, and then strokes her soft fur. She purrs with contentment and nuzzles into him.

"So, tell me," Sana says as she sits onto her chair, cross-legged. "Let's talk it through."

"Harlande, these killings are getting serious, as you know," Satoru begins. "Now, dead bodies are not just appearing—it's the citizens who are dying. Shinrin is falling apart."

Sana tries to reassure him. "Prince Takashi, you are trying your best."

He does not seem to hear her. "And *I* sent Albert to Qieta," Satoru continues. His words are rushed, and his voice is thick with worry. "I thought only of what might help our kingdom. I didn't think what may happen to him. The possibility of Qieta being dangerous did not even cross my mind. How could I send him somewhere that I barely know anything about?"

Sana stays silent, sensing that the prince needs to get all of this out at once.

He plunges his hand into his robe and pulls out a folded piece of parchment. "A while ago, I sent him a Kaidara, but he did not respond immediately," Satoru says. "I wondered what was taking him so long, but when he finally responded, this is what I got back." He unfolds the piece of parchment and shows it to Sana.

Sana glances at the message and a hand flies up to cover her mouth. It is a two-worded message that looks as though it was smeared with blood.

YES. HELP.

"Albert is my brother," Satoru rambles. He holds his head in his hands. "How could I do this to him?"

"First of all, calm down," Sana tries to reassure him again once it is clear he has run out of steam. But she, too, is shocked. *Things are truly getting out of hand.*

"After I got this message, I thought long and hard about what to do," Satoru says. "I could send an army of our soldiers there right now, but how long would that take? A month? No, that is too long. Instead, I should be the one to go right this minute. But even that would take too long. Not to mention, I cannot leave this kingdom unattended." He shakes his head again.

Sana takes a moment to absorb this information. "Can you be sure that this message is from him?"

Satoru looks up at her. "To the best of my

knowledge, it is," he says quietly.

"Well, sending an army there may take too long, but we can start this sooner than later," Sana suggests. "The sooner we send help to him, the faster they will be able to reach Sir Leon."

"Right," Satoru replies, his voice still thick with worry. He leans back in his chair and closes his eyes briefly.

"That will be a good start," Sana says, "and then we can try to figure out what else we can do. We need more time to think." Sana shuffles on her chair, wondering what all is happening. The situation is very unsettling.

"I wish my brother was here," Satoru whispers. "Every time I encountered a problem, he always had an answer."

Sana looks at Prince Takashi. She cocks her head to one side, suddenly wondering about his past. She realises that she barely knows a single thing about the man in front of her—the great ruler of Shinrin.

Just like her, he must have his very own story to tell.

"I miss him," he whispers.

"It seems it's not easy, being king," Sana whispers. She looks at him with sincerity in her eyes. "You must carry a lot of weight on your shoulders. I cannot imagine your responsibilities, nor the pressure you are under every single day as the sole ruler of a kingdom as large as this," Sana continues.

Satoru opens his eyes. He picks up the grey cat and lays her gently on the ground before glancing at Sana again. His expression is soft, and his eyes are light, emerald jewels, like the waters of the lakes. His pupils are wide, and his gaze lingers on her. He stands suddenly and walks toward her. "Harlande . . ."

Sana looks up at him and blinks.

The prince gently grasps her hands, taking her by surprise. His long, ivory-and-golden sleeves drape around his wrists. He edges a little closer towards her.

Suddenly, Sana is not sure where to look. She turns her head slightly, her round eyes wide as she stares back at the prince.

"You are something, Harlande," Satoru whispers. The warmth from his grasp is radiating into Sana's hands. "I know nothing of you, yet I am grateful we have met." He continues to look right into her eyes. "And right now, I am grateful you are here." His lips turn up into a small, soft smile. There is something very raw, yet vulnerable, about this moment.

Sana stares on, not knowing what to say. His hands are very warm, and it is a fact she keeps getting stuck on—this warmth from another human.

"Thank you for your words," Satoru says. "I shall go and order our soldiers to be sent to Qieta right now."

"And after that, get some sleep," Sana replies, blinking back at the prince and unsure what else to say. "You may be Prince Takashi, but your poor brain still needs to rest."

Satoru manages a small laugh.

"Then," she continues, "tomorrow, your mind will be more prepared to better think of how to help Sir Leon."

Pain crosses through Satoru's eyes once more. "Sleep now, Harlande," Satoru whispers. He nods at her and lets go of her hands. He makes his way towards her door, then stops and looks back.

Sana smiles at him. "Night, Prince Takashi."

Satoru nods again and smiles before making his way out.

Long after he has left her, his warmth on Sana's hands linger on.

CHAPTER TWENTY-SEVEN

Chamber of Memories

A SMALL, MAROON BIRD LANDS on Satoshi's wrist. She peers up at him with round, beady eyes, and chirps before dropping a tiny scroll into his hand.

Satoshi glances at his palm before opening the scroll and scanning the message. He rises from his chair and strides toward the exit of his haven.

✾

The guards greet Satoshi as he reaches the entrance of King Rheinallt's room.

"Lord Azrael!" they shout in unison before bending forward into deep bows. They then pull open the circular doors so he can stride through.

King Rheinallt sits on his throne, facing Satoshi and resting his chin in his hand. His appearance has become much more human-like since the last time they met. His facial features are well-proportioned, and his long, black hair is pulled into a high ponytail. His skin, although much tighter, is still maroon. A few scars are etched over his cheeks and chin.

"Lord Azrael." King Rheinallt smiles. "Good of you to come so quickly."

"You possess something worth showing to me?" Satoshi replies.

"Indeed, I do," King Rheinallt replies. "It is a blessing to have you visit Incarae once again, especially within such a short amount of time."

"I see a slight improvement in that lamentable visage of yours," Satoshi comments.

King Rheinallt gasps. "My! Did Lord Azrael just compliment me?" He flicks his long hair over his shoulder. "Indeed. The spoils from those Katek creatures are turning me back into what I should be. I thank you, my lord."

Satoshi nods, his facial expression flat.

"And as soon as I get my hands on the one," King Rheinallt continues, "I shall break free from this."

"Patience, Rheinallt," Satoshi replies.

"Anyhow," King Rheinallt says as he rises from his chair, "now that I have regained the ability to walk, I will take this opportunity to show you something."

The king slowly takes a step forward and groans. He struggles to move. He pants and tries again. Pain crosses over his features as he takes a moment to brace himself on his thighs.

Satoshi shakes his head and tuts. "Is this feeble attempt at walking truly the best you can muster?"

The king laughs and a sound of contentment escapes his lips. "Harsh words as always, my lord," he replies. "How I do adore it." He pauses before speaking again. "I have not used these legs in . . . who knows how long?"

It is another moment before he tries again. This time, he makes it a few more steps, and then suddenly, he strides forward without any more struggles.

"Ah, it feels good to move," the king says. "Now come with me, my lord."

The two of them exit the king's chamber and walk

down several dark, eerie corridors, turning at right angles every so often. The guards bow to them as soon as they walk past.

Soon, they reach a glass door. It is large, rectangular, and engraved with various patterns of leaves and flowers. The way the engravings bend causes different colours to be reflected—the light from the candles hits them from multiple angles.

"Open the doors," King Rheinallt commands.

The guards on each side salute and follow his orders instantly.

Satoshi steps inside. This room is extremely large and spacious, and the contrast of light against the dark surroundings he has just travelled through causes him to squint. He holds a hand over his eyes, adjusting to the brightness.

The room is covered with glass. The floor, the ceilings, the walls—everywhere he looks is cyan-blue glass. There are rows and rows of glass shelves that are each home to several square indents. Each indent houses a small glass bottle.

Satoshi steps towards the closest shelf and peers at one of the bottles. It is azure in colour and engraved with elegant, swirling patterns. It is shaped like a large jewel: thinner at the top and broader at its base. A golden stopper sits on the top. Something pale and silver swirls around inside, like smoke. Beneath the bottle is a golden plate with Qietian symbols on it.

Satoshi recognises these symbols as someone's name. "This is?" he asks.

"Welcome to the Chamber of Memories," King Rheinallt says. He smiles and looks around, taking in the beautiful, yet fragile, room they are in. "I am glad to finally be able to show you this." His footsteps echo through the room as he walks between a row of shelves. "Come, Lord Azrael," he says.

Satoshi follows behind. "Why have I only been enlightened to the existence of this room now?"

"I should think I need to have a few secrets to keep you interested," the king replies. "By what other means might I tempt the great lord to grace me with his presence more often?"

Satoshi shakes his head and sighs.

The king comes to a stop. "It's a strange concept, isn't it? To think that everything one has ever known and experienced is in here."

The king reaches towards one of the bottles on the shelf, then stops just before touching it. This bottle is the colour of rose, and it gleams back at them.

Satoshi peers around as the multiple colours of the

glass bottles reflect off his eyes. He wonders if what he is looking at is real.

"Enlighten me. What purpose do these serve, especially when they merely occupy this space?" Satoshi asks. "What is the consequence if someone attempts to claim one as their own?"

"Ah," King Rheinallt replies. He stops for a moment and gazes at Satoshi. He closes his eyes and exhales. "Your deep, exquisite voice is making it rather arduous to maintain my focus."

Satoshi raises an eyebrow and King Rheinallt snaps back into reality.

He clears his throat. "With something as precious as this, one should think it wouldn't be so easy," the king says. His hand, which was hovering in front of one of the glass bottles, edges forward.

Suddenly, it is as though he hits a barrier. The king is unable to move his hand forward any further. His fingers touch some sort of clear film that dents and vibrates, but it does not allow his hand to reach through.

"It protects itself," the king explains.

Satoshi does not respond. He takes in what he is seeing.

"And how is the above?" King Rheinallt asks.

"The usual."

"I hear an intruder has come," the king says.

For the slightest of seconds, something crosses over Satoshi's eyes. It is almost as if he feels some pain. In an instant, however, the feeling is gone, and he stares ahead, his expression unfazed.

"Mm," Satoshi replies.

"Nothing too hard for you to handle, I'm sure," King Rheinallt says. He smiles.

"Do tell me, what is the purpose behind presenting this room to me?" Satoshi asks. "I fail to discern its relevance."

"My, I thought the lord would be impressed," the king answers.

Satoshi remains silent.

"Look at what I have access to here," the king continues. "The above, or Qieta I should say, may be something, but down here in Incarae, I have just about everything."

"How is this, by any stretch of imagination, your definition of everything?"

"I am so close, Lord Azrael. So close to it. I shall rule and make the world right once more."

Satoshi sighs. "Wake up, Rheinallt."

Suddenly, the king turns to face Satoshi. He narrows his dark eyes, but then his face softens. "You still call me

Rheinallt," the king says.

Satoshi stares back at him, his expression indifferent.

"How many years has it been? I long for the day you call me Edward again."

"Your words elude my comprehension entirely," Satoshi says.

A pain sparks inside Edward's eyes. Suddenly, his original, youthful aura of innocence seeps through his facial features as he blinks his deer-like eyes. He gazes at Satoshi and his throat tightens up.

In an instant, Edward is back on that bench by the shores, looking into the violet crystals of Satoshi's eyes for the very first time. A memory—*the* memory of their first encounter—Satoshi's playful and captivating demeanour—the way his vibrant voice rings like music in his ears and—

Just like that, the memory is gone. However, the lingering feelings remain, clinging onto him like a film he cannot shake off. King Rheinallt blinks back the ache that is twisting up inside him.

"When I finally find the one," he continues as he covers up a break in his voice, "I will be just about complete. And I believe now, with your help and the Katek, I am almost there. I shall rule like I was always meant to. The world will be just. I only have one more thing I desire, Lord Azrael."

Satoshi looks at him, waiting for what he is about to say.

"You already know what it is, my lord."

Surely, he is not talking about me? Satoshi frowns. "Trust you to utter something so nonsensical and absurd."

"Lord Azrael," King Rheinallt says. "Look in front of you. Look at what I have. Look at what *we* could have. Is it so difficult to accept?"

"I believe what you want is different to what I seek," Satoshi replies bluntly.

"Must I spend my whole life convincing you that I am the one for you?" King Rheinallt asks. There is sadness in his eyes. "Everything I have ever done was because—I mean, I have only, and will only ever lo—" The king stumbles over his words until they are a jumbled mess.

Satoshi puts up a hand and stops his attempts at speaking. He continues to frown. His eyes tell the king that he has had enough. "If this is what you wanted to show me," Satoshi says, "then I believe I have seen enough. I shall leave."

"Wait, Lord Azrael," King Rheinallt pleads.

Satoshi turns back towards the door. His long, raven hair and black robe swirl around him as he does so. He begins to make his way out.

"Lord Azrael!" King Rheinallt repeats.

Satoshi does not look back. He takes long strides and walks straight out of the Chamber of Memories.

CHAPTER TWENTY-EIGHT

Determination

EMIKO HOLDS OUT HER HAND and helps Sair as he climbs up the wall of her dorm. He swings a leg over the balcony but loses his balance and nearly trips.

“Woah,” Sair says as he rights himself.

“Be quiet,” Emiko hisses as she pulls him inside frantically and slides the window shut. Every time he comes, she worries that someone will notice. It is only a matter of time before the Academy realises that they are hiding a wild, magical creature in her dorm.

"Easy, red head," Sair says, sighing. "It's not like I want to be here."

"Well, here you are, so quit talking," Emiko replies, frowning.

"Is this some sort of temperament you have, red head?" Sair asks, frowning in return. "Fiery hair means a fiery temper?"

"Oh, quit it, will you?" Emiko hisses again. "Did you bring them or not?"

"Calm down, woman." Sair tuts as he takes his cloth bag and turns it upside down. Something rolls onto the carpet with a thump. When he pulls the bag away, there are three dead rats on Emiko's floor.

"Sair!" Emiko exclaims, then covers her mouth in fear of being overheard. "Can you not throw them onto my carpet like that, please?" she whispers harshly.

"Make up your mind, woman," Sair says, shaking his head. "Do you have a problem with everything I do? I did you a favour, for God's sake."

The two of them glare at each other for a moment.

Something chirps.

Sair snaps his head in the direction of the sound and walks around the small curve of Emiko's room. Emiko follows behind.

"Hello, little guy," Sair says as he crouches by the cage and pokes his finger between the bars to stroke the young Cerus's head.

The Cerus wags his tail happily and sticks out his tongue. The feathers on his wings rustle as he shakes them out.

The cage he is in now took Emiko and Sair a few days to build. Since discovering the creature, Emiko has hidden him in her room, and Sair has come every so often to bring supplies and check how the creature is doing.

"He's not so little anymore, is he?" Sair asks as he looks back towards Emiko. He sits on the carpet and crosses his legs.

It is true. It has only been a few weeks, and the creature has doubled its original size.

"Yes, Yuki has grown a lot already," Emiko replies.

Sair makes a face. "Yuki?" His nostrils spring wide in irritation. "You named him that?"

"You have a problem with it?"

"Yes. All this time, I've wanted to call him Tornado," Sair replies.

Emiko sighs and shakes her head, ignoring his statement. She unlocks the cage and Yuki springs out of it onto the carpet. He sniffs around and leaps towards the rodents on the floor, devouring them in an instant.

"Mm, tasty," Sair comments in the background.

They watch the young creature in silence.

After a while, Sair speaks again. "I don't know how we are going to keep him in here once he's an adult," he says. "His mother was big enough for someone to ride. Now imagine a male Cerus—he'll be even bigger."

"We'll figure something out," Emiko replies, trying to reassure herself.

The Cerus wanders back to Sair and bats his paws against Sair's legs playfully.

"I thought they were supposed to be ferocious," Sair says as he strokes the creature's fur. "He likes me."

"Anyway," Emiko says, changing the subject. "You already have the key to my window. So, if I ever happen to be running late from class or something and you need to come over, you can get in here. Just remember to tap on the glass like we agreed and don't barge through without warning."

"Yes, yes," Sair says, making a face. He tussles with the young Cerus some more, until suddenly, his face changes. His silver eyes are wide, and he looks at Emiko.

"What?" Emiko asks.

Sair stands. He feels all around his robe and plunges his hands into his pockets. He then looks around the floor and glances back in the direction he came.

"What is it?" Emiko repeats.

"I-I, uh—" Sair blinks as he plunges his hands into his pockets once more, the movements slightly more frantic. "I swear it was in here—"

"Don't tell me you dropped my key," Emiko says, her nostrils flaring.

"I swear—"

Emiko sighs with irritation. "Such nerve!" She gets up and walks to the hooks by her door, then throws on her cloak.

"Where are you going?" Sair asks.

"To find my key, what do you think?" Emiko replies with annoyance. "When was the last time you had it? Whereabouts were you?"

"I can go myself, red head," Sair mutters. "I'll find it."

"It is nearly sunset, Sair," Emiko says. "So, stay here until nightfall—that way, you'll be harder to spot when you climb out of the window. It stresses me out enough each time you come."

"Uh . . . right," Sair says. It is clear he is still feeling panicked and guilty about losing her key.

"So?" Emiko asks. "Where did you have it last?"

"I uh—I think I went to the forests around the palace

with it. You know, the ones right next to the Academy?" Sair replies. "I found the rodents there."

"Very well," Emiko says. "I will head there now. *You* stay here and look after Yuki, all right?" She glares at him.

Sair blinks back at her, still as stone, then nods slowly. "Honestly, you scare me sometimes, red head."

Emiko ignores him. She opens her door and steps out.

✾

Emiko looks all around, hoping she will spot her key. As she had noted, the sun is beginning to set, and it is a big, orange yolk in the sky.

She looks ahead and her heart sinks. The Academy's paths are so large and, although she can guess which paths Sair may have taken, the possibilities are endless.

Honestly! Trust this guy to drop my key!

Emiko continues down the Academy paths, scanning left and right. Soon, she enters the forests of the palace. The orange glow from the setting sun falls through the gaps between the trees, casting down a beautiful light.

The sound of nearing horse hooves reaches her ears.

Emiko turns, immediately picturing that it is Sir

Leon riding on his magnificent ivory stallion through the forests. Her heart beats hard inside her chest.

But when she looks up, it is not Sir Leon. It is a strikingly handsome man with long, raven hair. He is perched on top of a midnight-coloured horse.

The young man nods as he and his horse trot past. "Excuse me, milady." He wears a luxurious black-and-golden robe, as well as a golden headpiece. He looks to be in a hurry.

Emiko watches as he disappears onto the palace grounds. *My goodness . . . was that Prince Takashi?* She thinks in awe. Something inside her tells her to follow him.

She hastily runs behind him, scanning the ground in case she happens to spot her key.

Emiko reaches the public palace gardens and stands behind one of the rose hedges. Through the crossing branches, she watches as Prince Takashi hops down from his horse and greets a man who is standing there.

This young man has short black hair and a trimmed beard. He bows to the prince. "Your Majesty."

The prince nods in return. "Hello, Ryota."

"You have sent out the soldiers, Your Majesty?" Ryota asks.

"Yes. I went to do the final checks. I have sent the

very best—twenty to start with. They will depart for Qieta as soon as possible."

Emiko gasps. *Qieta? Isn't that where Sir Leon went?*

"Great news, Prince Takashi," Ryota replies.

"In the meantime, I must think of something else to ensure this will succeed. I would do anything to go myself, but I cannot leave the kingdom unattended," the prince replies. He shakes his head. There is worry in his eyes.

"Prince Takashi," Ryota says, "you are doing your very best. Shinrin is dealing with several crises. Trust that we will do everything we can to help Sir Leon."

Emiko's heart sinks as soon as she hears his name. What could have happened?

Prince Takashi's answer heightens her worries. "Albert is in danger." He closes his eyes for a moment and gulps. When he opens them again, they are dark with sadness and fear.

Emiko's heart sinks further. *Sir Leon is in danger?*

Something cracks in her chest. Panic begins to consume her and immediately, tears form in her eyes. She stumbles from behind the rose bush, uncaring of the branches and thorns that catch on her uniform.

The prince and his guard immediately look towards her.

"S-Sorry," Emiko apologises as she nears. She wipes a tear from her eye.

"Milady?" Ryota asks. "May I help you with something?"

"Sir Leon is in danger?" Emiko asks, her anxiety rising. She looks at the prince and his guard, her face full of worry.

"I'm sorry, milady," Ryota says, "but it appears—"

"I love him," Emiko states. Her words are strong and firm. She leans in further, and her breaths become rapid and shallow. "Please, tell me what is going on."

Prince Takashi stares at her and blinks. "Your name please, milady?" he asks.

"Emiko. Emiko Tanaka."

"Oh," the prince says. "The granddaughter of Mr Kenta Tanaka, yes?"

"Y-Yes," Emiko says between shallow breaths. There is a weight crushing her chest. "My grandparents—they—they, uh—came to meet you, Your Majesty."

"So, they did," the prince replies. "Come, sit down." He gestures towards one of the benches in the palace gardens.

Emiko stumbles forward and her foot catches against a loose part of the ground. She nearly falls, but

Ryota reaches out his hand and steadies her.

"Careful, Milady," Ryota says as he helps her to sit down.

Emiko takes a seat, wiping additional tears from her eyes.

"I am sorry to see you in this state," Prince Takashi says gently. "Please, do not cry now." He reaches into his extravagant robe and pulls out a white handkerchief.

Emiko takes it with both of her hands. There is a small emerald leaf embroidered on it.

"I didn't know Albert had a lady," Prince Takashi whispers.

"Oh—I'm not—We aren't—" Emiko gasps as she wipes her eyes. Her cheeks warm up under her tears. "I mean, I just . . . care for him. A lot. He doesn't—"

Ryota puts a hand on her shoulder in an attempt to comfort her. Emiko stops talking and stares at the ground with watering eyes as she tries to control her breathing. Worry and embarrassment vie for control of her heart. It hurts.

"I see," Prince Takashi says. He looks away as Emiko turns to look at him. Pain is reflected in his eyes. "I can see you care for him a lot, Miss Tanaka." He pauses. "I do, too."

There is silence.

"I received a message from Albert. It said little apart from, 'Help'. Albert is not one to panic in unexpected situations, so to receive something like this from him tells me that he is in urgent need of aid."

"Oh, Sir Leon," Emiko says. She holds her face in her hands, bunching the handkerchief against her cheeks. "What could have happened to him?"

"I have sent an army of soldiers to Qieta," Prince Takashi says, "but it will take quite some time for them to get there and then report back." He sighs.

Emiko's eyebrows turn into a frown, and she leans towards the prince with extreme determination. "I will go," she says. Her amber eyes burn into the prince's.

The prince leans away slightly, taken aback. "Milady?"

"I will go," Emiko repeats. "I have to. I must."

Prince Takashi looks at Ryota and Ryota looks back at him.

"I understand you care for him, milady," Ryota begins, "but I'm not sure a young lady on her own will be able to do much. It is far too dangerous." He rubs his nose.

Emiko stands abruptly. There is a fierceness inside her that cannot be tamed. She is in love with Sir Leon, and she will do everything she can to ensure that he is safe, even if it means travelling to an island a million miles away on her own.

"I insist, Your Majesty," Emiko states.

"I'm afraid I cannot endanger a young lady like that," Prince Takashi says after a moment's pause.

"I do not need your permission," Emiko says suddenly. "This is my decision." She takes a step forward.

Ryota panics and reaches out a hand to stop her. "Milady—"

"Your Majesty, I am currently studying Animal Studies at Furukawa Academy," Emiko says as she sidesteps Ryota's hand. "You must have a way to inform them that I will be absent due to an important mission."

Prince Takashi is further taken aback. He looks at the young girl and his expression is full of worry. "Milady, this is unwise."

"I thank you for your concern, Your Majesty," Emiko says, "but I shall be making my way to Qieta. Sir Leon needs me." She bows to the prince and his guard, then turns briskly to run out of the palace gardens.

Prince Takashi and Ryota stare at her retreating back. Ryota turns to look at Prince Takashi, and the prince stares back at him.

Without saying a word, both shake their heads and sigh.

CHAPTER TWENTY-NINE

A Lost Voice

SAMUEL PLACES THE TRAY ON the grand, royal dining table. Using both of his hands, he carefully lifts up the large, ivory bowl of pumpkin soup and places it between the king and queen, who are sitting opposite each other. He then turns an upside-down bowl right-side up, ready for the king to use.

Just as he does the same for the queen, a weakness in his hand overwhelms him. He knocks the bowl over and his heart leaps with panic. Immediately, he reaches out to try and catch it before it falls to the floor.

The queen stops the bowl in its tracks—the numerous jewels and bangles around her wrists clatter against the ivory as she grips the dish. She glares at Samuel, her piercing, crimson eyes filled with disgust. She wrinkles her nose and tuts. "How useless," she comments. Her red, painted lips flatten unkindly.

"My dear, let us not begin our meal like this," the king says.

Samuel looks at the king, hoping that he will come to his defence. His hope is short-lived and his heart sinks as soon as the king continues speaking.

"These servants are merely our objects to use as we please, my dear," the king says to his wife. "This one is proving to be rather incompetent, however. Perhaps he can be the next one we feed to the devil." He glares up at Samuel, his sharp, dark eyes penetrating his soul.

Samuel cannot decide between holding the king's gaze or looking away.

"Come here." The king beckons to Samuel with a short, stubby finger.

Samuel walks towards him reluctantly, his heart beating hard inside his chest. *What does the king want?*

"Hold out your hand," the king demands. His full,

black-and-grey beard frames his small mouth and bobs as he speaks.

With apprehension, Samuel holds out his right hand.

Without warning, the king picks up a golden spoon laying in front of him and strikes it hard against the bony part of Samuel's wrist. Samuel flinches, knowing that, after a split second, the pain is going to throb like nothing else.

"Now, this will teach you to be more careful. If you drop dishes on my wife again, perhaps I will chop off your hand next time." The king snickers. "You do realise that you are lucky to still be alive?" He raises an eyebrow at Samuel. "Now, work to prove your worth, or I shall take you next."

Samuel immediately bends forward into a deep bow, using it to convey his deepest apologies. He cannot speak, after all.

"Now, get out of my sight and leave us to enjoy our meal," the king states.

The queen looks at Samuel with the same expression of disgust from earlier, then turns to her husband and smiles sweetly.

Samuel trudges towards the side wall of the royal dining room and stands still. He will have to stay here and serve the royal Keskan leaders their meals until they are finished.

This is going to be a very long evening.

"So, my dear," the queen begins, "tell me how our deal is proceeding with the underworld." She helps herself to some of the pumpkin soup. Her extraordinarily long, painted, golden nails must be an utter hindrance to everything she does, but it does not seem to bother her.

Samuel looks to the floor and away from the queen's claws. To him, the royal crimson carpet reflects the blood of all the victims the king and queen have sold and sacrificed.

He then glances up, catching sight of his own wobbly reflection in the golden doors in front of him—there is a leathery belt fastened in a cross over his neck with a spherical, ruby gem in its centre. It is a constant reminder to him that he cannot speak.

Since the day he endured an unspeakable amount of torture from the masked men, Samuel had been ordered to give up his title as a soldier; his injuries were so great that he was now considered far too weak to hold his position.

He was thrown right into the Keskan palace—home to the king and queen—to work as a servant. Since coming here, he discovered that there are many servants here just like him, those made to work for these royal leaders.

The servants are all in similar situations—all too weak to be a physical threat. Not only that, but the dreadful belt was forcibly tied around each of their necks and reinforced with ancient, dark Keskan spells. Due to it, the servants are forbidden to speak or convey messages by any other means.

This way, the Keskan secrets never leave the palace.

Each time Samuel tries to voice something, his tongue becomes horribly heavy and seals completely to the roof of his mouth. Speaking in this circumstance is absolutely impossible. When he tries to write down things he has heard, his palms burn as though they are on fire, making him drop whatever he is holding instantly.

Samuel leans against the wall and sighs. How is he going to get out of this place? Where was Sir Meness taken to? Where is his sister? Is it possible to tell anyone what is happening?

"Our business with the underworld is fine as always, my dear," the king says. "So long as we keep the trade going, our wealth will never cease. Speaking of, I have noticed that a few of the servants may not last much longer. Perhaps we can take them next."

"Did you not say that they preferred strong, healthy bodies?" the queen asks. "Pity that Suyin hasn't taken any new soldiers recently."

Suyin? Is that not Princess Lore's name? Samuel wonders. He stares at the floor.

"Her soldiers are the perfect food, but any organ is better than no organ at all," the king says. "Perhaps it is time they stop being so picky." He wipes his shiny forehead with his sleeve.

"We do have to be careful though, my dear," the queen says as she brings a spoon of pumpkin soup to her lips. "We want to stay on their good side."

"Do not worry about that," the king says, mirroring his wife's movements and then swallowing his bite. "I know what I am doing. They will always need more organs, and we are one of the few places that is willing to supply them."

The queen swallows another spoonful. She sighs. "And now, they are asking for more children?"

"We have plenty of those to dispose of."

"We may have plenty, but we do not have an infinite amount, dear," the queen says. "We need those children for our mines."

The king leans towards her and smiles. The white

hairs from his moustache and beard poke out like whiskers. "If we need more, we shall send our soldiers to capture more. Do not worry your little head with things like that."

Samuel's heart stops. *So, the soldiers that Princess Lore previously took were fed to the devil by her parents? And the servant children who have gone missing also suffered the same fate?* He stares at the king and queen, unable to stop himself from frowning deeply.

The king and queen are evil. Pure evil.

Please do not let Sir Meness and his sister meet their ends in this way as well, Samuel prays to whoever is watching over him. He blinks hard and then shuts his eyes.

He must find a way to get out of here.

. . . No.

First, he must gather as much information as he can before he tries to flee. He shall take advantage of the fact that these royal leaders believe their secrets will not escape the palace.

Then, he will find a way to escape. He made a promise to Sir Meness, and it is a promise he shall keep.

He shall find Sir Meness's sister and reunite them at last.

CHAPTER THIRTY

Beneath the Stars

SATORU SITS AT HIS DESK, looking through his paperwork as usual when something moves in the corner of his eye. He looks up at his ceiling, at the girl perched there. "Mutoren?"

She is dressed in black from head to toe and hanging from his ceiling. Her wooden mask is pulled to the side of her head and she smirks before jumping down. She lands on his desk without a sound.

"Excuse me, Mutoren," Satoru says, wondering why

she is here, "you're standing on my paperwork."

"Oh, am I now?" she asks. There is a playful edge to her voice.

When she looks at Satoru, his heart immediately begins to skip. *Why is she here?* A fluttering feeling begins inside his stomach and intensifies.

The Mutoren swings her legs around—knocking a filled vase and the flower she'd gotten him to the floor—and lands in front of his desk. She leans towards him and Satoru is taken aback. The way her braided hair falls softly in front of her shoulders is making his breathing go strange.

"I have something," she whispers, the playful edge still lingering in her voice. She reaches around her neck and pulls a small jewel out in front of her. "Does this look familiar?"

Satoru looks at what she is holding—there is a golden chain around her neck and a small emerald leaf dangling from it. It is his necklace. "You—"

"Come get it," the Mutoren teases. She turns and walks away from him.

Satoru gets up from his desk and follows.

Suddenly, he treads into a patch of water from the spilled vase and slips. He tumbles forward just as the Mutoren turns in surprise and also loses her balance; the two of them land on the floor in a heap.

Satoru catches himself with his hands just before he falls on top of her. He is now only inches away from her face. She is looking at him with a softness he has never seen before. Something inside his heart throbs further.

"This is where we first met," the Mutoren whispers. "Just like this." She smiles.

Satoru's cheeks start to burn. He hastily pushes himself away, but something is firmly pressed against his back, stopping him in his tracks.

It is the Mutoren's hand, and she is pushing him back towards her.

"Stay like this," she whispers. The Mutoren trails her fingers into his hair, twists them around the strands that fall in front of his face, and tucks the hair behind his ear. "You are rather handsome, Satoru," the Mutoren whispers.

Satoru stops breathing. He is about to faint. *Did she just call me by my first name?* The heat from his cheeks is absolutely blazing. The way she said his name is creating music in his ears.

The Mutoren smiles wider at him, her fingers still playing with his hair. As he tries to remember how to breathe, her face closes in towards his.

Their lips are about to touch—

Satoru jolts awake. He is drenched in sweat and his breathing is hard and heavy. He wipes his forehead frantically. He then scrambles out of his bed, trips, and falls to the floor.

It was a dream. A very intense dream, to say the least.

Briskly, Satoru stands and immediately catches sight of his desk. The vase is still on the surface with the flower inside. The image of Harlande smiling up at him from the floor immediately hits him.

"It was only a dream!" he exclaims before he clambers towards his windows. He pushes them wide open, breathing heavily.

"Your Majesty!" a guard on his balcony shouts. "Are you all right?"

It is still night, and snow is falling outside. The guards are dressed in extremely thick clothing, taking their shifts in turns to try and keep warm.

Satoru stares ahead as various emotions run wildly through him. He has no idea what is going on, and he has never felt anything like this before.

"It is a bit hot in here, is it not?" Satoru asks out of nowhere.

His guard stares back at him, half of his face hidden in the thick layers of fabric wrapped around his neck. He blinks in confusion. Snowflakes are clustered on his eyelashes.

"Right, I'll be going, then." Satoru closes the windows and draws his curtains.

The sweat is beginning to dry and feel sticky. Satoru stumbles into his bathroom and turns on the water, drawn by an urge to immerse himself in a bath. He shrugs off his night clothes and plunks himself into the tub. He leans back and stares at the ceiling as warm water flows around him and the tub fills up.

His heart is still beating out of control.

Despite his best efforts, he finds himself recalling the dream. In it, she is looking back at him. She has a confident smirk and the grace of a fighter, even when she is stuck on the ceiling like a spider.

His heart throbs again. Satoru closes his eyes.

I have officially gone mad.

✱

Later that morning, Satoru is sitting properly at his desk in his study. He is dressed in a fern-coloured robe—one embroidered with silver patterns—and he is struggling to concentrate.

He looks at his door and the image of Albert bursting through springs to his mind.

Satoru's heart is heavy. He remembers when Albert

first told him about the killings, and how he tried to find ways to stay in Shinrin for Satoru's protection.

Satoru sighs. Perhaps he should have listened to Albert.

He has now sent two troops to Qieta, warning them to also look after a young girl named Emiko Tanaka if she appears. There is not much he can do to stop her from going. She had such a fierce determination in her eyes, and Satoru could not argue against it. But now he feels like it is his responsibility to ensure that she is safe.

Responsibilities after responsibilities. Satoru sighs again. What else can he do apart from sending his soldiers to Qieta? He would give anything to know what is happening with Albert right now. He wants to go to Qieta himself, but he knows that is impossible.

Satoru leans back in his chair and closes his eyes.

More things have piled on top of the issue with Albert, as well. Recently, the analysis of the ashes from the monster he and Harlande saw in the Oku Forests came back with nothing helpful. The report claimed that there was nothing special about them—they were just ashes. Plain ashes, like what would come from something that was burned.

They have no new details and no extra clues.

This case of the killings is driving him to the edge.

He has not been able to find a single answer, and his best friend is now in danger. Just the thought makes him want to throw up.

Satoru prays inside his mind. *Please, be safe. Please, Albert.*

And then there is Akalin, who is also missing. Satoru's heart sinks even further. *Why is everything going so wrong?*

One small fortune is that there have been no new monster sightings since the last. He ordered for the majority of the lakes in Shinrin to be drained, and that seems to have halted the attacks. The rivers have been closed off and citizens are forbidden to go anywhere near them. Satoru prays that this will keep them safe for now.

Suddenly, there is a *tap tap* on his window.

Satoru turns to see a Ketu. He stands immediately and opens his window. The bird hops inside and opens her wings. Satoru opens the scroll and scans the message quickly.

Yoo-hoo, Satoru.

I was captured in Keska, which is where the Hinoki children were sent. They have been enslaved and are forced to work in the mines. I have found an underground organisation that is trying to overthrow the Keskan Empire, and I am with them at present. I have yet to find Aiyla.

Please do not reply to my message. Don't send any soldiers here. Let me seek out more information. This is a dangerous place. I do hope you and Albert are doing well. Do not worry about me. Keep Shinrin in your safe hands like you always do.

Regards,
Akalin

"Oh." Satoru gasps. He reads the message again, over and over.

Akalin—his friend, his brother, his comrade—is alive.

It is a strange feeling. He is unsure whether to be ecstatic that Akalin is alive or horrified that he was captured in an unknown land.

Keska? Satoru thinks. *Isn't that the land that paid a large sum of money to be removed from all the maps?*

From his knowledge, the land became more and more private over the years, and now, they strictly control everything that is going in and out of their kingdom. They are so private that they have almost disappeared from Neputa completely.

He makes his way to a nearby shelf and pulls out all the atlases he can find. He flips each of them open. Sure enough, there is no Keska to be seen . . . apart from in one atlas.

This particular atlas of Neputa is quite old. It had once belonged to his brother, Satoshi. On it, sitting quite some distance to the Northwest of Shinrin is Keska, a small, jagged island.

Something lights up in Satoru's mind. *Didn't Brother Satoshi meet the princess from this land, many years ago?*

Yes, he had. Satoshi had come into his chamber to tell him about how ladies kept asking to take his hand and how he found it so tiring. He said that he was content just being by himself.

One of the ladies who wanted to marry him is from this land. Satoru is sure of it.

Should I send my soldiers to Keska as well—no, Akalin explicitly told me not to.

With a sigh, Satoru closes the atlas and puts it back on his shelf. He walks back towards his chair and sits.

This feeling of uselessness is eating away at him. He cannot do anything to help Albert directly. His friend, Akalin, is stuck in Keska and he cannot send his soldiers there. Brother Satoshi broke his promise and never returned. His parents disappeared.

Once again, Satoru feels terribly alone. He holds his face in his hands and squeezes his eyes shut. After a moment, he turns to face the window once more. The Ketu is still on his windowsill.

Satoru writes a quick message to Master Kinali. He and his wife will be overjoyed to know that their son is still alive.

✾

Satoru makes his way to the Central Training Ground. Even from afar, he immediately notices her.

Harlande.

She is practicing her forms and her movements are fluid, like water. Today, she wears a maroon outfit and her sleek black hair is tied into two buns with red ribbons.

Satoru makes his way up the high, wooden beams that overlook the grounds. He sits down in the centre seat and rests his chin in his hands.

Soon, soldiers begin to march into the clearing. Sana immediately stops and bows as the men line up. They bow back.

They salute in unison. "Knight Lishuah!"

Satoru watches intently as Sana begins another

training session alongside the soldiers. It appears that she has become quite accustomed to her role as a knight. Her leadership is impressive. She is firm yet encouraging.

Satoru finds himself admiring her soft, fluid movements and the way she holds her forms with strength and impeccable posture. He smiles. Warmth radiates from his heart.

At a time like this, when he feels so alone, he is suddenly grateful, once again, that she is here.

He waits for the training session to finish. Once the soldiers begin to exit the training ground, Satoru makes his way down the steps.

"Lishuah," he calls out.

Sana looks at the prince and bows. "Your Majesty."

"Well done," he says.

Sana nods at him. "Thank you for your kind words."

"I was wondering if you had some time tonight?" Satoru asks. His heart rate suddenly accelerates inside his chest. "I wanted to speak with you."

"Oh," Sana replies, surprised. She nods again. "That would be great. I also wanted to speak with you."

Satoru blinks. *She wants to speak with me, too?* He wonders what she has to say.

"Then tonight, after nightfall. At the palace porch?"

Satoru asks. He wonders why his heart is squeezing so hard inside him.

Sana nods a third time. "See you then, Prince Takashi." She bows and exits the training ground along with the soldiers.

✲

Satoru kneels on a cushion on the palace porch. It is situated right at the back of the palace, facing the back gardens. Wooden floorboards extend out from the main building and the trees and plants in the distance make it a particularly tranquil place to be.

The sun set not too long ago, and the sky is slowly fading into the night. Despite it snowing only yesterday, tonight is pleasantly mild. A few stars have started to appear in the sky.

Satoru wears a pale blue robe embroidered with navy patterns. The sleeves are long and drape onto the ground. He takes off his headpiece to make sure the golden tassels are untangled, then pops it back on his head.

Satoru looks at the small wooden table next to him. He asked the palace kitchens to prepare some of the finest jasmine tea. The teapot is currently sitting on a round stone that is supposed to keep it warm.

He wonders when Harlande will arrive.

He looks at the ceiling and scans it, wondering if she will suddenly appear up there. He thinks through what he wants to say.

"Hello," Sana says.

Satoru's head snaps forward briskly. His heart skips a beat. He has never seen her like this before.

She walks towards him like a normal human being, far removed from the Mutoren. Instead of the usual fighter-style fabrics or simple clothing she wears, today she has on a beautiful, long, lilac-and-violet dress. She is glowing.

There are silver gems that sparkle in the fabric as she moves, and her smooth, dark hair is half tied around both sides of her head into small braids, then secured with lilac ribbons. The rest is let loose and drapes softly over her shoulders.

Satoru stares at her. His eye twitches. "Good evening," he manages to say.

Sana smiles. She kneels on the cushion next to the table.

"I thought you would appear on the ceiling," Satoru says. He cannot look away from her.

"I don't think I can do that wearing this," Sana replies, lifting an arm and showing him how the sleeves drape towards the floor, just like his. "I do prefer to enter a place from the ceiling, though." She laughs. "Crawling across the ceiling is more my style."

Satoru wonders why she looks so different today. The warmth inside him pulses and deepens. Did she dress so beautifully because she was coming to see him?

"You, uh, look different," Satoru says, losing all of the formality in his voice.

"Thank you for the compliment," Sana answers. She looks up into the night sky and Satoru notices a sadness in her eyes. "I never do anything like this," she says quietly. "But something told me I should make the most of everything while I am still able to."

The sadness in her eyes deepen. A small ache throbs inside Satoru's heart, overshadowing the warmth. He wonders why she looks so sad and what her words mean.

"So, I decided to do something different while I still have some time left." She turns and smiles at him. "It just so happens that I was coming to see you."

"Right," Satoru answers.

"Do I look like I belong more in the palace now?" she jokes.

"You always have," Satoru finds himself saying. It surprises him. He looks away suddenly and remembers the tea. "Please." He gestures to the small cups in front of them and pours some tea into hers.

The aroma of the jasmine drifts into the night air.

Sana takes her cup and thanks him. She takes a sip. "You know, I commend you for wearing these things all day," she says. "It's harder than it looks."

"Oh," Satoru replies. He finds himself staring at her again and forces himself to turn back to the tea pot. He pours himself some tea.

"You wanted to speak with me?" Sana asks.

"Oh—yes." Satoru snaps back into the moment. "I was looking into sidium poisoning after your recent illness. I know you haven't stepped out of the palace grounds as such, but I've come to learn that animals can carry traces of it as they roam around in the wild. It doesn't affect them the same way as it does humans, so I thought that, perhaps your cat—"

"It's all right," Sana interrupts quietly. "I know where it came from."

Satoru wonders what she means. "You do?"

"Yeah," she replies. She does not say any more.

"Where?"

Sana sighs. The sadness returns to her eyes once more. She looks into the distance and something on her face tells Satoru that she is debating whether to elaborate.

Eventually, she sighs again. "It is a part of my life, I guess." She says nothing more—it is clear she has decided not to give him more information. "Thank you for tending to me when I was ill." She smiles, although it does not reach her eyes.

He takes a sip of tea. "That's—you're welcome," he says.

The two of them look into the night sky some more.

"Will you ever tell me why you stole the great treasures of Shinrin?" Satoru asks quietly all of a sudden. He does not want to push, but this question sparks inside him every time they meet.

Sana continues to look at the night sky, pain joining the sadness in her eyes. Her emotions swirl in the reflections of the starlight. The usual, indifferent mien of the Mutoren is completely gone. Right now, Satoru only sees a beautiful young lady who has experienced pain in her past.

"I stole them for protection," Sana answers after a long while.

Satoru stays quiet. Protection from what? What would make someone go to such extreme lengths, to the point of becoming infamous?

"I see sadness in your eyes, Harlande," Satoru says instead of asking his questions.

"And I see curiosity in yours," Sana answers. She takes a sip of tea.

"You are something, Harlande," Satoru comments.

"So, the sidium was what you wanted to speak with me about?" Sana asks, changing the subject abruptly.

"Y-Yes."

"Well, you have your answer. Was there anything else?"

"Y-Yes," Satoru repeats, wondering why he is stuttering. "Harlande, I am impressed by your skills and I believe you give your position the respect it is due. I was wondering if you would like a permanent place in the palace." Satoru's heart pounds inside his chest as he waits for her response.

Sana looks away. "Oh, you believe so?"

"I do."

"How long would the role go on for?" she asks.

"As long as you wish," Satoru answers, wondering why she is asking.

"I'm not sure I am the right person to ask, then," Sana replies. "I may not be able to hold this role for much longer."

Satoru frowns. "I'm not sure I understand what you mean. Harlande—"

"This reminds me," she interrupts. "I wished to

speak with you, too."

Satoru nods, allowing the interruption and hoping she will explain herself.

"I wanted to ask for a few days away from the palace. I believe I need to see my family. I have something important I must do," Sana states.

Satoru's heart stops for a moment. "You do?" *Please, not another person leaving my side.*

"Yes. I have come to ask for your permission," Sana says.

"You don't need my permission to go and see your family," Satoru answers, although pain is increasing in his heart. *I will be abandoned again.*

"It is my duty to ask," she says. "After all, I am your temporary first-hand guard and a palace knight."

"It is courteous of you to ask," Satoru replies. He does not want her to go. He wonders what it is she must go and do. "When will you be going?"

"Soon, I guess," Sana says. "I will let you know. Thank you for your understanding and permission."

"Very well."

Sana finishes her tea. She suddenly stands.

"You're going?" Satoru asks immediately, standing with her. He truly does not want her to leave. Not right now.

"It's probably best I do," Sana replies. "It is late now, and as always, your brain needs to rest."

"I enjoy your company, Harlande," Satoru says. His words do not falter. He is not stuttering now. He looks her straight in her eyes. "But if you must go, I understand. Just, if you need anything, let me know and I will help you," Satoru adds.

"That is kind of you," Sana says. "I shall bid you goodnight, then."

Satoru has an urge to embrace her, but he is unsure whether he should.

In a second, he decides that he should.

He steps forward and pulls her into his arms. He holds her tightly and wonders why the ache is throbbing so hard inside his chest. She is so small and delicate—he towers over her. He does not want to let her go, but he knows he must.

"Good night, Sana," Satoru whispers. He blushes, although Sana cannot see it. When he says her name, it is soft and it sends a warm pulse through his heart.

He wishes this moment would last forever.

✽

That night, Sana returns to her guest chamber and sits in front of the mirror. She begins to untie the lilac ribbons from her hair.

It is weird, knowing that she is nearing the end of her life.

She must go home and tell her family about the Kurai and about her role as the Mutoren. They are not going to be happy with what she has done, but it is only right for them to know. She owes them this knowledge before her life comes to an end. She must make sure they are protected as much as possible from both the Kurai and these new monsters.

There is a knock on her door. She hops down from her seat and pulls it open gently.

Healer Aoki steps inside and bows. "Knight Lishuah," he says, "my apologies for coming so late in the night, but I have your results. I am sure you do not want to wait any longer."

"Oh," Sana says, her heartbeat accelerating. "Please tell me."

The palace healer takes a seat. "Knight Lishuah," he begins, "from my calculations, you do not have any Soltair left inside you."

Sana does a double take. "I'm sorry?"

"I analysed your blood several times, and the calculations tell me that you were most likely last dosed with Soltair when you were around ten years old. Since then, the fortnightly injections you mentioned do not appear to have taken place. As such, there is not a single trace left inside of you," Healer Aoki explains.

Sana stares at the palace healer, wide-eyed. *How is this possible?* "A-Are you sure, Healer Aoki?" Sana asks in disbelief.

"I am certain, my child," he replies.

"Th-Then, what you mean is . . . I am not nearing the end of my life?"

"You will live on naturally until you are nice and old, just like any other lady, Knight Lishuah," Healer Aoki replies.

Sana bursts into tears. She does not bother to hide her emotions. She begins to sob.

Healer Aoki stands and puts his arms around her. "There, there," he says gently, patting her on her head as she cries like a child. "This is good news."

"Please—it is all right—" Sana says between breaths. "Thank you . . . for letting me know. Please—you may go—it is late."

The palace healer releases her and bows. "Don't cry now, my child," he says, before he makes his way out.

After Healer Aoki leaves, Sana flops onto her bed and allows herself to sob her heart out, just like she did when she buried Seiji's arm next to the Akamatsu

Windmill.

"Seiji," Sana cries into the bedsheets. "All this time, you knew, didn't you?" The tears form damp circles onto the fabrics of her bed.

Seiji was fifteen when he started practising independently, which would have made Sana ten years old at the time. It seemed that, as soon as he was able, and practising without oversight, he stopped injecting her with the toxic substances. He must have somehow developed a substance that had the same side effects as the Soltair—such as the high fever which she experienced each fortnight—so that the masters would not become suspicious.

Perhaps this is why I often came last in the training sessions—I never received the heightened effects the Soltair supposedly gives! Sana manages a small laugh between her sobs. She scrunches the bedsheets into her fists.

But knowing Seiji, Sana is sure that he did the same for her team-mates: Yuka, Izumi, and Eric. None of them would have received the Soltair, either. She is sure of it.

It feels strange remembering their names. She wonders how they are doing. Are they still in the Kurai?

Sana sobs some more, overwhelmed by the kindness that Seiji is still showing her, so many years after his death. “Oh, Seiji.”

How could someone like him ever exist? What did she do to ever deserve him?

Whereas his life was so unjustly taken from him at such a young age, he had allowed her to escape the evil Kurai. He was now helping her to live on—to escape the death from the sidium, the Kurai, and even the Soltair.

“I promise you,” Sana manages, sobbing into her bed some more. “I promise you Seiji. I will live a long, happy, and healthy life.

CHAPTER THIRTY-ONE

Eldi

SINCE ALBERT DISCOVERED THE SECRET passageway between his cell and the blind man's, he has been going to visit him each day. And since the man did not know his own name, Albert had suggested the name *Eldi*, for his hair, as it means fire in Cernese. Albert explained to him that he himself used to be called *Gullna* when he was a child.

Albert grasps onto Eldi's hand as he is pulled out of

the passageway once again. It has become much easier to get in and out of this tunnel, especially after he and Eldi went inside and widened the passageway with various tools Eldi had hidden over the years.

"You're getting used to coming in and out of there, my child," Eldi comments as Albert pats down his knees.

"Very much so," Albert agrees.

"My wife would be pleased to know you're here," Eldi says. "After all, our hard work didn't go to waste."

"I am grateful for what you both have done," Albert replies, thinking about what Eldi told him. "You say your wife was the one occupying my cell many years ago?"

"Correct," Eldi replies. "We dug out this passageway over the years in secret, using various utensils and tools we managed to steal from what was brought to us each day." He pauses, and his lip trembles. "I do miss her so."

"I am sorry," Albert replies.

"When she fell ill, she told me that one day, another human being might appear, and when that day comes, there will be hope once more," Eldi says. "I didn't want to believe it, especially after she passed, but then you came along."

Albert makes his way towards the wall facing his own cell. He traces his hands over the Qietian symbols

Eldi engraved on the wall. This was the strange sound he had been hearing all this time, each day. *If only I could understand them.*

“I see you have new engravings once more,” Albert says.

“Yes, my child. But as always, I cannot remember what they mean,” Eldi replies.

The man told him that, each day at a particular time, he gets urges to write about memories that cross his mind. He etches them into the walls as quickly as he can, but soon afterwards, he forgets what they are. He is also unable to understand his own words, even if he traces them with his fingers.

“Come, my child.” Eldi beckons to Albert.

When Albert nears, the man lifts a large piece of cloth that covers one of the walls of his cell, revealing a deep, long tunnel. Albert steps inside and follows Eldi until they reach the furthest end.

“I believe we are nearly there,” Eldi says to Albert as he hands over a metal tool he had built from cutlery.

During their many years in captivity, Eldi and his wife dug through this tunnel in hopes of getting out of this prison. Now that Albert is here, they have been advancing through the escape tunnel at a rapid pace.

“You still don’t remember why you and your wife

were imprisoned, good sir?" Albert asks as he chips away at the wall alongside the middle-aged man.

"I am afraid not," Eldi replies. He, too, is chipping away at the wall.

"Do you remember our plan, Eldi?" Albert asks.

"That, I do," he replies.

"Remind me, good sir," Albert says. He wants to check that he has not forgotten.

"Over the next few days, you are to pretend that you are falling ill. You will refuse to have any of your food. However, rather than letting you grow weak, I will share the food I get in my cell," Eldi explains. "However, we will only do this if we have managed to successfully open the passageway to the outside."

So far so good. "And then?" Albert prompts.

"The 'ghost' who comes to tend to you each day will soon realise that you are not eating. Then, after a few days, you will lie still inside your cell, pretending that you are dead. The 'ghost' shall enter to check on you." Eldi chips away at a section of the wall and absently brushes some gravel aside. "In that instant, you will fight and threaten him into telling you what is going on. We will hold him hostage until we get out of here and run to safety," Eldi finishes.

"Exactly that," Albert agrees. He carries on chipping

away at the walls. He is filled with hope. He and Eldi shall escape this prison. They shall find Liuana Pharlos. They shall find Satoshi too, and finally find out what in the world is going on.

At last, he shall return to Shinrin, back to Prince Takashi's side.

CHAPTER THIRTY-TWO

Déjà Vu

THE NIGHT AIR IS CRISP as Satoru climbs onto his roof and sits. It has been a while since he last came up here. Although it is still winter, tonight, it is not snowing. He takes his flute out from its case.

Satoru peers down at his cherished possession, turning it round and round in his hands. He traces over the golden rings and the fine wooden engravings, pleased that it was fixed so seamlessly. He is embarrassed when he thinks back to the night when the Mutoren appeared behind him and witnessed him breaking his beloved instrument.

But that very night was when he began to feel differently about her.

Satoru has not yet had a chance to play his flute since it was fixed. He decides to play it tonight, to see how it is and to help clear his mind. He brings the mouthpiece to his lips and closes his eyes.

Sana Harlande lingers on his mind.

His fingers move almost on their own as a light, soulful tune echoes through the night air. The more he plays, the deeper his emotions expand. He enjoys how the music takes him to another place, one away from everything that is bothering him.

"Hey," comes a voice.

Satoru stops. He opens his eyes and glances behind him. *She's here?* Is he reliving his memory? Even the way they are greeting each other is exactly the same as that night. It is informal yet comforting.

"Hey," Satoru finally replies.

Sana sits next to him. She is back in her usual clothes as she wears simple brown shirt and trousers. Her hair is pulled into a ponytail. "I see it is fixed," Sana says, glancing at Satoru's flute.

"Oh, yes," Satoru replies. He looks away, still embarrassed by the fact that she saw him in such a state that night. "This is the first time I'm playing it since . . . then."

"It sounds lovely," she says.

"What brings you here?" Satoru asks. Deep inside, it does not matter. He is glad that she is here. He puts his flute back into its case and rests it on his lap.

"I wanted to let you know that I will depart tomorrow morning," Sana says. "I shall be back within a few days, however."

"All right." Satoru notices that she appears relaxed today. There is a soft gleam in her eyes and the clear sadness from the other night has disappeared. He decides to try his luck. "Did you have a think about my offer?" Satoru asks gently.

Sana looks at him. "About the role?"

Satoru nods.

"I did." She swings her legs as they dangle from the roof. "Perhaps I will take it. But I need some more time to think about it. I will let you know after I come back."

"I am glad to hear that." Satoru does not hide his smile. "Take all the time you need."

Sana smiles back at him. She twiddles her thumbs.

Satoru wonders why she seems particularly happy

today.

"You look well," Satoru comments.

"Mm," Sana replies, looking into the distance. "The world is beautiful."

Satoru snorts. Why is she talking in such an abstract manner? What happened to the audacious and daring, yet minimally worded and direct Mutoren?

"Did you eat something off?" Satoru cannot help but mutter.

"Sorry?"

Satoru bites his lip. "You seem . . . different."

"Perhaps I am," Sana replies. "Perhaps I am not. Who knows?" She shrugs happily and swings her legs some more.

Satoru laughs. What has gotten into her today?

"You are something, Harlande," Satoru finds himself saying once again. He pauses, and then, drawn by something unexplainable, he lets his tone go serious. "In fact, you are everything, Sana," Satoru says.

His heart begins to thump inside his chest. The more he looks at her, the faster his heart beats. *Why did I just say that all of a sudden?* Something dies a little inside him.

Sana's legs stop mid-swing. She blinks at Satoru. "I'm sorry, but did *you* eat something off?" As she repeats his words, her nostrils widen.

Satoru looks at her face and bursts into more laughter. He braces himself, holding onto the rooftop with both of his hands as he leans back and laughs some more.

Soon, Sana finds herself laughing along with him. The prince's laughter is loud, radiant, and incredibly contagious.

As the two of them laugh, a weight is lifted from Satoru's shoulders. He takes a breath as they quiet down.

"Prince Takashi?" Sana asks as she catches her breath.

"Prince Takashi has a name," Satoru says, copying what she said to him that night on this rooftop. His ears perk up, wanting to hear her say his name.

"Yes, Stomach-ache," Sana answers.

Satoru looks at her and his mouth immediately turns back up into a smile. In moments, he begins to laugh once more. This girl surely knows exactly what he is talking about, and she responded so smoothly. She is quick-minded and witty indeed.

"So?" Satoru asks. He thinks about the way she said his name in his dream, and his heart skips a beat.

"So, Prince Takashi," Sana says as she stands up, "I believe I should go. I need to pack and get ready for tomorrow."

"Oh," Satoru says. Disappointment settles inside him. He looks at Sana and wishes that she would stay a moment longer. He wonders when he will see her next. Then, he pushes that all back and offers her a pleasant nod. "Have a safe journey," Satoru says. "I hope your family are healthy and that I will see you soon." He puts the case containing his flute to the side.

"Thank you." Sana smiles. She walks towards the edge of the roof and, just before she leans backwards like she did that time many nights ago, she looks at Satoru. Her round, dark eyes peer into his very own.

Satoru finds himself gazing back, arrested by the fond mischievousness in her gaze.

"Good night, Satoru," Sana says. She leans back and disappears into the night.

Satoru's heart skips another beat. He stands briskly and then squats at the edge of the rooftop like a child, peering into the darkness. He stares, starry-eyed, into the night, the echo of her voice saying his name ringing in his ears. His breath creates mist in the cold, crisp air.

"Good night, Sana," Satoru whispers, although she is gone.

He stays there, squatting at the edge of the roof for a bit longer, listening to the echo of her voice bouncing around in his mind.

CHAPTER THIRTY-THREE

Waiting

A NINE-YEAR-OLD SATORU snuggles up to his brother as they lie in bed at night. Satoru buries his head into Satoshi's chest as the dampness from his tears seeps into the fabric of his brother's clothes.

He insisted on invading his brother's bed since Satoshi is due to leave tomorrow. Tomorrow is the day Satoru has been dreading since his parents broke the news. He wants nothing more than to spend every last possible second with his brother.

"Hey, hey, stop crying now," Satoshi whispers as he lies on his side, gently patting Satoru's head. "If you keep that up, you're going to wash us all away!"

"Why do *you* have to leave?" Satoru protests as some more tears roll down his face. Even his brother's humour cannot sway him right now. "Why can't someone else go?"

"Hey, don't be like that now," Satoshi whispers.

"How long will you be gone again?" Satoru asks as he scrunches up the fabric of Satoshi's shirt and looks at his face.

"It's hard to say, Brother," Satoshi says quietly, still patting Satoru on his head, "but I should think I will be back in a few months. A year at the latest."

"A year!" Satoru exclaims. He howls into his brother's chest.

"Hey," Satoshi whispers again, "there's no need to cry right now."

"Can't you—why not tell me—I just want to know where you're going!" Satoru sobs. He is struggling to speak through his tears and his breathing has become shallow and difficult to maintain.

"I'm going on a little adventure, Brother," Satoshi whispers. "A mission, so to speak."

"Yes, but to where?" Satoru presses.

There is a silence. Satoru hears his brother sigh quietly. He looks up once more and notices a sadness settled deep in the violet colour of his eyes.

Satoshi blinks a few times, trying to dissipate the watery film sliding over his eyes. "Satoru," he finally says, "you know the shrine on the outskirts of the palace?"

"The one up all those steps?"

"Yes, the red one that is 'up all those steps,' indeed," Satoshi answers. "Whenever I make it back, I will return there before nightfall on that day."

"But you don't know the exact day?" Satoru asks. He wipes tears from his eyes.

"I'm afraid not," Satoshi whispers.

"But you will be there?"

"Yes."

"Promise?" Satoru presses.

Satoshi laughs. "I promise, Brother," Satoshi replies. He pauses again. "Hey, it's not like I'm leaving forever," he suddenly says.

Satoru sniffs. He has been crying so hard that his nose is running quite uncontrollably.

"Brother," Satoshi says softly, "some children wait years for their brothers and fathers to come back from battle. When you think of it this way, you'll realise how lucky we are. I will be back before you realise."

"I will miss you so much, Brother Satoshi," Satoru says. He squeezes his eyes shut and leans into his brother once more.

"I will, too," Satoshi whispers. He pats Satoru on his back. "But when I come back, you will be all grown up and moody and you won't talk to me anymore," Satoshi teases.

"No, I won't!" Satoru cries. "I'll always want to talk to you!" He begins to sob once more.

Satoshi allows his brother to cry. He does not say anything else and continues to pat Satoru on his head. They lay like that for a bit longer.

Once Satoru's crying has calmed, he pulls away slowly to catch his breath. A stringy strand of snot connects his nose to the fabrics of Satoshi's shirt.

Satoshi bursts into laughter. "Brother, you got your snot all over my shirt."

Satoru laughs through his tears, embarrassed. He wipes his nose with his sleeve and chuckles more as his brother says, 'Eww.'

As his breathing settles, Satoru whispers, "Come back soon, Brother Satoshi."

"Be good, Brother," Satoshi responds.

As they lay together in the dim light of the room,

Satoru slowly drifts to sleep, his breathing loudly rattling through a nose blocked from crying.

Satoshi's eyes remain wide as he stares ahead of him. He looks down to see his dear little brother sleeping soundly, his fist still tightly grasping the fabric of his shirt.

✾

After Satoshi leaves, nine-year-old Satoru makes his way to the palace shrine every single day at sunset. Although his brother said he would be away for a few months at least, something inside Satoru hopes that Brother Satoshi will return much sooner.

Only seven days had passed so far and yet it felt like a century.

Days turn into weeks and weeks turn into months. Each time Satoru sits by the shrine, his ears perk up at the smallest sounds. His eyes widen as he imagines Brother Satoshi walking up the steps or appearing behind one of the large, red poles of the shrine.

To his disappointment, however, there is nothing there each time.

Soon, the months turn into years.

✾

A ten-year-old Satoru sits by the steps of the shrine, just like he has done every single day for the past year.

A ten-year-old Albert sits next to him, holding his face in his hands. "I wonder when he will come back," Albert says, looking into the distance.

The sun is beginning to set and it is forming pink and orange streaks across the sky.

"Me too," Satoru says. He mirrors Albert's position, holding his own face in his hands and staring into the sky in the same direction.

"It should be soon, should it not?" Albert asks. "Didn't he say a year at the latest?"

"He did," Satoru says. Brother Satoshi made a promise, and he is not one to break them.

But something is sinking inside his little heart, harder to ignore with each day that passes.

"Don't be sad, Prince Takashi," Albert whispers as he notices the sadness in Satoru's eyes. "I'm sure he went to do something important. There is no one quite like our Brother Satoshi."

"There is no one quite like him indeed," Satoru agrees.

He sighs as they watch the sun continue to set. Soon enough, the late afternoon sky becomes one of dark night.

Satoru stands as some frustration expands inside him. “He’s not coming,” Satoru states. He rushes down the steps.

Albert panics as he follows behind him. “Wait!” he shouts.

Satoru does not slow. He storms down the steps with frustration and blinks hard. He does not want Albert to see that he is crying.

✾

Back in the present, Satoru slowly makes his way up the mossy stone stairs on the outskirts of his palace. The sun is starting to set as he heads towards the great shrine.

He reaches the grand, scarlet structure. Two strong poles hold up a slightly upward-curving arch. He looks up at the shrine and exhales. It forms mist in the evening air.

“Brother Satoshi,” Satoru says as he gazes up at the shrine. “I am seven-and-twenty today.” He sighs.

Since that day when he stormed down the steps at ten years old, Satoru stopped coming to the shrine every day. He would come every few days, and eventually, it became every few months.

“I am still waiting, Brother Satoshi,” Satoru says quietly. “Are you coming?”

His voice is heavy with sadness and grief. The palace is so large, and he truly feels so alone. He sits on the ground and leans against one of the shrine's poles. He watches as the sun goes down and the sky turns from an evening of orange to a night full of stars.

"I guess not," Satoru says quietly.

He stands and slowly makes his way down the stairs, emptiness in his heart.

CHAPTER THIRTY-FOUR

Hostage

THE COLDNESS OF THE CELL floor seeps into Albert's back as he lies in the far corner. He and Eldi have carved through the entirety of the escape tunnel. Now, they can walk through it and step into the open Qietian night if they so wished. However, the prison is likely to be heavily guarded, and the last thing they want is to be re-captured right when they finally escape.

As such, Albert lies on the floor, waiting to enact

their plan. He has a sharpened spoon tucked in his sleeve, ready to act as a knife. Over the past week or so, he refused all the food he was offered. Secretly, he was sharing Eldi's portions.

Today, he will pretend that he is dead so that the 'ghost' who visits daily will come inside to check on him. Albert and Eldi will hold him hostage until they find their way back to safety.

An orange glow appears. Although Albert is turned away from it, he can still see the glow reflecting off the wall he is facing.

The time has come. The 'ghost' will come and bring him another bowl of food.

The glow remains. Albert senses that he must be standing in the doorway, wondering why Albert is laying on the floor, unmoving. Soon, there are footsteps and the glow disappears.

The 'ghost' is inside the cell, and he is coming towards him.

Their plan is working.

The 'ghost' crouches and leans towards Albert. He pauses before reaching a hand towards Albert's shoulder and turning him around.

As soon as Albert is facing the 'ghost', his sapphire eyes are wide and blazing. In a second, Albert springs to his feet, loops his arm around the neck of the 'ghost', and squeezes. He can feel his frightened swallow and heavy breathing through his strange, white fabric.

"Do not move or I will break your neck," Albert threatens as he pulls his new hostage's arms behind his back with his other hand and presses him against the wall of the cell.

The hostage makes a sudden movement as he attempts to turn and lunge at Albert. Albert's leg immediately straightens and he strikes a hook kick at the man's head, all while still holding onto his arms.

The hostage drops to the floor and groans.

Albert ties up his arms with ripped up pieces of clothing, made by Eldi and his wife back in the day. He secures the knots tightly.

There is an ache in his legs. He may be the first-hand guard of Shinrin, but he has not fought in a very long time.

"Do not try anything," Albert threatens as he presses the back of his knife against the hostage's neck. He orders him to stand and pushes him through the secret passageway towards Eldi's cell.

Once they reach Eldi's cell, Albert immediately pushes the hostage into the dark escape tunnel—the man's breathing is shallow and frightened.

Albert presses the knife to the man's neck once more as Eldi follows behind. "Tell me why we have been imprisoned," Albert hisses into the man's ear.

The hostage turns his head from side to side. Albert can tell that he is panicking.

"Speak!" Albert orders.

"I-I am just—I'm following orders," the man stammers. It is a young voice. Perhaps the man is around his age.

"I know," Albert snarls. "Whose orders are you following?" *Is it Satoshi?*

"I-I shan't speak his name—" the man stammers again.

"I order you to speak!" Albert leans in again threateningly. He pushes the back of the knife so hard against the man's neck, it makes him yelp.

He gasps. "I . . . can't."

"Is it Azrael?" Albert asks forcefully.

"I-I . . . don't—I don't know!"

"Move." Albert pushes the man forwards, deeper into the tunnel. It does not look like he is going to get anything out of him. He sighs as he forces the man to continue ahead.

"My child," Eldi whispers from behind, letting Albert know that he is still there.

"Follow on, good sir," Albert whispers back.

The three of them trudge through the darkness and, after a while, they reach the open Qietian night.

Albert gasps once the breeze hits his face. He gazes up at a night sky full of stars, in disbelief that they have truly made it out. He has been inside the claustrophobic cell for God knows how long. He looks around frantically, expecting an army of soldiers ready to attack them, but there is nothing at all.

Only the tranquillity of the Qietian night greets them.

Eldi closes his eyes as he takes in a large breath. Under the moonlight in the open night, Albert can see him much more clearly. He is truly unkempt. His copper-and-grey hair is long and tattered, and his bushy beard is in the same state. The rough fabric he is wearing is torn and falling apart. This is the sight of a man who has been imprisoned for the last twenty years.

Albert looks around, trying to work out where he is. The truth is, he does not know where to go. Eldi does not remember much of anything about the Qietian geography—the only thing he did mention was that the Spiritual Towers should be the safest place in the land.

Albert remembers how Sir Xandyr and Liuana Pharlos had urged him to go to the Spiritual Towers when Azrael appeared. They also said it was the safest place in the land. He wonders if they will be there.

It is unsettling to be in a completely unfamiliar environment in a weakened, lost state like this. Everywhere seems unsafe, and Albert's guards are up at their highest.

To Albert's surprise, he spots the Spiritual Towers in the distance. He tears the fabrics covering the hostage's head to reveal who is underneath. Albert finds himself looking at a frightened young man.

"Pl-Please don't—kill me," the young man says between panicked breaths.

"I will decide what to do," Albert replies coldly.

Deep inside, Albert is frightened. He has no idea what is going to happen to them. He wonders if an army of soldiers will turn up any moment now. He will not be able to fight against so many of them at once. Especially not in his current state. Eldi is still gazing around through the grey film of his eyes, trying to take in the surroundings he cannot see.

"I sense more light," Eldi says as he continues to gaze around.

"Good sir, I see the Spiritual Towers," Albert says.

"Then, let us make our way there," Eldi replies.

Albert holds onto Eldi's hand with one of his own

while his other hand grasps onto the knife that he continues to point at the young man.

The frightened young man walks ahead obediently, trembling.

✽

After quite some time, Albert and Eldi, along with their hostage, make it to the Spiritual Towers. A sense of familiarity brings Albert the smallest sense of reassurance. He looks around, trying to see if anyone is around.

As it has been for the whole journey, his heart beats hard inside his chest. He prays that there will not be a sudden army of soldiers, waiting to capture them.

Albert and Eldi stumble their way through the maze of ivory pillars. Their hostage is forced to move with them. Everywhere they turn, there is no one to greet them . . . until suddenly, as Albert makes one more turn, he finds himself right in front of the old man.

Liuana Pharlos rushes towards him, holding onto his silver staff. "Sir Leon!" the old man calls out. "Oh, you're alive!" His eyes are wide as he hobbles over in disbelief. "Where have you been?"

A small wave of relief rushes over Albert. *Finally, help is here.* "Liuana Pharlos," he replies through heavy breaths, "I-I have no idea what is going on, but I was imprisoned. I believe it is not safe for me to be here. I need to return to Shinrin at once," he urges.

"Oh, my child, this is not a place for you to be at all," Liuana Pharlos agrees. "I did not expect Lord Azrael to rise out of his haven. It is unsafe for you here. We need to get you out of Qieta as soon as possible." The lines on his forehead deepen as he talks.

Albert's mind is jumbled as he thinks of Brother Satoshi. He has too many questions, but there is no time for them at this moment. "Please, where is my horse? Do you know when the next boat will depart?" Albert asks.

"Your stallion has been safe with us while you were gone," Liuana Pharlos reassures. "I am so very pleased that you are alive." He exhales. "Please, let us make our way. We shall head to the boats immediately."

"Oh, I thank you, Liuana Pharlos," Albert replies, adrenaline still pulsating through his body. His heart is beating heavily inside his chest.

There is hope. He has almost escaped back to Shinrin.

Albert follows behind the old man, still holding onto his hostage.

Liuana Pharlos turns briefly and finally takes note of the two unfamiliar faces. "These are?" Liuana Pharlos asks, as they continue toward the docks.

"The good sir is coming with me," Albert says as he glances towards Eldi. "However, I believe this man works for Azrael." He nudges the young man. "We are holding him hostage." Albert takes a breath. They are walking quite quickly, and he is very out of shape.

"Do not let the hostage go, young Sir Leon," Liuana Pharlos urges. "I fear that Azrael will sense that you have escaped, and he could be here again any minute now."

"Oh, Liuana Pharlos," Albert starts, his mind spinning at the thought of Brother Satoshi, "How long has Azrael been in Qieta for?"

The old man does not have time to answer him. They near the edge of the spiritual grounds and Albert immediately notices the ivory steps that enter into the Qietian waters. This is where he first arrived.

"Young Sir Leon," the old man says, "please, go ahead and seek out the boats while I go and fetch your horse. This will save time."

Albert nods frantically.

"Be careful, my child," the old man urges. He briskly walks back in the other direction.

Albert turns to Eldi and hands him the young hostage. "Good sir, please keep him with you while I go and seek out the boats. If any of Azrael's people come, you know what to do."

Eldi nods frantically.

The young hostage turns his head from Albert to Eldi in a panic. He is trembling. "Please, I am innocent," he begs. "Please, don't do this to me."

Albert does not give him a second glance. He turns towards the waters and desperately looks for a boat that may be able to take them off the island. He notices a few and—

There is a young boy with a paddle standing next to one, just like when he first arrived.

Just as Albert is about to stride towards the young boy, there is a sudden, loud yelp. Albert turns to see that a short spear is now impaled through the young hostage's back. Eldi, who is now trembling, is still holding onto him.

Liuana Pharlos's hand is still on the handle of the spear. He holds it there for a moment more before pulling it back out. The sound of the spear being yanked out of the young man's flesh sends a chill right through to Albert's core. Blood splatters all over the ivory floor.

The young hostage, whose white fabric is now completely drenched in blood, falls as a lifeless heap onto the ground. Eldi's torn fabric is also soaked through with red. He clutches his chest as he too, slowly drops to the ground.

"How amusing," Liuana Pharlos says as he wipes the head of the spear on his own hand. It leaves a thick, red trail on his palm. The wise, gentle glint in his eyes has transformed into a sinister glare.

"A foreigner trying to escape our island with a man who has lost his mind?" He snickers, his voice now thick and malicious. He looks at Albert and the corners of his thin, aged lips turn upwards into an evil sneer.

Small, incomprehensible sounds of shock and confusion escape from Albert. He is trembling and sweating. *Did I just jump from the frying pan straight into the fire?*

"There are no boats for you here. Shinrin shall never see their first-hand guard ever again," Liuana Pharlos says wickedly. "Farewell now, Sir Leon."

About the Author

Dr. Ting-Wei Wu, known by her peers as Tina Wu, was born in Taiwan and moved to the United Kingdom in 2001. As a little girl with a big imagination, The *Quest for Qieta* series has lived in her mind since she was sixteen. At last, over a decade later, she has put pen to paper to bring the universe of Neputa to life.

www.thequestforqieta.com

Message To Reader

Thank you for reading my story until the end.

You may have enjoyed it and may be keen to find out what happens next. Or you may not!

As an author, I love to tell stories. But there will be no point in my stories if there is no one around to listen. That is why, you, as the reader, matter a lot to me.

I humbly ask for a few minutes of your spare time, to write a review on your thoughts. Not only will it mean a lot when I see in which hands my book may have landed into, it will mean even more to hear what you thought about it. Please, be honest!
I promise I will not be offended.
cries in a corner

Once again, thank you, from the bottom of my heart.

Acknowledgments

Thank you to my dear family for your encouragement and constructive ideas, and for being my number one supporter since day one.

Printed in Dunstable, United Kingdom

80213781R10214